THE CURSE OF THE
GLOAMGLOZER

Also available in The Edge Chronicles:

The Twig sequence
Book One: Beyond the Deepwoods
Book Two: Stormchaser
Book Three: Midnight over Sanctaphrax

Cloud Wolf
Special publication for World Book Day 2001

Praise for The Edge Chronicles:

'My favourite in the series is *Midnight Over Sanctaphrax*, because you've packed so much into such little writing space and the only words I can describe this book with are, this is the best book in the world. The illustrations by Chris Riddell are absolutely brilliant and amazingly life-like'
Joe, Leicestershire

'I love your books… I went off reading because there weren't any good books left; because of your books, I read a lot more'
Adele Celia, South East London

'The pictures looked as if they were going to come to life. It only took me five days to read *Stormchaser* because it was so thrilling. I stayed up till midnight reading it and the same with all the others' *Harry, South East London*

'I really love the Edge Chronicles because every page seems to draw the reader in, making him/her want to read on'
James, Rutland

'I can't wait to read the next book' *Umara, Glasgow*

'*Beyond the Deepwoods* is a fantastic book full of enchantments and adventure with brilliant illustrations and a magical storyline. The characters in the story really came to life and after I had finished reading it I felt like going through it again because I missed them so much' *Tom, East Sussex*

'*Beyond the Deepwoods* is my most favourite book I've ever read' *Harry, Cornwall*

'I also love the excellent funny illustrations by Chris Riddell, which complement your vivid descriptions of the characters and goings on in the Deepwoods perfectly' *Robbie, Norfolk*

'I loved your books even though I am dyslexic… I cannot wait for the next one to come out' *Johnnie, Richmond, London*

'So good I read it at play and lunch-times at school!'
Rachel, High Wycombe

'When I started reading the first book, *Beyond the Deepwoods*, I found it so unpredictable and full of suspense that I couldn't put it down! This then inspired me to read the next two books... The way in which the books are written transforms the magical, fantastical but dangerous world in which Twig is living into an amazing reality' *Diane, Middlesex*

'All three books were magnificent! I haven't read any good books like yours in ages! I loved everything about them. The names, the characters, the pictures and the story itself. It's very hard to say which book is my favourite!' *Nadia, Berkshire*

'I've just read the first Edge Chronicles book. It was fantastic! ... By the way, I never liked books until my friends told me about yours' *Michael, New South Wales, Australia*

'I have read all the Harry Potter books and I thought that I was never going to find a book that could possibly be better than them. Well I was wrong, your books are way better. They really make me get stuck in and use my imagination' *Harriet, Norfolk*

'Our mums have said that we talk about your books in our sleep' *Jacob* and *Chris, Hertfordshire*

'Last year when I was looking around my local library, I spotted *Beyond the Deepwoods*. I took it home and started reading it straight away. It's totally fantastic! I couldn't put it down! It's a truly fantastic book with brilliant characters, an adventurous storyline and Chris Riddell's illustrations are superb!' *Victoria, Cornwall*

'For Sky's sake, bring out a fourth one!!!' *Sam, Somerset*

THE CURSE OF THE
GLOAMGLOZER

THE EDGE CHRONICLES

Paul Stewart &
Chris Riddell

DOUBLEDAY

LONDON · NEW YORK · TORONTO · SYDNEY · AUCKLAND

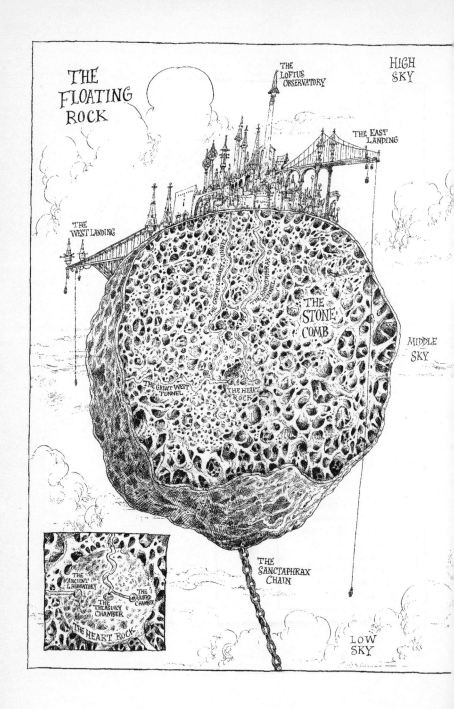

THE
FLOATING
ROCK

HIGH
SKY

THE
LOFTUS
OBSERVATORY

THE EAST
LANDING

THE
WEST LANDING

THE GREAT LIBRARY TUNNEL

THE SANCTAPHRAX TUNNEL

THE
STONE
COMB

MIDDLE
SKY

THE GREAT WEST
TUNNEL

THE HEART
ROCK

THE
SANCTAPHRAX
CHAIN

THE
ANCIENT
LABORATORY

THE
GUARD
CHAMBER

THE
TREASURY
CHAMBER

THE HEART ROCK

LOW
SKY

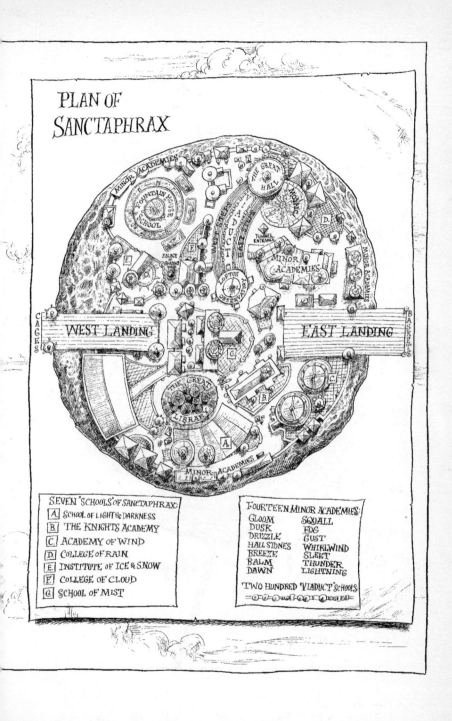

TRANSWORLD PUBLISHERS
61–63 Uxbridge Road, London W5 5SA
A division of The Random House Group Ltd

RANDOM HOUSE AUSTRALIA (PTY) LTD
20 Alfred Street, Milsons Point, Sydney,
New South Wales 2061, Australia

RANDOM HOUSE NEW ZEALAND LTD
18 Poland Road, Glenfield, Auckland 10, New Zealand

RANDOM HOUSE (PTY) LTD
Endulini, 5a Jubilee Road, Parktown 2193, South Africa

Published 2001 by Doubleday
a division of Transworld Publishers

3 5 7 9 10 8 6 4 2

A catalogue record for this book is available
from the British Library

ISBN 0 385 602014

Printed in Great Britain
by Mackays of Chatham plc, Chatham, Kent

For Joseph, William, Katy, Anna and Jack

INTRODUCTION

Far far away, jutting out into the emptiness beyond, like the figurehead of a mighty stone ship, is the Edge. Shrouded in mist and bordered by open sky, it is a place of forests, swamps and rocklands.

There are many who inhabit its various landscapes; from the trolls, trogs and goblins of the perilous Deepwoods to the phantasms and spectres of the treacherous Twilight Woods, from the bleached scavengers of the Mire to the white ravens of the Stone Gardens. While in Undertown – that seething urban sprawl which straddles the Edgewater River – there are creatures from all over the Edge who have travelled there to discover what they hoped would be a better life than the one they left behind.

Not all the inhabitants of the Edge live with their feet on the ground however. Some – the citizens of the great floating city of Sanctaphrax – live with their heads literally in the clouds. Dwelling and working in their sumptuous palaces and lofty towers, they are academics, alchemists, sub-acolytes and apprentices, plus, of course, all those who make their lives of research and study possible: the guards, the servants, the cooks and cleaners.

Secured by the great Anchor Chain to the centre of Undertown below, the rock upon which Sanctaphrax has been constructed is still growing. Like all the other buoyant rocks of the Edge, it started out in the Stone Gardens – poking up from the ground, growing, being pushed up further by new rocks growing beneath it, and becoming bigger still. The chain was attached when the rock became large and light enough to float up into the sky.

Over the years, successive generations have built more and more impressive buildings upon it; ever grander, ever higher. The once-splendid Great Library and erstwhile Palace of Lights are now dwarfed by the College of Cloud, the palatial School of Light and Darkness, the Twin Towers of the Mistsifters and, of course, the magnificent Loftus Observatory. The latest additions to the Central Viaduct – that grand marble walkway which spans the air between the Observatory and the Great Hall – are the most grandiloquent and ornate so far.

Overseeing it all, is the Most High Academe, an individual chosen by the Sanctaphrax academics for his intellect and independence. In the past, this post was filled by one of the earth-study librarians. Today, with the sky-scholars in control of Sanctaphrax, it is from their ranks that the current Most High Academe has been selected.

His name is Linius Pallitax. He is a father and a

widower. In his enthronement speech he spoke of the need for the sky-scholars to work with the ousted earth-scholars once again for the betterment of all. What he is to discover, deep down inside the floating rock itself, is that when the earth and sky come together for the wrong reasons, then there is no room for the greater good, but only for the greatest evil.

The Deepwoods, the Edgelands, the Twilight Woods, the Mire and the Stone Gardens. Undertown and Sanctaphrax. The River Edgewater. Names on a map.

Yet behind each name lie a thousand tales – tales that have been recorded in ancient scrolls, tales that have been passed down the generations by word of mouth – tales which even now are being told.

What follows is but one of those tales.

CHAPTER ONE

THE PALACE OF SHADOWS

The great vaulted entrance-hall to the Palace of Shadows was silent save for the hiss of the wind and the soft, yet echoing, footfall of the immense insect-like creature that teetered unsteadily across the marble floor. High up above, beams of dim light streamed in through a circle of arched windows and criss-crossed the shadowy air. And as the floating rock of Sanctaphrax – fixed in place by the Anchor Chain – turned slowly in the breeze coming in from beyond the Edge, so the light swooped and the shadows danced.

The spindlebug paused for a moment at the foot of the sweeping staircase and looked up. The skin, as translucent as the high arched windows above, revealed blood pumping through veins, six hearts beating – and last night's supper slowly digesting in a see-through belly. The light glinted on quivering antennae, and on the goblet and oval-shaped bottle of cordial which stood

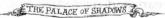

THE PALACE OF SHADOWS

on the burnished copper tray clutched in the creature's claws. The spindlebug was listening intently.

'Where are you, master? Where are you?' he murmured to himself.

He cocked his wedge-shaped head to one side. The antennae quivered impatiently. They picked up the soft murmur of voices throughout the vast building: the inconsequential chatter of the old woodtroll nurse, the soft humming of a girl – the young mistress – intent on some absorbing task, and there, unmistakable, from up in the master-study, a dry cough.

'I hear you, master,' the creature responded. 'I'm sure you could do with a little pick-me-up to go with the news I bring,' he trilled to himself. And with the goblet clinking against the bottle, he began the long climb up the staircase.

It was a staircase the spindlebug knew well – but then he knew every single nook and cranny of the sprawling Palace of Shadows well: its hidden chambers, the murder holes, the corridors that led nowhere, the great balcony from which, for centuries, High Academes had stood to address the plotting, scheming academics below. What was more, the creature knew all the palace's secrets, his antennae picking up the whispers, the gossip, the rumours and cries.

He stopped at the first landing, wheezing heavily, breathlessly aware that he wasn't getting any younger. Indeed, even for a spindlebug, he was old. A hundred and eighty years had passed since he had first hatched out in the underground gardens of a gyle goblin colony, far away in the Deepwoods. So long ago, so very long ago . . .

The slavers had come. They'd destroyed the precious fungus beds and enslaved the spindlebugs who tended them. But not Tweezel, oh no. He was a young bug then, fast, quick-thinking. Hearing the slavers breaking through the walls, he had hidden himself away, making himself invisible in the shadows. Then he had fled into the Deepwoods, keeping to the shadows; always listening, always on his guard. Shadows were his friend.

Tweezel reached the second landing, the place where he'd first laid eyes on his new master – Linius Pallitax, the youngest Most High Academe anyone could remember – and his young wife. She had been standing by the entrance to the robe-chamber, Tweezel remembered, laughing at her husband's ill-fitting new robes and the Great Seal of High Office round his neck. Big with child, and so pretty and full of life, she had seemed out of place in the dusty old palace.

Tweezel stopped.

But soon after had come that terrible night, when her cries of joy became cries of pain. He didn't like to think about it: the woodtroll nurse running back and forth, the terrible screams from the birthing-chamber, the sobs of the young master. Pitiful sounds. Terrible sounds. And then, silence.

Tweezel shook his head and climbed to the third landing. He still remembered how long the silence had seemed to last and how impenetrable it had been. Despite his sensitive antennae, he had had no idea what had happened. The seconds had ticked past, one after the other ... And then all at once, shattering the deathly silence, had come the most wonderful sound of all – the sound of a baby crying. The sound of the young mistress.

Linius Pallitax had suffered a terrible tragedy: he had lost his wife in the throes of childbirth, yet he had also brought life back into the Palace of Shadows. It had been, Tweezel thought, almost like the old days when he'd first come to the great floating city, and the palace had been a noisy, bustling place, bursting with life.

Back then, the academics of Sanctaphrax had been primarily earth-scholars, fascinated by the flora and fauna of the Deepwoods. Why, even he, Tweezel, had been considered a marvel! The High Librarian himself – the greatest earth-scholar of all – had found him starving in the slums of Undertown and brought him up here to the palace. Oh, happy, *happy* memories!

In those days, of course, the Palace of Shadows had been known as the Palace of Lights and, with its countless windows of coloured glass which bathed everything inside in jewelled light, it had been the most magnificent building in all of Sanctaphrax. And he, Tweezel, the strange creature seemingly made out of glass, had been appointed its custodian.

The ancient spindlebug reached the fourth landing and paused to catch his breath. But times had changed. The sky-scholars had begun to take over. Earth-study was no longer fashionable, it seemed. All over Sanctaphrax, the towers of sky-scholarship had begun to sprout; taller and taller they grew, reaching high into the sky. With the completion of the College of Cloud, the Palace of Lights had finally been surrounded totally, and thrown into deep shadow.

The Great Purges had begun soon after; earth-scholars had been expelled from Sanctaphrax in wave after wave, and Tweezel's magnificent palace had become the Palace of Shadows. Tweezel sighed. There had followed the lonely years. The old librarian had died and a sky-scholar had been elected new Most High Academe. He had chosen to live in one of the magnificent new towers, and Tweezel had been left on his own to look after the empty palace as best he could.

But shadows were his friend. He had stayed, and listened, and waited.

And then – some sixty years later – Linius, the young Professor of Mistsifting, had become the Most High Academe. Just another sky-scholar, Tweezel had thought. But he'd been wrong. Linius was different. He respected the old ways. He had moved back into the palace, stood on the balcony and called for an end to the rivalry and faction fighting, and the beginning of a new era where earth-studies and sky-scholarship would complement one another, rather than compete.

The sky-scholars hadn't liked that one bit – then or now. They muttered, they plotted – Tweezel heard them – but what could they actually do? Linius was the Most High Academe.

Tweezel stopped at the door of the master-study and knocked three times.

'Come in, Tweezel,' came a weary voice.

'I bring news of Wind Jackal, master,' said Tweezel, entering the smoky room. 'He sends word of his estimated time of arrival.'

'Which is?' said Linius.

'Three hours, master.'

'Wherever are you taking me, Maris?' Linius chuckled as, still blind-folded, he found himself being steered across the floor by his daughter, his injured left leg dragging slightly as he went.

'Stop!' his daughter commanded, and Linius felt her little fingers teasing at the knot behind his head. The silken scarf fell away. 'All right,' she said. 'You can open your eyes now.'

Linius did as he was told. He rubbed his eyes and looked down to see a half-finished mosaic spread out on the table before him. He rubbed his chin thoughtfully.

A soft beam of muted yellow light swept across the shadowy room as the great floating rock turned. Maris held her breath.

Would he like the picture she had made with the fragments of sky-crystal, or would he have preferred her to do something original?

When she'd started out, making a copy of the ancient Quadrangle Mosaic had seemed like such a good idea, and Maris had spent several hours the previous day down in the airy marble square in front of the Great Hall taking detailed measurements of the intricate design. The circumference of the concentric circles. The angle of the lightning bolts. Getting the irregular series of calibrations just right. Later, she had turned the figures into a sketch, which she was now using to make as accurate a reproduction as she could.

Her father picked up the sketch, glanced at it, laid it aside and returned his attention to the incomplete mosaic. 'It's . . .' He hesitated, his brow furrowed.

Maris swallowed anxiously. She *should* have done something original. A caterbird, perhaps. Or a league ship – no, a sky pirate ship, soaring over the Sanctaphrax spires. Or maybe the white ravens circling the towering Loftus Observatory . . .

'It's *wonderful!*' he breathed. He leaned across the red-oak table and tousled his daughter's hair. 'You're a clever girl, Maris.'

Maris smiled. It was all she could do not to purr out loud and her hand trembled as she tried to decide exactly where to place the piece of yellow sky-crystal she was holding.

'What about over there?' Linius suggested, and pointed to a gap in one of the zigzag lightning bolts.

Maris slipped it into place as, from outside, there came the sound of a bell chiming five. She looked up and smiled shyly – but her father had turned away and was staring out of the tall glass balcony-doors, a puzzled frown on his forehead.

'It fits perfectly,' she said. 'Thanks.'

'What? I . . .' Linius muttered absent-mindedly. Then, turning back, he noticed the completed lightning bolt. 'Oh, I see.' He paused. 'Tell me, Maris, why *did* you decide to make your mosaic in the shape of the Great Seal?'

'The Great Seal?' she repeated, surprised.

'Yes, child,' said Linius, a little impatiently. He raised the heavy chain of office which hung round his neck and let the medallion it supported swing back and forwards in front of her.

23

'Oh, *that*,' said Maris. 'Yes, it does look similar. But my picture is of the Quadrangle Mosaic.'

'I can vouch for that,' a voice piped up from the other side of the great room. 'Three hours we spent there yesterday. Blowing a gale it was, and so *cold*!'

Linius turned round and peered into the shadows. 'Welma Thornwood,' he said, 'is that you?'

'No, it's the Queen of the Wodgiss Parade,' the voice replied sarcastically.

Linius smiled. How different from the academics Deepwooders were. No airs, no graces, no false compliments that became whispered insults the moment your back was turned. With Welma, the old woodtroll nurse, what you saw was what you got.

'Mind you,' Welma went on, 'far be it from me to complain. If three hours of standing around in the bitter wind is what it takes for a daughter to get her father's attention, then so be it.' She cleared her throat quietly. 'No offence intended,' she added.

'None taken,' said Linius. He knew there was truth to her words. The time-consuming responsibilities of high office had driven a wedge between a father and daughter who, before, had always enjoyed such a close relationship.

The floating rock of Sanctaphrax turned once more, sending the shadows darting round the vast room. Welma Thornwood was briefly bathed in the dim yellow light. She was seated in a hanging-sofa with her embroidery frame on her lap and Maris's pet wood-lemkin on her shoulder.

'Of course, the mosaic will look even better when it's

finished,' she said, without looking up from her needle-work. The shadows swallowed her up once more. 'And since Maris has promised to complete it as soon as possible, it would be so nice if you didn't leave it *too* long before your next visit.'

'Quite, quite,' said Linius, who hadn't heard a word. With his stave back in his hand to support his weight, he was looking over his shoulder at the balcony-doors. The long, lace curtains fluttered in the breeze. 'Curious,' he muttered to himself. 'I could have sworn Tweezel said three . . .'

At that moment the lemkin on Welma's shoulder began jumping about on its leash and shrieking furi-ously: a high piercing cry followed by a staccato cough which – had it been back in the Deepwoods rather than in this floating palace – would have alerted others of its kind to imminent danger. *Waa-iiiii – kha-kha-kha-kha-kha . . .*

'Calm yourself, Digit,' said Welma, tugging it closer and stroking its trembling neck and shoulders. 'Come on, now. Quieten down.'

But the lemkin would not quieten down, and when Welma tried to hold it in her lap, it scratched at her legs and slapped her face with its prehensile tail, so hard that it left an angry white weal on her cheek.

'*Aargh!*' she cried out in pain, and let go of the end of the leash.

The lemkin leapt to the floor and bounded towards the door, its large eyes narrowed and mottled blue fur bristling.

'Digit!' called Maris, dashing after it. 'You naughty thing, you. Come back here.'

'*Waa-iiii – kha-kha-kha-kha,*' the lemkin shrieked back.

'Come back!' Maris demanded again, angry now. 'At *once!*' She glanced round at her father anxiously. He'd never approved of her keeping a pet in the palace, and the last thing she wanted to do was give him an excuse to get rid of it. But oddly, he didn't seem to mind what was going on – in fact, it didn't look as if he'd even noticed.

And then Maris saw why. On the other side of the tall, glass balcony-doors, a mighty sky pirate ship was slowly descending from the sky. Its sails fluttered, its brasswork gleamed in the golden light of the setting sun. It was magnificent. What was more, from the curve and carvings of its shiny polished bow, she recognized it as the *Galerider*.

As she continued to watch, the sky pirate ship dropped anchor. The next moment, a gangplank was lowered onto the balustrade, and the *Galerider*'s elegant captain descended.

Maris's heart sank.

Not that she had anything against the sky pirate captain – in fact of all her father's friends, Wind Jackal was probably her

26

favourite. Uncle Windy, she'd once called him. He was funny – and sometimes he would do magic tricks for her. No, it wasn't Wind Jackal she was disappointed with, but her father – and herself, of course, for being so stupid!

When Linius had entered the room earlier that afternoon, unannounced and out of the blue, Maris had been so happy to see him that she hadn't questioned his reasons for coming. She'd simply assumed he wanted to spend some time with his daughter.

She now knew that she'd been wrong, and she remembered how distracted he'd been; forever checking the time and glancing out of the windows. He hadn't come to see her at all. He'd simply been waiting to keep an appointment with one of his Deepwoods friends.

'*WAA-iiii – kha-kha . . .*'

'Digit!' Maris cried in a sudden fury. 'Will you be quiet!'

'*. . . kha-kha . . .*'

Welma lunged forwards and swiped at the screeching, scratching creature, knocking it firmly away from the door. Maris seized the end of the leash and wrapped it round and round her hand. At the same instant, the door opened and the angular head of the spindlebug looked round furtively.

'I've brought the master's cordial,' he began, 'together with . . .'

'*YAAOOOW!*' the lemkin howled with a mixture of pain, rage and frustration.

Tweezel paused. 'Wh . . . where is the young mistress's little pet?' he asked breathlessly.

'You're quite safe,' said Welma. The spindlebug noticed the furious lemkin writhing in Maris's grasp and winced. Welma smiled. 'Shame on you, a great big spindlebug frightened by a little wood-lemkin.'

'I . . . that is . . .' Tweezel's antennae quivered uneasily. 'A new message came for the master, the Most High Ac . . .'

'Yes, yes, get on with it!' said Welma impatiently. The old spindlebug could be painfully slow at times.

'The message comes from Wind Jackal, captain of the sky pirate ship, *Galerider*.' Tweezel cleared his throat. 'He regrets that unforeseen circumstances have delayed him, but hopes to arrive no later than two hours after the time I originally informed the master would be the time of his official appointment . . .'

'As usual, you're too late,' said Welma, interrupting him for a second time. She nodded towards the now open balcony-doors, where Linius Pallitax was warmly greeting Wind Jackal behind the flapping white curtains. 'I dare say the captain will be able to deliver his own message,' she added sniffily.

'This is most irregular,' the spindlebug muttered miserably. 'I haven't announced him yet ...'

'Oh, well, never mind,' said Welma, who had never found the glassy creature's behaviour anything less than bizarre. 'But I'd go if I were you,' she added, 'before Digit breaks free again.' The lemkin screeched, louder than ever. Tweezel drew back his head and Welma closed the door. 'Ridiculous creature,' she laughed. 'Haven't announced him, indeed! Why, Wind Jackal is the master's oldest friend. Now, Maris,' she said, turning to her charge, 'hurry up and clear everything away. Your father's got work to attend to.'

But Maris was not listening. Idly stroking the now purring lemkin under its chin, she was staring out on to the balcony where a third person had joined her father and Captain Wind Jackal. Although dressed up in sky pirate gear, with a longcoat and parawings, he was a mere youth – little older than Maris herself judging by his height and build.

Yet when he caught her gazing at him, the look he returned with his deep, dark eyes was sky-wise beyond his thirteen or so years. To her horror, Maris realized she was blushing.

·CHAPTER TWO·

QUINT

'It has been a long while, Linius,' said Wind Jackal as he pumped the Most High Academe's hand up and down. 'Too long,' he added. 'I noticed you were limping.'

'Oh, a little accident, no more,' said Linius. 'It's on the mend.'

'Glad to hear it,' said Wind Jackal. He looked round to inspect his ornate surroundings and nodded appreciatively. 'Sky-fortune has clearly shone down upon you.'

'You, too, Wind Jackal,' said Linius, nodding at the *Galerider* which hovered above them. 'That's certainly a magnificent vessel.'

'Sails from the costliest woodspider-silk,' the sky pirate captain confirmed. 'And the finest lufwood timber that money can buy.' He shook his head. 'Mind you, the whole sky ship could do with an overhaul. You wouldn't believe what we've been through on our journey here. Storms, gales, turbulent fog – and then the most almighty sky battle you could possibly imagine! It was us against the *Great Sky Whale*.'

'The *Great Sky Whale*,' Linius murmured. Such matters as sky battles seemed far removed from his life of study and research – yet even *he* had heard of the *Great Sky Whale*. The slave-ship's terrible reputation went before it.

'We were lucky to escape with our lives,' said Wind Jackal. 'Eh, Quint?'

From her hiding-place behind the billowing curtains, Maris watched as the youth stepped forward. He looked so horribly sure of himself, and when he spoke his voice was big and confident.

'But we did escape, Father,' he said, his dark eyes flashing gleefully. 'And with enough black diamonds to pay for the *Galerider* to be overhauled a hundred times over!'

'Well said, lad,' Wind Jackal laughed, clapping his son on his shoulder. He turned to Linius, and tapped his prominent nose conspiratorially. 'That accursed Leagues-master, Marl Mankroyd, got more than he bargained for, I can tell you. He'll think twice before trying to ambush Wind Jackal the sky pirate captain again.'

Quint chuckled throatily. 'That is, if he ever makes it back to Undertown at all.'

Wind Jackal looked back at Linius. 'He had a little "accident" with his flight-rock,' he explained. 'It got chilled and . . .'

'Hurtled upwards into open sky,' Linius completed for him. 'Why, you wily old skycur!' he said and embraced his old friend a second time. 'I see you haven't changed a bit. Welcome to the Palace of Shadows – to you, Wind Jackal, and to you, too, Quint.'

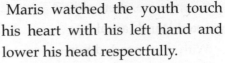

Maris watched the youth touch his heart with his left hand and lower his head respectfully.

'So, Quint, my lad,' Linius went on, 'you were three years old when I last saw you. How old are you now? Twelve? Thirteen?'

Quint raised his head. 'Seventeen next year,' he announced.

'Wishing your life away again, Quint?' said Wind Jackal, and cuffed his son lightly round the head. 'He's fourteen,' he said.

Maris stifled a snigger.

'But it's true,' said Quint, a little sulkily. 'I'll be fifteen later this year and sixteen next year, at which time I shall enter my seventeenth year and . . .'

'I see young Quint here has quite a head for creative counting,' said Linius, amused. He looked the youth up and down.

'So, tell me, Linius,' said Wind Jackal, his face growing more serious. 'Why such an urgent summons, eh? What's on your mind?'

Linius smiled. 'All in good time, old friend,' he said, and called back through the open doors to his daughter. 'Maris? Are you still there in the balcony-chamber?'

Heart racing, Maris scampered from the curtain and over to the table where the half-finished mosaic lay. 'Y . . . yes, Father,' she called back, hoping he wouldn't hear how breathless she was.

'Come here, then, child!' said Linius. 'You haven't yet greeted Wind Jackal.'

With her head down, Maris left the shadow-filled room and stepped out onto the balcony. She smiled at Wind Jackal.

'Sky above!' the sky pirate captain gasped as he moved towards her. 'Who is this tall and elegant vision before me? Surely it can't be Maris.' He placed his finger under her chin, and tipped her head upwards. 'Can it?'

Maris beamed. 'It *is* me,' she said.

Wind Jackal shook his head in disbelief. 'But it's not possible,' he said, then added, 'though there's *one* way to find out. My little Maris always kept a single gold piece in her ear.' He reached forwards and grazed her cheek with his hand. 'And here it is!' he announced. 'It *must* be Maris.'

He slipped the coin into her hand.

'Thank you,' Maris whispered shyly. She was beginning to feel self-conscious being the centre of attention, particularly with Wind Jackal's son, Quint, staring at her so intently. 'I didn't . . . I mean, I wasn't expecting . . .'

She looked down at the gold piece.

'Of course you weren't,' said Wind Jackal.

'Maris,' said her father, 'Wind Jackal and I have some important business to attend to. I wonder if you'd be so good as to entertain our young guest here.' He paused. 'His name is Quint.'

'Quint,' said Maris slowly, pretending that she was hearing it for the first time. She glanced at him quickly. His eyes, she noticed, were not black, but rather a deep indigo, like the darkest storm clouds that sometimes swirled in from beyond the Edge. 'You'd better come with me, then,' she said.

As the two of them disappeared into the building, Wind Jackal turned to Linius. 'She is growing up to resemble her mother closely,' he said softly.

Linius nodded sadly. 'I confess that sometimes I find it difficult even to look at her. And it isn't just her appearance . . . The way she purses her lips. The way she chews the tips of her hair. I mean, how is it possible that she should have the mannerisms of a mother she never even knew?' He shook his head.

Wind Jackal placed his hand on Linius's shoulder. 'Do not forget, my friend,' he said, 'I, too, have had my share of loss.'

Linius swallowed guiltily. 'Forgive me,' he said. 'I've had a lot on my mind. I did not intend to be so thoughtless . . .'

Wind Jackal nodded. 'It hasn't been easy,' he said.

'I'm sure it hasn't,' said Linius. 'That's what I want to talk to you about. Please sit.'

The sky pirate captain took a place beside the Most High Academe on the wrought ironwood bench at the edge of the balcony. The shadows of the neighbouring towers fell across them, deepening the mood.

'Losing your family like that must have been hard, Wind Jackal,' Linius said.

'It was, Linius, it was,' said the captain. 'But I saved one – and I haven't let the lad out of my sight since. The pair of us travel everywhere together. Quint and me, and the *Galerider* . . .' He paused.

'I have a great favour to ask of you, old friend,' said Linius. He rubbed his injured leg tenderly.

'Anything, Linius. You know that. Just ask.'

'This leg of mine,' said the Most High Academe. 'It's brought home to me the fact that I can't do everything myself. I have important work. Difficult work. And I need help with it.'

'I'm just a sky pirate captain,' laughed Wind Jackal. 'But anything I can do for the Most High Academe of lofty Sanctaphrax, I do willingly.'

'You can give up your son to me,' said Linius, quietly.

Wind Jackal stood up abruptly. 'Quint?'

'I need an apprentice,' Linius continued hurriedly. 'Someone I can trust to help me. You don't know Sanctaphrax like I do, Wind Jackal. It's a treacherous place. I cannot share my Great Work with an academic who would smile to my face and then betray me behind my back. I need a Deepwooder. Someone young, agile, eager to learn. I need a sky pirate's son as my apprentice.'

'This is quite a shock,' said Wind Jackal, sitting down again. 'After losing his mother and the young'uns on that terrible night, the thought of losing Quint . . .'

'You wouldn't be losing him, Wind Jackal, old friend,' said Linius reassuringly. 'He'd be with me, the Most High Academe of Sanctaphrax. He'd live here in the palace, be educated at the Fountain House with my own daughter and perform certain simple duties as my apprentice. Why, who knows? A fine lad like Quint – in due course, he might even secure himself a place in the Knights' Academy.'

'Yes, well, I don't know about that,' said Wind Jackal, who understood all too well the perils of life as a knight academic. His eyes moistened. 'I couldn't bear it if . . .'

'Wind Jackal, my old friend,' said Linius, taking him warmly by both hands, 'Quint will be safe here. Nowhere in all of the Edge could be safer. While the lad is in my charge, not a single hair on his head will come to harm. I give you my word.'

'A word I trust as much as my own,' said Wind Jackal. He smiled. 'You are offering my son a fine opportunity, Linius. I won't stand in the lad's way.'

'Thank you, old friend,' the professor said warmly. 'You don't know how much this means to me.' He cocked his head towards the open balcony-doors, from where the low buzz of conversation was coming. 'He seems to be making himself at home already.'

'Put it back!' Maris snapped.

Quint turned the curious yellow crystal over and over in his hand. 'But what *is* it?' he persisted.

'It's a sky-crystal, if you *must* know,' said Maris impatiently as she snatched it from his hand. 'My father created them in his laboratory.'

'He must be very clever,' said Quint.

'He is.' Maris sniffed. 'Recognized by all in Sanctaphrax as the most brilliant academic of his generation. That, after all, is why he was made Most High Academe.' She returned the crystal to its place in the mosaic. 'Please don't touch anything again,' she told him primly. 'I am making this picture for my father. On my own.'

Quint shrugged. He didn't like the bossiness in her voice, or the fact that she clearly thought herself superior to him. But he said nothing. *Better answer with silence than with indignation*, as the saying went. And while Maris continued to select the beautiful crystals and slot them into place, her back turned pointedly towards him, he wandered off to look round the rest of the room by himself.

When he'd first come in through the balcony-doors, it had been too dark to see properly. A 'chamber', the Most High Academe had called it – and that was what he'd expected to see. Somewhere small, somewhere cosy.

Yet now his eyes had become accustomed to the curious shifting shadows, Quint found himself standing in a vast hall with tall pillars, lofty arches and magnificent crystal chandeliers. And though there were indeed a few armchairs and hanging-sofas clustered round a rug at the far end of the room beside a cavernous fireplace where a tiny lufwood stove burned, they looked ridiculously small and out of place, and served only to emphasize the grandeur of the great stately room.

He was about to ask Maris more about the exact function of this curious Palace of Shadows when a voice piped up from the hanging-sofa in front of him. 'It's rude to stare!' it said.

Quint started back. 'I . . . I'm sorry, I didn't know anyone was there,' he said. He peered into the shadows and saw a short, roly-poly creature – a woodtroll, by the look of her – sitting on a hanging-sofa, her stubby legs sticking out before her.

He stepped forwards and held out his hand. 'My name is Quint,' he said, and added formally, 'I am honoured to make your acquaintance.'

Welma giggled as she put her embroidery aside and jumped down onto the floor. 'The honour is all mine,' she replied as etiquette demanded, and shook his hand. 'My name is Welma Thornwood.' She smiled. 'It is a long time since I have come across a youth with such fine manners.'

'Then it must be a long time since you came across the son of a sky pirate captain,' said Quint, glancing round to see whether Maris was listening. She should know she wasn't the only one with an important father.

'A sky pirate captain,' said Welma, clearly impressed.

'The bravest, the finest and the noblest sky pirate captain who ever took to the sky,' said Quint.

Poised over the mosaic with a piece of red crystal in her hand, Maris groaned. It was bad enough having been asked to entertain such an obvious roughneck in the first place, but for Nanny to be taken in by a couple of oily phrases! Couldn't she see how rough he was underneath? How uncouth? How . . .

'Oh, is that a wood-lemkin?' she heard Quint exclaim, and turned to see Digit leaping down from the chandelier and onto the back of Welma's hanging-sofa.

'Why, don't you like them?' Welma asked. 'I can tie her up if you'd prefer.'

Maris held her breath. Could this be a chink in the youth's otherwise impenetrable armour? she wondered.

Of course it couldn't! With a broad grin plastered across his face, Quint reached a hand out towards the screeching creature and rubbed his thumb and fore-fingers together. Instantly soothed, the lemkin jumped up into his arms and began purring with pleasure. Her hopes dashed, Maris turned away petulantly.

'I love lemkins,' Quint was saying, 'and this one's an absolute beauty. Does she have a name?'

'Digit,' said Welma.

Quint smiled down at the creature and tickled it behind the ears. 'You like a good tickle, don't you, Digit? Oh, yes, that's *nice* ...' The lemkin went helplessly floppy and purred all the louder.

Maris scowled. First her nanny. Now her pet. She just wished that Wind Jackal and her father would hurry up and finish their business and the sky pirate captain would take his horrible son and go. At the other end of the room, Welma was having other ideas.

'If you're staying,' she said, 'I'll see about some refreshments. What do you fancy?'

Quint looked up. 'Anything at all,' he replied. 'Except for one thing. Pickled tripweed. I know it's a woodtroll delicacy but I'm afraid I can't stand the stuff.'

'What a coincidence,' Welma laughed. 'Neither can Maris.' She bustled off and, as she reached the door, Digit leapt down from Quint's arms and scampered after her. 'It's her tea-time, too,' she said. 'I shan't be long. Just you make yourself at home.'

With Welma and the pet lemkin gone, the huge hall fell into awkward silence. Quint paced over to the walls to have a closer look at the inlaid panels. The footfall of his boots echoed eerily.

Maris wanted to abandon her mosaic work for the day. The fading light was making it difficult for her to see the exact shades of the sky-crystals. But if she gave up now, she'd have no option but to talk to Quint – and she had no intention of doing that.

Unaware of Maris's irritation, Quint stopped by the walls and traced his fingers lightly over the intricate marquetry. Each of the panels was decorated with delicate patterns picked out in different coloured woods. Twists and coils and plaits were carved into the timber in great interlocking swirls and raised lattice-work sections, each one cornered with curlicues and containing complicated and unfamiliar emblems. A flower and coiled rope. Three crossed ladders. A series of concentric circles split up by a seven-pointed star . . .

The panelled wall was quite unlike anything Quint had ever seen before. 'It's amazing,' he whispered softly.

'It's amazing ... amazing ... zing...' his echo repeated excitedly.

Maris could bear it no longer. Spoiling her afternoon was one thing, but so obviously enjoying himself was quite another! There he was, all bluster and rough edges. He'd come in, ruined her mosaic, spellbound Welma, bewitched Digit ... She groaned angrily.

Quint spun round. 'Are you all right, Maris?' he asked.

'Yes, I ...' she began, embarrassed by the concern in his voice. 'Just clearing my throat,' she said, and did it again. 'The echo makes it sound worse than it is.'

Quint nodded. 'It's the best echo I've ever ... HEARD!'

HEARD ... HEARD ... *heard* ... heard ...

The pair of them burst out laughing, and the sound of their laughter mingled with all the other noises as Quint crossed the hall to the table where Maris was still working on the mosaic. He put his hands up defensively.

'I won't touch,' he said. 'Promise!'

'I should hope not,' said Maris with mock severity.

Quint frowned. 'Can you actually see *any*thing?' he asked.

'It is a bit dark,' Maris conceded. 'The thing is, I promised my father I would complete it for him as soon as possible.' She looked up at Quint. 'You couldn't light my lamp for me, could you?' she asked. 'Only I'm not allowed to.'

'Me?' Quint gulped and, for a split second, Maris saw fear – raw and blind – flash across the young sky pirate's face. The next moment, he was in control once more. 'Light your lamp?' he said jauntily. 'Yes, I can do that.'

Maris looked at him closely. Even in the shadows, his skin was glistening with sweat. 'If it's too much trouble, then don't bother,' she said meanly. 'Welma will be back in a moment.'

'It's fine,' said Quint. 'How does she do it? Fire-sticks? Flint-flames?'

'She usually takes a piece of flaming wood from the stove,' said Maris. 'The tongs are on the hook.'

Quint nodded, grabbed the lamp and turned away. Face set grimly, he crossed the floor to the little stove standing in the middle of the huge fireplace. His heart was thumping. His legs felt like lead. Out of the corner of his eye, he thought he saw something glinting scuttle across the floor – though when he looked, there was nothing there.

The lufwood was burning well; deep purple and very hot, it bounced around buoyantly inside the stove. Trembling uneasily, Quint placed the lamp down on the floor. Then he unhooked the tongs, crouched down and flipped the front catch of the stove up. The iron and glass door swung open and Quint was struck in the face by a blast of scorch-ing air.

'It's all right,' he whispered to himself. 'The f . . . f . . . fire's *in* the stove. Don't panic. J . . . J . . . . Just reach in with the tongs, take out a single piece of burning wood and light the lamp. You'll be f . . . fine, Quint. Absolutely fine . . .'

On the other side of the room, Maris's brow furrowed with consternation. The curious echoes and acoustics of the vast room being what they were, she had heard every faltering word. For whatever reason, Quint was clearly petrified of fire. Perhaps she'd gone too far.

Suddenly, she found herself running towards him. 'It doesn't matter,' she shouted out. 'Quint, leave it!'

But by then, Quint was already pulling a length of burning wood from the stove. His sweaty hands were shaking so badly he could barely maintain his grip on the tongs. And when Maris cried out, her booming voice gave him such a jump that he let go of them completely.

The tongs clattered to the hearth. The burning lufwood log, however, neither fell nor flew away. Half burning, half smouldering, it hovered in mid-air inches away from Quint's eyes.

Mesmerized, he stared at it in horror, unable to move, unable to cry out. Fire. Fire! He could see the white-hot flames, coming closer. He could feel them getting hotter. He could smell that terrible stench once again. He could *taste* it. Burning hair, burning flesh. And he could hear it all. The hiss and crackle. The screaming, screaming, screaming . . .

'No! It mustn't happen again!' he cried out, and before Maris knew what he was doing, he had reached forwards and seized the burning log in his left hand.

'Quint!' she shrieked. 'What are you doing? Don't be a . . .' Quint thrust the log back into the stove and slammed the door shut. Maris swallowed. '. . . a fool,' she finished weakly.

At the same moment, the door behind them opened. Both Maris and Quint spun round guiltily. Welma was standing in the doorway, a laden tray in her hands. Digit jumped down from her shoulder and bounded towards them.

'I thought you could have toasted oakbread with hyleberry jam,' she said, as she pushed the door shut with her foot. 'With some hammelhorn curds and syrup for . . .' Her brows lowered. 'What *have* you two been up to?' she said suspiciously.

'N . . . nothing,' said Maris.

Welma sniffed the air. Her rubbery button nose twitched. 'Lufwood and . . . who's burned themselves?' she said sharply. 'Come on, show me.'

Quint held out his upturned hand. There were angry red sores and frayed blisters on his fingers and his palm.

The soft pad of his thumb looked particularly raw.

Maris gasped and bit into her lower lip. Welma put the tray down, seized the pot of hyleberry jam and dolloped a huge spoonful into Quint's hand. Quint looked at Maris, his eyes asking her whether the old woodtroll had gone completely mad.

'Jam, Nanny?' said Maris.

'*Hyle*berry jam,' said Welma, as she smoothed the sticky yellow substance over the burns. 'Hyleberry *salve* would be better, of course – but I dare say a little bark-sugar won't do any harm. There,' she said at last. 'Now if we wrap this napkin around it . . . So.' She looked up. 'It'll be as right as rain by the morning.'

'I give you my heartfelt thanks,' said Quint politely.

But Welma was no longer in any mood for his fancy words. 'And I'll give you a heartfelt kick up the back-side if I catch you playing with that stove again!' she said sternly.

'He was only trying to light my lamp for me,' said Maris.

'Ay, well, leave things to those who can,' said Welma. She stood up. 'I'd better fetch another pot of jam, then I'll – *I'll* – see to the lamp. Is that understood?'

'Yes, Nanny, Welma,' Maris and Quint chorused.

Only when she was out of the room did Maris turn to Quint. 'What happened?' she said. 'What did you see?'

'See?' he muttered.

'When you were staring at the burning wood.'

Quint shook his head, unable to speak. He took a deep breath, and swallowed away the lump in his throat. 'I was once in a fire,' he began. 'A terrible fire.'

'I didn't know,' said Maris in a quiet voice.

'The Great Western Quays fire,' said Quint. 'It was no accident. It began in my house. My father's quarter-master, Smeal, decided it was time to become captain of the *Galerider*. He set the house ablaze. My father was away, but . . .' His voice broke. 'My mother, brothers . . . our nanny . . .'

'I'm so sorry, Quint,' said Maris.

'I escaped across the rooftops,' Quint continued. 'I always had a head for heights. But I couldn't save them . . . I . . . couldn't . . .' Quint put his head in his hands, his voice sob-cracked and small. 'The fire . . . the smoke . . . the heat . . .'

Maris stared at him. She was beginning to under-stand just how brave he'd been to agree to light the lamp, to put his hand inside the stove, to grasp the burning log . . . A rather alarming thought suddenly struck her. All the things he'd done, he'd done them for her.

Maris tingled uneasily inside. With her father acting so oddly of late, she already had enough on her plate to contend with. She glanced up at Quint, still shaking from his ordeal, and sighed. The sooner Wind Jackal came and took him away, the better.

The lamps and torches had *all* been lit by the time Wind Jackal and Linius Pallitax finally re-entered the balcony-chamber. Night had fallen and a chill, spiralling breeze was giving the crew of the *Galerider* a hard time keeping her stationary above the balcony of the Palace of Shadows.

'There's a storm brewing,' said Wind Jackal.

'A sleet storm,' said Welma Thornwood, pulling a face. 'I can feel it in my joints.'

'Then we must conclude our business as soon as possible, so that Wind Jackal can depart,' said Linius, plucking at his fingers nervously. 'Sit down, everyone, please. I have something to announce.'

Maris and Quint sat down on adjacent chairs, with Quint taking care to keep his makeshift bandage hidden – there would be time for explanations later. Welma sat back in her hanging-sofa, the lemkin on her knee. The sky pirate captain stood behind Linius, who cleared his throat.

'Wind Jackal and I have made a decision,' he said. 'Quint is to be enrolled in the Fountain House. He will study skylore and cloudcraft; he will learn the rudiments of mistsifting, windgrading, raintasting, fogprobing . . . His schooling is to commence tomorrow morning . . .'

'But, but . . .' Quint objected. He leapt to his feet, red-faced and flustered.

'Don't interrupt,' said Wind Jackal sharply.

'Maris will be responsible for showing him the ropes,' Linius continued, and shot his daughter a warning glance that *she* was not to interrupt either.

'But, Father,' Quint shouted, 'an academic life is not for me . . .'

'You need an education, lad,' said Wind Jackal

gruffly. 'You'll thank me for this one day.' His eyes
darkened. 'By Sky, if I'd had the chances I'm giving
you . . .'

'But I don't want . . .'

'And then, as my apprentice, there are the little tasks
that I will be asking you to do,' Linius butted in.
'Perform them well, and there could be a place for you
in the Knights' Academy.'

'No, no, *no*,' said Quint firmly. 'That's not what I
want. Father,' he said, turning to Wind Jackal, 'I'm a sky
pirate. Like you. Like Grandfather. And . . . And . . .'
Maris watched his lower lip trembling. All at once he
was racing across the floor to his father, arms open
wide. 'I don't want to be separated from you,' he
wailed.

'It won't be permanent,' said Wind Jackal, his own
mouth tugging at the corners with emotion.

'But we've been good together, haven't we?' Quint
persisted. '*Haven't* we? Sailing the skies together. You
and me . . .' He swallowed. 'You're the
only one I've got left!' he sobbed.

'Quint!' said Wind Jackal.
'You're to stop this.' He placed
his hands on his son's shoulders and looked him in
the eye. 'You're shaming us
both,' he said quietly.

Quint sniffed and
wiped his nose. 'I'm
sorry, but . . .'

'It's not going to be easy for me either,' Wind Jackal continued. 'I've come to depend on your cool head, your bargaining skills . . .' He paused. 'Besides,' he went on, his voice now little more than a whisper, '*you* are the only one *I've* got left.'

Linius, who hadn't managed *not* to hear what was being said, stepped forwards and stopped before them, resting against his stave. 'Quint, Wind Jackal,' he said, looking from one to the other. 'While Quint is here, he will be like my own son.' He smiled. 'What more can I say?'

'There is nothing more *to* say,' said Wind Jackal. He hugged his son, Quint, one last time, before letting go and marching stiffly back across the room to the balcony-doors. His elbow caught on one of the lacy curtains as he strode through the doorway. He did not look back.

Maris shivered unhappily. Things were not working out at all the way she'd hoped. By now, Quint should be gone. Instead, he had been left behind in Sanctaphrax to take up a place at the Fountain House school – and as if that wasn't bad enough, *she* had been put in charge of his well-being. She snorted with irritation. It just wasn't fair.

·CHAPTER THREE·

THE GREAT LIBRARY

Quint put his pen down and listened. Yes, there it was again. A howling and shrieking, discordant, distant – but coming closer, and closer, till the air was throbbing with the terrible noise.

'What *is* that?' he muttered. He glanced over at the tiny window. There was only one way to find out.

Scraping his chair back on the wooden floorboards, Quint jumped up, knocking the barkscrolls he'd been reading to the floor, and hurried across the room. As he flung the window open, what had been a raucous noise abruptly became a deafening cacophony. What was causing it?

Quint thrust his head through the small window as far as it would go and craned his neck backwards. A blizzard? he thought, surprised by the sight of the snowy banks of whiteness swirling round in the air. In such warm weather? And making so much noise? Then, catching sight of the gleaming eyes and glinting talons, he realized that it was a blizzard not of snow, but of feathers.

'White ravens!' he gasped. 'Hundreds of them.'

Of course, when in Undertown, he had seen the white ravens flocking before. Their eerie flights alerted the academics of Sanctaphrax that the flight-rocks in the Stone Gardens were ready to be harvested. Everyone knew that. But he'd never been so close before, nor heard them so loud. Even now, as they came spiralling down, down out of the sky, they were still maintaining their ear-splitting screech. Easing his feet off the ground, Quint squeezed himself a little further out of the window and twisted round until he was lying out across the sill.

He watched in awe as, in a great feathery drift, the flock of ravens came in to land on the roof of the Observatory.

'Incredible!' he murmured. 'Quite . . . *Ouch!*'

Something hard and bony had taken hold of his ankle, and was wrenching at it painfully.

'*Ow!*' he cried – though nowhere near loud enough to be heard above the din of the ravens. He kicked out with his feet. 'Get off me.' He wriggled awkwardly back-wards. The bony pincer-like objects suddenly grasped both his ankles.

'Maris,
if that's you,
I'll . . . *whooaah*,' he
groaned, as he found
himself being pulled back
into the room. The next
moment, the back of his head
knocked sharply against the edge of the
sill on its way down to the floor, which it
struck with a loud *crack*!

'*Unkhh!*' he groaned.

His ankles were released and his legs crashed down.
His eyelids fluttered, opened. The room gradually stopped
leaping about. 'You!' shouted Quint. 'Why in Sky's name
did you do that?'

'A thousand apologies,' said Tweezel, bowing stiffly. 'I
did not mean . . . That is, I thought you were in danger.'
He trilled with agitation.

Quint rubbed his head and winced theatrically. 'I'll be
fine,' he said.

'That is just as well,' said Tweezel, 'for I have been
requested to convey the following summons of atten-
dance by my master, who is also your professor and
who, as such . . .'

'What?' said Quint sharply.

The spindlebug solemnly closed the window to muffle the shrieking din of the white ravens. 'The Most High Academe wants to see you.'

'Now?' said Quint, climbing unsteadily to his feet.

'No,' said Tweezel. 'Fifteen minutes ago. Urgent, he said it was. *Extremely* urgent.'

Quint hurried towards the door. Over the last week he had heard, if not seen, just how angry the Most High Academe could be when kept waiting. He was just about to leave his room when Tweezel laid a pincer on his shoulder.

'Just one thing, young apprentice,' it said.

'Yes?' said Quint.

'The Most High Academe hates to be kept waiting.'

With his poky little garret a narrow staircase up from the vast balcony-chamber, and the Most High Academe's study two storeys below that, Quint hurtled down the stairs in twos and threes. He didn't want to be even later than he already was.

'Ah, there you are, lad,' said Linius, looking over his shoulder as, hot and breathless, Quint knocked and poked his head round the open door of the professor's study. 'Come in. Come in.'

Quint entered the room. He was relieved to find that the Most High Academe, who was seated on a tall battered stool at a cluttered desk overflowing with charts and scrolls, seemed in a better mood than he'd anticipated – although he looked strained and tired. Quint hadn't yet discovered that Tweezel would always lie about the time, so that those he was called to summon were always on time.

'And close the door,' Linius added. His voice dropped to an urgent whisper. 'I don't want a single word of what I'm about to say to go beyond these four walls. Is that understood?'

Quint nodded calmly as he pushed the door shut, but inside his heart was racing. What *was* the professor about to say?

The professor swivelled round completely. 'So, Quint,' he said, 'how are you finding Sanctaphrax?'

'It . . . it . . .' he said, at a loss to know where to start. Everything was so bewilderingly different from what he was used to on board the *Galerider* – from the unspoken, yet rigidly upheld, pecking-order of the steamy refectory to the intrigue, whispers and lies that took place on the Viaduct Steps. And then there was the Fountain House school: the archaic rules he inadvertently kept breaking in Wilken Wordspool's classroom – and the lessons themselves, so long, so repetitive, so tedious . . .

Just then, the white ravens outside, who had been silent for a while, started up once again. His words were lost to their raucous clamour.

'What was that?' the professor shouted back, his hand cupped to his ear.

'Noisy!' Quint shouted back. 'I find Sanctaphrax very noisy.'

'I agree,' Linius nodded earnestly. He stood up and, limping slightly, crossed to the windows and closed them all. 'Shamefully noisy for a so-called place of learning, I would say.' He turned and smiled. 'How would you like to go to the quietest corner in all of Sanctaphrax?'

'I think I should like that very much,' said Quint.

'Very good,' said Linius. He plucked at his fingers, making some of the joints crack. 'It concerns one of those *little tasks* I mentioned the day your father dropped you off here. Do you remember?'

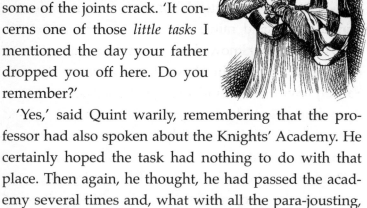

'Yes,' said Quint warily, remembering that the professor had also spoken about the Knights' Academy. He certainly hoped the task had nothing to do with that place. Then again, he thought, he had passed the academy several times and, what with all the para-jousting, pummelball, and one-to-one combat that was going on inside, it was probably the noisiest place in all Sanctaphrax.

'The place I want you to visit,' said Linius Pallitax, 'is the Great Library.'

Quint's brow furrowed. 'The Great . . .' He paused. 'I don't think I know where that is.'

'Very few academics do, I'm afraid. It was an ancient centre for earth-studies. These days it is most unfashionable. Nobody goes there any more,' said the professor, and tutted unhappily. 'Sky above, have we really come so far?' he murmured. 'Here I am, Most High Academe of a place where the very presence of the Great Library is ignored.'

The High Academe's eyes had a faraway look in them. He seemed to be talking to himself. 'Oh, it was a sad day indeed when the schism between earth-studies and sky-scholarship first occurred.' He glanced round nervously, as if worried that someone might be listening. 'Don't misunderstand me, lad. I am not saying that sky-scholarship is not invaluable. After all, were it not for the windtouchers and raintasters and, yes, the mistsifters also, we wouldn't know about stormphrax. And without stormphrax to weight down the floating rock, then Sanctaphrax itself would break its moorings and then everything would be lost. And yet . . .' his eyes misted over, 'the old scholars of earth-studies had accumulated so much knowledge . . .'

Quint listened closely, trying to take it all in.

'About the properties of plants, the qualities of minerals, the secrets of trees. And living creatures! They listed and sorted and classified and categorized the Deepwoods more precisely than even the Professors of Light and Darkness grade luminosity. And that's saying something, I can tell you!'

Quint looked suitably impressed.

'The problem, my lad, is that the knowledge they accumulated over the centuries is being lost. Despite my best efforts to revive it, earth-studies is ignored and the place where its wealth of information is stored – the Great Library – has been abandoned and left to fall into utter neglect. Even as we speak, the priceless barkscrolls and tomes it houses are crumbling to dust.' He sighed. 'And it is knowledge we cannot afford to lose . . .'

'Can't we go and tidy the place up a bit?' Quint suggested. 'Sort things out?'

'Oh, Quint,' said Linius wearily. 'You haven't a clue what you're saying. A hundred academics could work there for a thousand days and still barely scratch the surface.'

'Then, what do you want *me* to do?' said Quint.

Outside, the departing white ravens flashed past the windows. Agitated, the professor began plucking at his fingers again, one after the other. 'I want you to fetch me a barkscroll,' he said.

'Is that all?' said Quint, smiling.

The colour drained from the professor's face. 'This is no laughing matter, lad,' he said coldly. 'I would go myself, but my leg is still not up to it.'

'I'm sorry,' said Quint. 'I didn't mean . . .'

'I cannot impress upon you enough the importance of your task,' the professor continued. 'If you fail, then . . .' A shudder ran the length of his body. 'You must not fail.'

Quint nodded solemnly. Linius looked up to see the flock of white ravens, still streaming past his windows.

'Listen well,' he said. 'Tweezel will give you precise directions to the Great Library. Once inside, the layout is complicated to the uninitiated, but not impossible to negotiate. It is set out like a forest – filled with trees of knowledge, so to speak. Each tree has a core subject – *Aquatic Vegetation*, *Earth Organisms*, that sort of thing. You'll find the exact academic discipline on a small plaque nailed to the trunk. The core subject you are look- ing for is *Aerial Creatures*.'

'*Aerial Creatures*,' Quint repeated, committing it to memory.

'You are to climb into that tree,' said Linius. 'The higher you climb, the more branches you will come to. By following the words and symbols carved into the bark, you must climb up the relevant branches – each one representing a branch of the subject – until you home in on the barkscroll I need.'

'It sounds complicated,' said Quint.

'That is why you must listen carefully,' said Linius. As he spoke, the stragglers of the huge flock flapped past the windows and a plaintive cawing began. 'Oh, no,' he whispered nervously, 'I shall be late again.'

'Late for what?' asked Quint.

'As Most High Academe, it is my duty to bless the ritually purified academics who are about to harvest the flight-rocks,' he said. 'They may not go to the Stone Gardens until I have.' He wiped his sweating brow on his sleeve. 'So much to do and so little time,' he muttered and, once again, Quint couldn't help but notice how exhausted the Most High Academe looked.

'Then tell me exactly how to find this barkscroll,' said Quint. 'And quickly.'

'You must take what is known as the negative ascent,' the professor explained. 'At the first fork you will come to *bird* and *not bird*. Take *not bird*. At the second fork, *reptile* and *not reptile*. Take *not reptile*. At the third fork, *mammal* and *not mammal*.'

'And I take *not mammal*,' said Quint.

'Precisely,' said Linius. 'Do this so long as the option

59

allows. Then it becomes more tricky – and the branches rather slender – so do use the walkways and hanging-baskets provided. You need to find two twigs, one marked *legendary* . . .'

'Legendary,' said Quint.

'The other marked *celestial*.'

Quint nodded.

'Hanging from the point where these two cross, you will find the barkscroll I need.' He breathed out noisily. 'Now have you got all that?'

'I think so,' Quint said. '*Aerial Creatures. Not, not, not,* as far as I can go. Then *legendary* and *celestial*.'

'Well done,' said Linius. 'You make it sound easy. I only hope you don't find it too difficult in reality.'

'You can count on me,' said Quint confidently.

'I hope so,' said the professor darkly. 'As I said before, Quint, *you must not fail*. So, keep your mind on the task at hand at all times and do not let yourself be distracted.'

He turned and picked up his stave. 'Now, go, lad. And Sky speed be with you.' He sighed. 'I must go and see to my blessed academics.'

Head spinning with Tweezel's directions and the professor's instructions, Quint stepped outside the Palace of Shadows. It came, as it always did, as quite a shock to Quint when he stepped outside to find that it was still the middle of the afternoon – and sunny. Since the Palace of Shadows was completely surrounded by tall buildings which kept it in the shade, daylight was a constant twilight and even the sunniest day seemed overcast. As he emerged from the narrow alley onto the broad central concourse opposite the Central Viaduct, he had to raise his hand to shield his eyes from the dazzling sun.

'Which way?' he muttered, and answered himself in the same breath with Tweezel's words, 'At the southern end of the Viaduct Steps.'

A week earlier even this would have confused him, and he remembered how Maris had laughed at him when he'd headed in completely the wrong direction to the West Landing. The thing was, the compass directions of Sanctaphrax had been fixed before the floating rock had become buoyant. Now that the great rock was floating in mid-air and turning constantly, the so-called *southern* end could have been anywhere – except that Quint had recently learnt that the towering Loftus Observatory was at the southern end of the Central Viaduct, and it was that way he headed, skirting along its West Steps.

In the week he'd been in Sanctaphrax, Quint had learned a lot about the great floating city. His school day started at the unearthly hour of six in the morning, but finished at one, which meant that his afternoons were free. Every one, he had spent walking around, getting to know the various schools, colleges and faculties, familiarizing himself with its avenues and walkways; its bridges and landing-stages, large and small. The Viaduct Steps, in particular, fascinated him.

High above, the Central Viaduct itself was a magnificent structure, forming the main thoroughfare between the Loftus Observatory and the Great Hall. Lined by some two hundred small towers of the lesser academic faculties – anything from bark-reading to moon-chanting – it stood astride twenty-four mighty pillars. Beneath and between these were the Viaduct Steps, east and west sloping.

At first, Quint had paid little attention to the shifting groups of clustered academics on the marble steps. But as the days passed, he started to notice the same characters in the same places doing the same things, and began eavesdropping on their conversations.

The twelfth West Steps, for instance, was the place where young apprentices would furtively swap exam papers and gossip about their professors. The eighteenth, in contrast, was a place where academics with a grievance would air them publicly, and often to a huge audience. While on the other side, the eighteenth *East* Steps hosted fromp-fighting and illicit gambling . . .

On this particular afternoon, however, with the urgency of the Most High Academe's instructions still

ringing in his ears, Quint did not dawdle – tempted
though he was. He hurried on past staircase after staircase of feverish activity without once pausing, round the
base of the Loftus Observatory, and stopped in his
tracks. His jaw dropped.

How in Sky's name did I miss *that*? he wondered, staring at the vast wooden structure before him. He noted
the simple design: a low circular wall surmounted by a
tall fluted roof like a giant umbrella, all topped off with
a modest observation tower. Unlike its tall, showy neigh-
bours – which, in every way, put the ancient library into
the shade – it simply did not stand out.

Quint crossed the shadow-filled square and disappeared into the still deeper shade beneath the great
roof. No-one noticed him walk round the curving wall or
stumble across the concealed door. And no-one saw him
enter.

'Wow!' he gasped. If the outside of the Great Library
had surprised Quint, then the inside left him utterly
breathless. It was vast, yet deserted. It was cool and
silent. It smelled faintly of pine-sap with an ominous
hint of leaf-mould. It was like nothing he had ever ex-
perienced before.

The 'trees' that Linius had described were massive
vertical columns of wood set into the packed-earth floor,
with pegs up their sides to serve as hand- and footholds;
the 'branches' were an intricate system of arches and
cross-beams far, far up above his head. There were plat-
forms and decking attached to the trunks at various
heights, and ladder-ways and pulley-ropes with

THE GREAT LIBRARY

hanging-baskets connecting one tree to another. And suspended on wires from the 'twigs' were the bark-scrolls themselves. Some hung individually, like leaves. Others hung in bunches, fifty or so at a time, in large holders. Some, having fallen away completely, had turned the floor into a scene reminiscent of the Deepwoods in autumn.

Quint crouched down, retrieved a scrap of barkscroll and unrolled it carefully on the ground. As he did so, he thought he saw several shining things – objects or crea-tures, it was not clear – gliding across the floor. But when he looked round, there was nothing to be seen.

Returning his attention to the barkscroll, he smoothed his hand over its leathery parchment surface and looked at it closely. The text – all neatly written in a minute, feathery script, and accompanied by annotated sketches and charts – concerned banderbears, or rather the pale *sytil* moss which grew in their thick fur and gave the huge lumbering Deepwoods-dwelling creatures their green hue. The detail was phenomenal.

'And this is just a scrap from one single barkscroll,' Quint muttered, amazed. 'One of countless thousands,' he added, looking up at the hanging holders. 'The sheer amount of knowledge! What an incredible place this Great Library is.' He climbed to his feet. 'But don't let yourself become distracted,' he reminded himself sharply. 'Just find the barkscroll the professor wants and get it back to him as soon as possible.'

This, he soon discovered, was much easier said than done. Not only were there more than a hundred of the

tree-pillars to check through, but the plaques which
differentiated them were written in a curling script
which Quint found almost impossible to decipher.

'S-o-c-i-a-l G-e-s-t – *Social Gestures*,' he said, tracing his
fingers over the unfamiliar letters. He moved on to the
next. *G*— No, *C-a-r-n* . . . *Carnivorous F* . . . *Flora*. And the
next. And the next. Gradually the letters became easier
to read. The *A*s were like *S*s, the *F*s were like *T*s, the *C*s
were like *G*s. He moved more and more quickly from
tree-pillar to tree-pillar, searching systematically for the
one core subject he had to find.

But as the time passed – half an hour, an hour, two
hours – Quint became more worried and his searching
increasingly frenzied. What if he'd somehow missed the
one he was looking for? What if he couldn't find it before
sundown? – there didn't seem to be any working lights
in the library.

The professor's doom-laden words echoed round his
head – *You must not fail!* – over and over, like the tolling
of a bell. But what if he *did* fail?

'Pull yourself together,' he told himself. 'It *is* here. And
I *shall* find it.' There were still ten tree-pillars to go. Quint
ran from one to the other reading off the plaques but, as
he feared, not one of them bore the name *Aerial Creatures*.
If his calculations were correct, then he was right back
where he'd started from.

He crouched down by the one in front of him. 'Yes,
that was the one,' he muttered to himself. '*Social Gestures*
. . . Except. Hang on a moment.' He leaned forwards for
a closer look. 'I don't believe it!' he exclaimed. 'This *is*

the one! *Aerial Creatures*. I can see it now. And to think that it was the very first one I looked at!'

Furious with himself for his mistake, yet relieved beyond words to have finally found the right tree-pillar, Quint wasted no time in scampering up the pegs. He was agile, with nimble fingers and an excellent head for heights. His burnt hand had healed well enough for him to climb with no discomfort and, having lived on a sky pirate ship for years – forever shinning up masts and negotiating sky-rigging – the ascent offered no difficulty. He was soon at the first fork.

'*Bird. Not bird*,' he read, the words carved into the wood in the same floral script.

As instructed, he chose *not bird* and continued. From this point on, although the climb was no longer vertical, because the pegs had stopped he needed to take great care not to slip and fall – especially since the light was beginning to fail.

Further up the professor's so-called 'negative ascent', the choices began to get weirder. At first, Quint gave it little thought, simply taking the *not* option each time, but it wasn't long before he was questioning exactly what sort of aerial creature the barkscroll dealt with. *Inevitable/not inevitable. Stable/not stable. Sane/not sane.*

'Unstable and insane,' Quint muttered uneasily, and he found himself wondering why the professor would want information on such an unpleasant-sounding creature. Did he have one? Did he want one? What type of a person *was* the professor anyway? And more important than any of these questions, where was the next *something/not something* to choose from?

Having fumbled about in the near darkness of the vaulting for the previous ten minutes without finding any trace of lettering carved into the bark, Quint was feeling worried. He was on a thin, almost horizontal branch, far, far above the library floor. Despite his natural agility, the situation was not good. Every time he moved, the branch swayed ominously. If it should break, he would tumble into the darkness to certain death below. He tried hard to remain calm.

'You must have reached the end of the negative ascent,' he told himself. He looked round awkwardly. In the darkness, he could just make out the shapes of various barkscrolls hanging around him. Some were on their own, some in the holders. As for finding which specific one the professor wanted . . . 'Find two twigs,' he had said. What were they again? *Legendary* and . . . and . . . and *what*? His head spun. His legs shook. He hadn't come so far to fail now – yet, try as he might, he could not remember . . .

'Blast,' he muttered and, though softly spoken, the word echoed round and round the circular building, desecrating the hushed stillness of the library before fading away. At the same time, the full moon appeared from behind the clouds and shone down through the windows of the crown-like tower above Quint's head. Light – wonderful silver light – flooded into the Great Library.

'*Celestial*,' said Quint happily. 'That was it. I . . .' As the narrow branch bucked and dived, he groaned queasily and clung on ferociously, his cheek pressed to the wood. Gradually, the swaying steadied. Quint looked round. Then up. Then down. 'Thank Sky for that,' he whispered.

In the silvery moonlight, Quint had seen that there was no longer any need for him to remain on the 'tree' at all. He was now up in the well-ventilated, pest-free environment – the air heady with the scent of pine-sap – where the barkscrolls hung. Here, where the librarians of old would have worked, were the ladder-ways and hanging-baskets on rope-pulleys which connected the trees, and gave access to the scrolls that he had seen from below.

With a sigh of relief, Quint edged back a little and lowered himself down into the nearest basket. A cloud of dust sparkled in the moonlight as it sprinkled down from the rope it was suspended from.

By tugging on the pulley-rope, Quint pulled himself further along, checking every twig-like protuberance he passed, as well as the occasional barkscroll. The fact was, the further he went and the more he saw, the greater his curiosity was becoming about these earth-studies academics who had devised such an intricate system of categorization *and* been fit and agile enough to use it. The search continued until, with a whoop of delight, Quint announced to the echoing air that he had found what he was looking for.

'*Legendary*,' he read off, 'and *celestial*.' He looked up and saw – just as the professor had said – that where the two of them crossed, a single barkscroll was hanging. Quint grinned. 'There you are!'

All those hours of searching, and finally he'd found what he was looking for. He tugged at the pulley-rope to manoeuvre himself forwards. The basket lurched, but stayed where it was. Quint pulled on the rope again, harder this time and, when that did nothing, once again. Still nothing.

'Cursed thing!' he muttered, and looked across at the barkscroll, so temptingly near.

'Maybe if I could just lean across . . .'

He climbed onto the edge of the basket and, support-ing himself on the attached rope, reached out. The gap was still too wide. Below him, the cavernous drop yawned. With his shaking hands shifting little by little along the rope, Quint stretched out still further. Closer and closer his fingertips came. They grazed the edge of the barkscroll, setting it turning.

'Just a little further,' he muttered.

The barkscroll continued to turn, infuriatingly slowly. Quint strained forwards, and waited for it to come right round. His eyes bulged, his arms shook, the tendons in his neck flexed. As the scroll came closer, he jerked for-wards. His fingers closed around the leathery tube. He'd got it. The barkscroll was in his grasp.

'Phew!' he whis-tled with relief, as he eased himself carefully back along the rope and dropped down into the basket. 'This place is lethal. It's . . .'

At that moment, there was a sharp tearing sound behind him. Quint spun round to see a knot of rope wedged into the pulley fraying, fibre by breaking fibre.

Within seconds the whole lot had taken on the appearance of a woodthistle's fluffy seedhead. Quint's elation turned to despair.

'Oh, no,' he muttered, his heart thumping in his ears. 'Oh, no.' He thrust the barkscroll down inside his shirt and clung on to the rope and the side of the basket. The last strands snapped. 'Oh . . . *Help!*' he screamed as the basket abruptly plummeted.

Down, down, down, boy and basket crashed through the branches, tearing the barkscroll holders from their moorings and sending the barkscrolls they contained fluttering off every which way. Then, twisting and turning, Quint lost his grip and tumbled out of the basket.

Falling! He was falling towards certain death . . .

. . . when all of a sudden and out of nowhere, a hand seized him round his wrist.

'Hold on!' a voice hissed close to his ear.

Quint tried in vain to crane his neck round to see who had rescued him. It was all happening too quickly. Yet he was aware of a dry, crackling sound and a ripe, juicy odour like the smell of rotting leaves. The next moment, he found himself being swung hard to one side.

Terrified, Quint screwed his eyes shut. For an instant he imagined himself to be back on board the *Galerider*, tossed about in a great storm. Then, with a jarring *thud*, he felt something solid beneath his feet and looked down to find he was on an aerial platform, high up in one of the trees.

But who had got him there?

Scrambling to his feet, Quint scoured the forest of tree-pillars for the character who had caught him as he fell. There was no-one there.

Quint frowned. 'You saved my life,' he murmured. He patted the rolled-up barkscroll, still safely tucked into his shirt, and grinned. 'In more ways than one.'

Although Quint knew he hadn't been quick, he had no idea just how long his task had taken him. By the time he reached the entrance to the Palace of Shadows, the new day had already broken and the far horizon was blushing pink and red.

He turned the great brass handle and pushed the heavy front door open. A mournful creak echoed round the hall. He stepped inside.

'Where have you been?' came a voice. He turned to see Maris standing in the centre of the entrance hall, hands on her hips.

'I . . . I was on an errand,' said Quint, 'for your father.' He reached down inside the shirt and pulled out the barkscroll. 'He asked me to fetch this for him.' He stepped forwards. 'I need to get it to him at once.'

'Oh, no you don't,' said Maris. 'You know how tired he's been looking.'

'But . . .'

'He was up working all night again,' she insisted firmly. 'He's absolutely not to be disturbed.'

'But, Maris!' Quint protested. He really couldn't make her out at all. Did she like him, or didn't she? Sometimes it seemed as though he couldn't do a single thing right.

'Just give it to me,' she said impatiently, her hand out-stretched. 'I'll give it to him the moment he wakes.'

Reluctantly, Quint did as he was told.

'Thank you,' said Maris primly. 'Now go and get washed and changed. You can't possibly come to class looking like that. Wordspool would throw a purple fit – and anyway, it reflects badly on my father and myself.'

'Class? Wordspool?' said Quint, confused. 'What time *is* it?'

At that moment, the bell at the top of the Great Hall chimed the three-quarters. 'A quarter to six,' said Maris. 'We've got fifteen minutes before school starts!'

CHAPTER FOUR

WELMA THORNWOOD

The kitchen was stiflingly hot. The air above the glowing cooking-range shimmered like water while the high vaulted ceiling was thick with swirling clouds of steam. Yet still Welma was not satisfied.

'More heat,' she wheezed as she pumped up and down on the stove-bellows, first with one foot, then with the other. Up down, up down. The compressed air hissed through the pipes. The fire roared.

Maris flicked away the hair which clung to her glistening brow and looked up. Having spent the whole morning cold and shivering in Wordspool's draughty classroom, she was now dizzy with the intense heat coming from the glowing stove. 'Does it have to be *so* hot?' she asked.

'If we . . . don't want our spiced scones to . . . end up like spiced stones,' Welma replied breathlessly. *'The hotter the fire . . .'*

'The lighter the dough,' Maris finished for her, and laughed. She'd heard the words on a thousand other

baking days. It was one of the many woodtroll sayings that Welma had brought with her from the Deepwoods, passed on – word of mouth – down countless generations. She'd been told it by her mother, who'd been told it by *her* mother, who'd been told it by *her* mother . . . and Welma – who had no young'uns of her own – had passed it on to her, Maris.

Welma looked round to see the young mistress perched on her step-stool at the round table, smirking from ear to ear. She tugged at her apron. 'Forgive me,' she said, 'but I thought you liked your scones crunchy on the outside and fluffy on the inside.'

'I do,' said Maris.

'And for that, we must do two things,' said Welma. 'One, ensure the oven is furnace-hot. And two . . .' Her gaze fell on the whisk idling in Maris's fingers. 'We must beat the mixture until it is frothy light.' Her eyes narrowed. '*Is* it frothy light?' she enquired.

Maris looked down into the bowl. The mixture slopped about in the bottom. 'Not quite,' she said, a little shame-faced.

'Then beat, child! Beat!' said Welma. 'While I see to the woodapples.'

Maris nodded, tucked the huge bowl into the crook of her arm and began whisking the creamy mixture furiously. Ever since she was little, of all the cakes, pastries and other assorted dough-bakes that Welma and she had made together, it was spiced scones that she liked most. Delicious on their own, with the traditional Wodgiss Night filling of woodapples steeped in honey and topped off with cream, they were sublime. It was Maris who had suggested they make some for Quint. Now, with her right arm aching and her left arm stiff, she was beginning to regret her generosity.

'So, how are you and the young sky pirate captain's son getting on, anyway?' asked Welma as she stirred the stewing woodapples.

Maris started. It wasn't the first time

she'd wondered whether her old nurse could read minds. If she hadn't already been so red in the face from the heat, she would have blushed with embarrassment. 'We're getting on all right,' she said.

'More than all right, if you ask me,' Welma persisted. 'After all, why else would we be making him Wodgiss spiced scones?'

Maris whisked the mixture more vigorously. Glops of it splattered down her front, on the table, on the floor. 'Like I told you,' she said, 'we're getting on all right.'

'Only you did say you thought he was a little . . .' Welma placed the lid back on the bubbling pot '. . . rough and ready.'

Maris snorted. 'Well, he is,' she said.

'Hmm,' said Welma thoughtfully. 'Your father certainly seems to think highly of him,' she added.

Maris's lips pursed. 'Does he?' she said, and began beating the mixture so violently that a huge dollop landed in her face. '*Ugh!*' she exclaimed and the bowl slipped from her arm and fell to the stone floor with a loud *clang*!

'NO!' Maris shouted and burst into tears. 'Oh, Nanny,' she sobbed. 'I'm hopeless! I'm useless! I can't do *anything* right!'

'Maris, my little sugar-dumpling,' said Welma, her face crinkling up with concern. She trotted across from the stove, wrapped her arms around Maris's waist and squeezed her tightly, warmly. 'There, there,' she whispered, as she reached up and wiped Maris's face clean with her apron. 'Don't fret so. It's only a bit of batter.'

'But I've ruined it,' said Maris. Scalding tears streamed down her cheeks. 'We're going to have to start all over again. Separating the snowbird eggs, sifting the barley flour, grinding the spices . . .'

Welma pulled away and glanced down at the floor. She shook her head. 'No we won't,' she said. 'Look!'

To her surprise, Maris saw that the ironwood bowl

had landed on its base. None of the mixture – frothy light as it was – had been spilt. She picked it up, placed it on the table and wiped her eyes.

'You see,' said Welma, taking Maris by both hands, 'things are never so bad as they first seem.'

Maris flinched. *Never so bad as they first seem*. The words echoed in her head. *Never so bad as they first seem*. She tore her hands away. 'No, they're not,' she laughed bitterly. 'They're worse! Far far *far* worse!'

'Why? How?' said Welma. 'What in Sky's name are you talking about, child? *What* is worse?'

'Everything!' wailed Maris. 'I mean, I try . . .' she sobbed. 'I try so *hard*. But Father never even seems to notice me. Whatever I do. I know it's not his fault. He . . . he spends so many hours on that Great Work of his, and – oh, Welma, I do worry about him so. He never even seems to sleep . . .'

Welma nodded sympathetically. She was only too aware of how much the young mistress worried about her father.

'And then *he* comes along. *Him!* That cocky little know-it-all son of a sky pirate, QUINT!'

'But you said you were getting on all right,' said Welma, patting her arm.

'We are,' said Maris. 'But now my father's got even less time for me. It's all "QUINT, can you do this? QUINT, can you do that?" ' She looked away. 'It's as if he'd rather have a son than a daughter . . .'

'That's *enough*, Maris,' said Welma sharply. She shook her head. 'All this carry-on! I mean, I'm not saying that the Most High Academe doesn't spend too much time on his work. He does. But that doesn't mean he loves you any the less. Work is work and family is family and . . .'

'And Quint is both!' she said. 'Work *and* family.'

'He's not,' said Welma.

'He *is*,' said Maris. 'Father includes him in everything. Sending him on errands, giving him tasks . . .' She looked up angrily. 'He's never given *me* a task!'

'He's made him his apprentice,' said Welma gently. '*That's* what apprentices do.'

'Yes, but what was it he told Wind Jackal?' said Maris, still fighting back the tears. ' "While Quint is here, he will be like my own son." *His own son!* You see! Work *and* family. He is both! And where does that leave me?'

'Maris, my treasure,' said Welma, 'if you don't mind my saying, you're sounding a bit jealous.'

'Jealous?' Maris stormed. 'Don't be ridiculous! Jealous of that oaf. I'm not jealous, I'm . . . I'm . . .' Her lower lip trembled. 'Lonely,' she said at last, her voice small and wobbly.

Welma shook her head sadly. 'Oh, Maris,' she whispered.

'I can't help it,' Maris blurted out. 'It's just the way I feel . . .'

'*What you feel is what you feel* – that's what we woodtrolls say.' She patted Maris on the shoulder. 'And *knowing* how you feel is the first step to *changing* how you feel,' she said. 'If you really want to.'

Maris shrugged. She still felt like crying. 'How can *I* change if nothing else changes?' she said. 'I mean, if

Father continues to work so hard and Quint takes all his attention the whole time . . .'

'Well,' said Welma, 'you must make things change.'

'How?' said Maris.

Welma's eyes twinkled. 'Let's look at this logically,' she said slowly. 'You feel your father ignores you. You can't seem to get close to him. And you're lonely. Quint, on the other hand, seems close to him, but is new here. He doesn't have any friends. I would think he was a little lonely himself. He probably needs someone his own age to talk to. So . . .'

'So, I ought to make friends with Quint?' said Maris.

Welma smiled. 'Let's just say that I don't think it's any bad thing us preparing delicious Wodgiss spiced scones for tea,' she said. 'So, come on then, Maris. You dollop out the mixture into the baking trays while I give the oven a final blast of the bellows, and . . .'

'And when they're in the oven,' said Maris.

'Yes?' said Welma.

'Can I scrape the bowl?' she asked.

Welma smiled so hard that her eyes disappeared and her button-nose creased back on itself. 'Of course you can, my little sugar-dumpling,' she said. 'Of course you can.'

In the upper gallery of the kitchen, far above the heads of the young mistress and her woodtroll nurse, stood a solitary figure, his head swathed in the clouds of steam. It was Quint.

Too tired after his long night in the Great Library to do any of Wordspool's homework, yet far too excited to sleep, he had taken to the palace corridors once again. The whole place fascinated him.

He'd just stumbled upon a music chamber. It was amazing. On the platform stood a klavinette – a keyboard instrument that seemed to produce sound by the internal plucking of its strings. Beside it were three chairs, each with a different instrument on it. One was a wind instrument, one was a string instrument, while the third was a combination of the two, with a bow leaning up against the back of a chair. It was made from the outer carapace of some giant barkbeetle, with a hollowed length of lufwood and woodcat gut. From what he could make out, it was designed to be bowed and blown at the same time.

What impressed Quint most was the fact that, thanks to the attentions of the faithful spindlebug Tweezel, the room was so clean. And not just clean – but *ready*. At any moment, that quartet of musicians could walk through the door, pick up their instruments and play as if nothing had ever happened.

And it was the same in the other rooms he stumbled across as he roamed the corridors, storey after storey, trying door after door. Room after room, each one lovingly tended to – yet so still, so unused.

There was the ground-floor Caucus Ante-Chamber – a wood-panelled room with leather chairs once used by the senior librarians who, following the death of the previous Most High Academes, would cluster together there until they had selected a new one. And on the third storey, the Gift Chamber where cavernous glass cabinets housed generations of officially received gifts – everything from a set of crystal woodgrog goblets to a stuffed and gilded banderbear. Further along the corridor was the Portrait Gallery with its paintings of Most High Academes – each one carefully dusted – stretching back down the centuries. Some were famous, like Ferumix the mathematician and Archemax, whose philosophical musings on light had once been considered heretical. Others were nonentities, forgotten even before the white ravens in the Stone Gardens had picked their bones and

set their spirits free.

Quint had stood looking at the portrait of Linius Pallitax for several minutes. It smelt of fresh paint and, from the dates on the plaque below, he could see that it was the first new painting to have been hung in decades – one more of the old traditions to have been reinstated by the current Most High Academe.

Certainly, the likeness was good; the hooked nose, the wispy beard and the ears, almost twisted at their tips, had all been faithfully reproduced. And as for the eyes, the artist had captured the expression in them perfectly – that sparkle of childlike eagerness, tempered by a haunted look of . . .

'What *is* that look?' Quint murmured. 'Weariness? Despair? Fear?' He shook his head. 'Or perhaps a combination of all three?' He sighed. 'But *you're* not going to tell me, are you?' he said to the portrait. 'I'll have to find out for myself.'

As Quint closed the door of the Portrait Gallery behind him, all thought of the Most High Academe vanished. The smell now filling the corridor was intoxicating. Sweet, fruity, laced with honey and spices – it reminded him so much of the oakapple cordial his mother had made all those years ago. Head raised and nose up, Quint followed the smell along the corridor, down the stairs, to the rear of the palace and through a small door . . .

'*Mmmm,*' he sighed. He had found the source of the mouthwatering smell. Clouds of it wafted round his head, billowing up from somewhere far below.

Quint walked forward to the stone balustrade and looked over. Between the clouds of steam, he could see several massive pieces of machinery. At first he thought he must have stumbled across some kind of workroom,

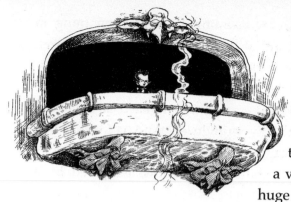

but a closer look revealed that – as the smell of cooking itself suggested – he was standing on the gallery above a vast kitchen. The huge machines were merely ovens, boilers and broilers, on a scale large enough to feed the army of academics and domestic staff who must once have filled the erstwhile Palace of Lights. Now, as the Palace of Shadows, the number it housed was down to five and, like so much else in this great building, the kitchen apparatus remained carefully tended but unused.

'But *someone's* cooking on *something*,' he murmured. He could smell the simmering oakapples. He could almost *taste* them.

Quint peered down. The steam was coming from directly below him. There must be a stove there, he thought, just out of sight – and he was about to move round to the other side of the gallery to check when . . .

'QUINT!'

Quint jumped.

'QUINT!'

The voice was coming from down in the kitchen. It was Maris.

'QUINT!'

There it was a third time. What had he done *now*?

He leaned over the balustrade and strained to hear what was being said. But it was impossible. He could just make out that she was talking to Welma – but the shouting was over now and their conversation no more than a murmured buzz.

Quint turned away, left the kitchen gallery and made his way back to his room. The anger and exasperation in Maris's voice when she had shouted his name had been unmistakable. 'She hates me,' he told himself flatly. 'It's the only answer. She hates me.'

He kicked the door to his bed-chamber shut and threw himself on the bed. 'Stuck-up little prig!'

'The thing is,' Welma was saying, 'as a Deepwooder, I must say that I'm all in favour of what your father is try-ing to do in Sanctaphrax. Those sky-scholars have got too big for their boots – what with their mistsifting and raintasting and big towers everywhere. Why, to listen to them you'd think the Deepwoods didn't exist. But they do, and there was a time when earth-studies mattered. The old librarians knew that, and so does your father . . .'

Maris listened, surprised, as she licked the whisk slowly clean. It was unlike Welma to mention the politics of Sanctaphrax, but ever since the trays had gone into the oven, she had talked non-stop.

'Oh, I accept that it can be handy to know when it's going to rain, but as a Deepwooder I know how im-portant it is to understand the properties of the creatures and plants of the Deepwoods,' she went on. 'To know what is and isn't edible, what should and shouldn't be

worn, what can and cannot be used for medicinal purposes . . . The librarians knew all about these things in
the old days. *Someone* has to prevent all the information
that has been accumulated over the centuries from
simply being lost.'

Maris nodded. She pulled the wooden whisk from her
mouth. 'I just wish that that *someone* wasn't my father,'
she said.

'I know, my treasure,' said Welma. 'He's taken a great
burden upon himself, that's for sure. And he's so determined to succeed that I fear for him.'

'What do you mean?' asked Maris.

Welma frowned. 'Do you remember that old story I
used to tell you?' she asked. *'The Tree That Said It Could
Fly.'*

A smile spread across Maris's face. 'I think so,' she
said.

'Tell it to me, then,' said Welma.

Maris laid the whisk down on the table. 'Well, it's
about a lufwood tree and a leadwood tree,' she said. 'The
lufwood tree keeps saying, "I shall fly, I shall fly, if it's
the last thing I do." And the leadwood tree keeps saying,
"Prove it!" '

Welma smiled and nodded encouragingly.

'The lufwood flaps its branches but it does not fly. It
spins its leaves but does not fly. It jiggles its roots but *still*
it doesn't fly,' said Maris. 'Then, just as the leadwood
tree is about to lose its temper with its boastful neighbour, the lufwood is struck by a bolt of lightning. It
bursts into flames and, being lufwood and buoyant

when on fire, it tears itself from the ground and rises up
into the sky.

' "I said I would fly," the lufwood calls down.

' "Yes, my friend," the leadwood calls back. "You said
you would fly if it was the last thing you did. And it is!" '
Maris looked up and smiled weakly. 'When I was small,
I used to think it had a happy ending,' she said. 'But it
doesn't, does it?'

'It depends how you look at it,' said Welma. 'The
lufwood's wish did finally come true.'

'Yes, but it was burning away to nothing,' said Maris.

'That's right,' said Welma. 'And do you remember the
moral of the story? *For in success can lie destruction.*'

Maris flinched. 'And you think my father is like that
lufwood. You think that he . . .'

At that moment, the heavy double doors to the kitchen
flew back on their hinges and crashed against the walls
behind them. Maris and Welma spun round to see Linius
Pallitax standing in the doorway.

His robes were dishevelled. His hair was matted. His
face was pale, drawn, puffy-eyed – and unmistakably
angry. 'Why did no-one wake me?' he demanded. 'I've
already missed most of the day.'

'B . . . but you were up all night,' said Maris nervously.
'You needed to sleep.'

'Even if it does mean turning nocturnal,' Welma
added wryly.

'When I want advice about when to sleep, I shall ask
for it,' he snapped. He looked round. 'Have either of you
seen Quint?'

'No,' said Maris. 'Not since . . .'

'Oh, for Sky's sake!' he roared. 'Do I have to do *everything* myself? I send him on an important, not to say urgent, errand – and what happens? He disappears!'

Maris frowned. 'Urgent?' she said. She fumbled in her side pocket for the rolled-up barkscroll. 'Is this what you need?'

Her father limped across the kitchen, snatched the barkscroll from her hands and opened it up. 'Yes,' he whispered. '*Yes!*' He turned on his daughter, eyes blazing. 'But why didn't Quint bring it straight to me?'

'Because . . . because I told him not to . . .' Maris stammered. Her face smarted, her eyes stung. 'You . . . you were asleep. I didn't want him to disturb you . . .'

'When did he arrive back?'

Maris hung her head. 'This morning,' she said, and swallowed. 'At about six hours.'

'Six hours!' he roared. 'Maris, this is absolutely in-tolerable! You must not interfere in matters you know nothing about . . .'

'But I only meant to . . .'

'Stop meddling in my affairs. Do I make myself clear?'

'Y . . . yes, Father,' said Maris, her voice breaking.

Without another word, Linius Pallitax turned on his heels and left. The double doors slammed shut behind him.

'You see?' Maris shouted, the moment he had gone. 'It's always the same. In his eyes, *everything* I do is wrong.'

'Oh, he didn't mean it, my sugar-dumpling,' said Welma. 'You could see how tired he looked. How out of sorts . . .'

'It's all that Quint's fault,' Maris went on bitterly. 'Bringing Father that wretched barkscroll. That's what upset him. That's what made him sh . . sh . . . shou . . .' She burst into racking tears. '. . . shout at me.'

'Come now, Maris,' said Welma softly.

But Maris was inconsolable. She pushed Welma aside and buried her head in her hands. With a slight shrug, Welma trotted over to the oven and opened the door. Maris heard her gasp, and looked up. Thick, black smoke was billowing from inside.

'We make a fine pair, we do,' said Welma. 'What with all this fuss and to-do, I forgot all about the scones.'

'They're ruined!' Maris howled.

'I could try scraping them,' Welma suggested.

'Throw them away!' said Maris. 'Quint doesn't deserve them anyway!'

Tears stinging her eyes, she ran from the kitchen and up the stairs. Tweezel was coming towards her, a tray held firmly in his translucent pincer-grip – but Maris ignored his respectful bow and brushed him roughly aside.

'Young mistress?' the spindlebug's creaky voice echoed round the stairwell.

Without hesitating, Maris rushed on – not to her bed-room – that would be the first place Welma would come looking for her, and she didn't want to be found – but to the balcony-chamber. Across the wooden floor she sped, behind the lacy curtains and out through the glass doors.

Panting with exertion, she stepped to the edge of the balcony and breathed in the warm, sticky air. To her right was the West Landing with its octagonal turrets; to her left, the Loftus Observatory, and below it – just visible through a narrow gap between the buildings – the Viaduct Steps, teeming with life.

'Sanctaphrax academics,' she murmured scornfully as she watched them. 'Like insects, scurrying here, scuttling there. Making alliances, breaking promises; plotting, scheming . . .' She sniffed and pushed her hair back out of her eyes. 'My father, Linius Pallitax, the Most High Academe of Sanctaphrax, is better than the whole lot of you put together.'

·CHAPTER FIVE·

THE VIADUCT STEPS

i
West Side: 18th Staircase

As the wind increased, a ridge of ribbed cloud sped in from beyond the Edge. The sky darkened. The air chilled. The lone academic with the wispy hair and wild eyes paused mid-sentence and wrapped his flapping gown around him. He straightened up and scanned his scanty audience with a dark, penetrating gaze.

'And worse than all that,' he repeated, 'is the food in the refectory. What exactly *is* being served from those great stew-pipes every day?'

'I dunno, but I'm sure you're going to tell us,' shouted a voice from the back of the small crowd and a group of mobgnomes began sniggering.

'They tell us it's tilder,' the academic continued undaunted. 'They tell us it's hammelhorn. They tell us it's snowbird. But I have it on the highest authority that it is none of these.' He paused for effect. 'I can tell you

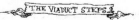
THE VIADUCT STEPS

now, that what we are being served daily is piebald rat, fresh from the sewers of Undertown.'

As one, the audience groaned. They'd heard it all before! If it wasn't piebald rats, it was muglumps from the Mire, or white ravens from the Stone Gardens – or some other creature considered equally inedible by all but the most barbaric citizens of Sanctaphrax. Once there had been rumours that even the recently deceased academics were ending up in the stew-pot. Disappointed that the speaker's revelations hadn't been more original, individuals in his audience began to drift away until only the heckling mobgnomes were left.

'I work in the kitchens,' one called out. 'I see the sides of meat coming in. Huge they are . . .'

'Have you seen the *size* of the piebald rats these days?' the academic countered.

'Rats don't have wings, neither,' shouted another.

'Down in the sewers, they come in all shapes and sizes,' the academic shouted back. 'Some have got two heads. Some have got lungs and live underwater. And some,' he announced triumphantly, 'have got wings.'

The mobgnomes looked at one another and shrugged. One of them screwed his finger into his temple. 'Sky-touched,' he muttered.

'As crazy as a square circle,' another added. 'The quality of speakers you get on the Viaduct Steps these days is really going downhill.'

They turned as one and trooped off together, ignoring the cries of the academic. 'Stop! Wait a minute!' he called after them. 'I haven't yet told you about the scandal of the Moon Observatory, or how the disappearance of seven fogprobing apprentices was hushed up – or what *really* goes on at the Convocation of Professors on Grey Thursdays . . .'

ii
East Side: 18th Staircase

Cursing the ranting buffoon behind him, Seftus Leprix moved away from the top of the Steps and headed down towards the raucous crowd. He needed to hear the odds and the form being called before finally placing a bet on one of the four fighting fromps.

'. . . and in the east corner, Bruto the Brave,' the fight-master – a swarthy lugtroll with a withered arm – was announcing as he scribbled on a blackboard. '4–1. In the west corner, Smarg the Mighty. 6–1. And finally, in the south corner, the current favourite, Magno the Claw. 3–1.'

All round the fight-master, a sea of hands reached towards him, each one clutching pieces of gold. 'Two on Bruto,' shouted one. 'Three on Magno!' demanded another.

Seftus Leprix smirked. If his insider information was to be trusted – and woe betide Jervis, his personal servant, if it was not – then the fromp to bet on was Wilbus the Sly in the north corner. Although untried and untested in Sanctaphrax, it had apparently won several vicious fromp-fights in the taverns of Undertown. And at 18–1, the odds were the best on offer.

With a brief flutter of his hands, he checked that his silver nose-piece was on straight. The ancient ceremonial object with its ornate curlicues and fine filigree mesh had formerly been worn by academics who, for purification purposes, wished to cleanse the air they inhaled. These days it was worn by academics who, for whatever reason, wished to conceal their identity. Seftus Leprix certainly did not want anyone to recognize him. After all, a fromp-fight was not the place for the Sub-Dean of the School of Mist to be caught spending his time and money. But then, old habits die hard.

He re-adjusted the silver nose, raised the hood of his gown and pushed his way through the crowd. 'Twenty on north,' he announced.

The gnokgoblin turned and looked at him from under lowered lids. 'Twenty, eh?' he said. For a moment, he hesitated; he did not as a rule conduct business with those whose faces he could not see. But then again, gold was gold. His hand darted forwards and seized the pouch of gold pieces being held out to him. He scribbled out a docket, returned it and turned back to the blackboard. The odds on the fromp in the north corner had shortened to 12–1.

When the bell at the top of the Great Hall chimed six times, the gnokgoblin closed the betting. The crowd fell silent. Seftus Leprix, who had remained near the front of the crowd, watched thoughtfully as the four fromps were uncaged. Although Wilbus the Sly looked younger than the others, what it lacked in size it more than made up for in naked aggression as it leapt about at the end of its leash – spitting, screeching, frothing at the mouth, trying desperately to get at the others.

'You *do* look fierce,' Seftus murmured to himself happily. 'And just as well, since it's too late to change my bet now.'

All four fromps were put on tethers, long enough for each of them to reach the fight-ring in the centre – but not so long that the creatures could get tangled up with one another. On their ankles now were razor-sharp spurs; on their prehensile tails, vicious spikes. Hunger and cruelty had turned the normally affable creatures into vicious killers and the fight would last as long as it took for one of the fromps to triumph over the other three.

'LET THE FIGHT COMMENCE!' the gnokgoblin roared, and lowered his raised arm.

Immediately, the air was filled with a cacophony of noise – wailing, screeching, howling. And that was just the spectators. Bruto the Brave from the east corner was the first to succumb as Magno the Claw's left spur sliced across its neck. The next moment, Magno's own neck was cut as Wilbus the Sly's tail-spike found its mark.

'Come on, Wilbus,' Seftus Leprix whispered as the vicious fromp turned its attentions on Smarg the Mighty from the west corner and the two of them flew at one another in a blur of bloodied fur and glinting blades.

The gnokgoblin scowled as Wilbus the Sly got the upper hand and glanced round furtively, as if he was preparing to bolt.

'Oh no you don't,' said Leprix, seizing the gnokgoblin by the scruff of his neck. 'You're not going anywhere.'

The pair of them watched the conclusion of the fight. It didn't take long. Within seconds, there was a howl of pain from the vanquished and a triumphant squeal from the victor. Wilbus the Sly had done it. Leprix brought his leering face up close to the gnokgoblin's.

'It's pay-up time,' he hissed.

iii
East Side: 9th Staircase

A slanting light fell across the ninth set of stairs of the east-facing Viaduct Steps, also known as 'the chankers'. This was the place where the sub-deans from all of the Sanctaphrax schools gathered together to discuss matters – for, with the complexities of their job, they had far more in common with one another than with others from the same school. The word itself came from an

ancient trog word, *shankir*, which was the name given to
the roosting grounds of the lesser woodowl – cunning
Deepwoods nightbirds that would, it was claimed,
gather noisily to plan their next hunting trip. Like the
woodowls, those academics who became sub-deans also
tended to be cunning, intelligent – and noisy.

'I see Seftus has decided not to attend once again,' the
Sub-Dean of the Raintasters commented.

'Too good for the likes of us,' said the Sub-Dean of
Cloudwatching.

'Like all those other confounded mistsifters,' the Sub-
Dean of Windtouching announced, and
sniffed. 'Ever since Linius Pallitax was
made Most High Academe,
they've been insuffer-
able.'

'And they've
been even
worse
since
Pallitax
moved
into the
Palace of
Shadows,'
a fourth
sub-dean
added.

'Lording it over the rest of us the whole time,' another complained. 'And the Most High Academe does nothing to stop it, despite all his fine words about how equal we all are.'

'Equal?' snorted yet another. 'That's a good one. The mistsifters get all the best preferments. They're all he cares about. The rest of us never get a look in.'

'It's iniquitous!' said the Sub-Dean of Cloudwatching.

'Invidious!' said the Sub-Dean of Windtouching.

'Something,' said the Sub-Dean of Raintasting darkly, 'must be done.'

iv
West Side: 12th Staircase

'Fifty gold pieces, and that's my final offer,' said the tall, bulbous-nosed apprentice.

'But, Skillix,' said the second apprentice, 'I told you, I haven't *got* fifty gold pieces.'

'Then stop wasting my time, *Runt*,' Skillix sneered and turned away.

Runnet winced. He hated his nickname. However, this was not, he realized, the time to complain about its use. With the important Mistsifting examination only two days away – and himself so ill-prepared – he needed all the help he could get. Skillix, he'd overheard, had come by a copy of the examination paper. If he could just get his hands on it, then he'd be able to prepare the answers

– and pass. If he didn't, he'd be thrown out on his ear. And if *that* happened, his father – a big name in the League – would disown him.

Runnet lunged forwards after the departing apprentice. 'Don't go!' he cried, clinging onto Skillix's robes.

'Get *off* me!' Skillix said, twisting round and swatting the young sub-apprentice away like a bug.

'You must let me have it,' Runnet persisted. 'You must . . .' He dragged a pouch from his pocket and jangled it loudly. 'Thirty-eight gold pieces there are here,' he said, 'and I can get you the rest next week.'

'The rest?' said Skillix.

'The other twelve gold pieces,' said Runnet. 'I'll . . .'

'Call it twenty and I might be interested,' Skillix interrupted.

Runnet's jaw dropped. 'Twenty?' he said. 'But you said . . . I can't . . . It's too much . . .'

'As you please,' said Skillix, and turned away again.

This time Runnet did not try to stop him. His eagerness to buy had alerted Skillix to the value of the paper he was trying to sell. They both knew that there were several apprentices in the School of Mist – apprentices with far more generous fathers – who would pay twice as much for the question paper once word got round that it was available. And, Runnet thought bitterly, word *would* get round.

'Oh, Gloamglozer,' he muttered miserably, and held his head in his hands. 'What in Sky's name am I going to do now?'

'So far as I can see, you have two choices,' came a deep, throaty voice from behind him.

He looked round to see a tall individual standing in front of him. He was dressed in ill-fitting academic's robes. A silver nose-piece could be seen glinting from within the folds of his baggy hood.

'Are you talking to me?' asked Runnet.

The academic glanced quickly over both shoulders, then nodded. 'I am,' he confirmed gruffly. 'I couldn't help overhearing all about your little . . . *difficulty*,' he said, 'and . . . that is . . . I am in a position to help you out.'

'You are?' said Runnet suspiciously. No-one did anything for anyone in Sanctaphrax without seeking something in return. He looked the academic up and down but, thanks to the false nose, was unable to place him, although there was something faintly familiar about the smell of tallow and woodcamphor coming from his robes.

'You are interested in the Mistsifting examination, are you not?' he said.

Runnet nodded. 'The final one,' he said.

'The very same,' said the academic, patting a pocket at his side.

Runnet gasped. 'You've got a copy of the question paper?' he said.

'Better than that,' said the academic. 'I've got the answers.'

Runnet was speechless. The *answers*! If he hadn't been able to afford the questions, then he certainly wouldn't have enough to buy the answers. If only he could . . . He looked up at the academic. 'H . . . how much are you asking for them?' he said, nervous of the answer.

'Thirty-eight gold pieces,' came the reply.

'Thirty-eight?' said Runnet excitedly. 'Yes, I can afford that. It's . . .'

The academic raised his hand. 'Thirty-eight gold pieces,' he said, his eyes narrowing, 'and a small favour.'

v

West Side: 24th Staircase

As the shadows grew longer and the lamps lining the Central Viaduct far above their heads were lit, the group of mistsifters on the twenty-fourth set of steps huddled closer together. Most of them were sub-acolytes and apprentices who, like sub-acolytes and apprentices all over Sanctaphrax, would gather to carp and complain about their professors. However, the presence of the school's dean, sub-professor and various readers, both senior and junior, lent extra weight to this evening's criticisms.

'He's so intent on *appearing* fair that he's forgotten all about us mistsifters,' one of the apprentices complained.

'Yeah,' said another, nodding vigorously. 'It's like he's going out of his way to prove that everyone's equal. Why, even that little scrot, Dervillus – you know, that *drizzle* character – has been promoted.'

'And since he's moved into that old palace, he's been even worse!' added a third.

'You're right,' said a fourth. 'I've even heard rumours that he's preparing to increase the power and influence of the Professors of Light and Darkness. And at *our* expense!' He glared round him. 'It's we mistsifters who should be up for preferments, not them!'

Runnet listened as a ripple of angry agreement went round.

A tall, senior reader with a waxed, white moustache raised his hand to his mouth and whispered to his squat neighbour conspiratorially, 'They're right, of course. Not that we'll ever be able to prove anything until it's too late . . .'

'No, that's the problem,' came the hushed reply.

Runnet turned towards them and tentatively held out a piece of folded parchment. 'I don't know if *this* counts as proof,' he muttered.

The short, stocky dean leaned forwards and took it from his hand. He opened it up. The senior reader peered over his shoulder, twiddling his moustache as he scanned the words on the parchment.

'Upon my spirit!' he exclaimed.

'Sacred Sky!' gasped the dean.

The apprentices broke off mid-gossip and looked round.

'It's *his* writing,' the dean was saying. 'Definitely. In my position, I get to see it enough.' He turned to Runnet. 'Who gave you this?'

'I . . . I found it,' said Runnet, his cheeks reddening.

'But how *could* he?' the senior reader broke in. He shook his head. 'Seftus Leprix isn't going to be happy.'

'About what?' the apprentices chorused as they clustered round, each one trying to see for himself what was written on the piece of parchment.

'Yes,' came a voice. 'What exactly is it that I won't be happy about?'

'Leprix old fellow,' said the dean. 'We were just . . .' He frowned, and handed him the sheet of paper. 'You'd better read this.'

As the others watched, the expression on the face of Seftus Leprix went through various changes – from bemusement, through horror, to utter outrage. 'I . . . I don't know what to say,' he spluttered.

'Don't you worry,' said the senior reader. 'We won't allow it to happen.'

'What? What? What?' the apprentices and sub-acolytes were clamouring. 'What's *happened*?'

The dean puffed out his chest, pulled himself up to his full height and turned to address them. 'According to this letter – written by the Most High Academe himself – he is proposing to make the Sub-Dean of the School of Light and Darkness *our* new sub-dean.' He shook his head darkly. 'It's the thin end of the wedge, you mark my words.'

'And what of Seftus Leprix?' asked Runnet, just as he

had been instructed to do by the character with the silver nose-piece. 'We won't stand idly by while he's dismissed.'

A murmur of rebellious agreement rumbled round the group of apprentices and junior readers.

'He is to become . . .' the dean paused and shuddered, 'a sub-*librarian*.'

'Can you believe it?' said the senior reader, his moustache trembling with indignation. 'Our so-called Most High Academe is planning on reviving the Great Library.'

There was a gasp of amazement. The Great Library, with its dusty scrolls full of mumbo-jumbo, belonged to the past; it had no place in Sanctaphrax these days.

Runnet spoke for them all when he cried out indignantly, 'What's the world coming to when earth-studies is preferred to sky-scholarship?'

Another ripple of anger went round the group of apprentices, and before long all of them were demanding that justice be done and action be taken.

'Before he gets rid of our sub-dean, perhaps *we* ought to get rid of *him*,' said one – half seriously, half tongue-in-cheek.

'Yeah,' said another, warming to the theme. 'After all, what use is he to any of us now?'

'No use at all,' another chipped in. 'In fact quite the opposite. Actual harm, he's doing the School of Mist.'

'And not just the School of Mist,' said another. 'Every sky-scholar of Sanctaphrax will suffer if his half-baked plans should go ahead.'

'Earth-studies scum!' grumbled someone else. 'We've got to stop him.'

'Yeah, well, if he was ever to suffer from an unfortunate *accident*,' said a young sub-acolyte with spiky red hair, 'I know just where it would be.'

'That precious low-sky cage of his,' said an apprentice.

'Precisely,' said the sub-acolyte, with a smirk. 'Bars can buckle. Chains can snap . . .'

Runnet looked round at his fellow mistsifters gratefully. The character on the twelfth staircase had promised him the examination answers if he could stir up trouble amongst the mistsifters. It had been easier than he'd hoped. These academics were a treacherous lot, he thought with a smile.

His task complete, Runnet turned and made his way down the Steps. Now all he had to do was pick up the examination answers from the mysterious professor, and learn them. Up in the sky, the East Star began to twinkle. And as a following breeze began to blow, he caught a whiff of something familiar – woodcamphor. And tallow . . .

·CHAPTER SIX·

THE LOW-SKY CAGE

It was approaching midnight yet, tired as he was, Quint couldn't sleep. He was up and pacing back and forth, his head spinning with question after unanswered question.

'Why *does* Maris hate me?' he muttered as he approached the door. 'What exactly does the Most High Academe want from me? What is so important about that barkscroll I fetched for him?' He twisted round on his heels and marched back to the window. 'Who *was* it that broke my fall and saved me from certain death in the Great Library?'

So many questions! He shook his head. Once life had seemed so simple.

Outside, small clouds drifted across the face of the waning moon. Small clouds and ... Quint paused and squinted. 'A sky ship,' he whispered.

'Oh, Father, why did you leave me here in Sanctaphrax
with its horrible schools of Gossip, Rumour and
Treachery, surrounded by shiftless academics – not to
mention Miss High-and-Mighty Maris? Why can't I be
with you, Father? Far away. With the moon in my eyes
and the wind in my hair . . .'

He sighed, and was closing the window when there
was a sharp rap at the door. 'It's not locked,' Quint
called, and turned to see the handle moving. 'You again,'
he said, surprised to see the spindlebug standing there
so late.

'Indeed,' said Tweezel, nodding dolefully. 'I'd turned
in for the night, only to be summoned by his Lordship's
bell the moment my head touched the block.' He sniffed.
'He wants to see you again.'

'Me?' said Quint.

'At once,' said Tweezel, his antennae quivering with
agitation. 'If not sooner. And take your cape,' he added.

'My cape . . .' said Quint, scanning the room for it.
'Will we be going outside then?' he asked.

'I wouldn't know,' said Tweezel. 'I'm just passing on
his Lordship's instructions.' He spotted Quint's cape in a
heap beside the desk and picked it up with one set of
long, glinting pincers. 'Here,' he said.

'Thanks,' said Quint. He slipped it over his shoulders
and made his way towards the door. As he passed
Tweezel, he paused. A row of round black objects were
moving steadily along the internal tubes and pipes
which led to the spindlebug's huge, transparent
stomach. 'A late supper?' he said.

'The young mistress baked them specially for me,' said Tweezel proudly.

'That was kind of her . . .'

'Spiced scones,' he explained. 'A trifle over-done, but delicious nevertheless.'

Quint smiled. 'Rather you than me,' he muttered.

'Yes, well, the young mistress appreciates my work around . . .' Tweezel began. But Quint had already gone. '. . . the palace.' He shook his head. 'Unlike some,' he grumbled.

Linius Pallitax, the Most High Academe of Sanctaphrax, was already pacing the landing by the time Quint reached the floor with the master-study on it. As well as his stave, the professor was holding an unlit tallow-lantern in his hand.

'*There* you are, lad!' he exclaimed and, seizing him by his arm, dragged him back along the corridor. 'Come, come, come,' he said. 'We have urgent work to do.'

'Is this to be another task?' asked Quint eagerly.

'It is,' said Linius. 'But let us wait until we are outside before we discuss the details. I'm all too aware that there is a whispering campaign against me. The last thing I want to do is fuel it with any ill-chosen remarks that might be overheard.'

'Even here?' said Quint surprised.

'Even here,' Linius confirmed darkly.

They continued along the corridor, down the stairs and across the hallway in silence. Outside, they went down the marble staircase and, having checked there was no-one lurking in the shadows, Linius turned left. Far in front of them stood the gleaming winch-towers of the West Landing.

Quint shivered. 'It's cold,' he said.

'The cloudwatchers are forecasting snow,' came the gloomy reply. Linius increased his stride. 'Which is why we must act as soon as possible.'

'I . . . I don't understand,' said Quint, wrapping his cape around him as he trotted to keep up with the professor.

'The cages are difficult enough to operate at the best of times,' Linius explained, 'but with snow and ice in the air, they can be positively perilous.'

'The cages?' said Quint. 'We're going down in one of the low-sky cages? I didn't think anyone used them any more.'

'I do,' said the Most High Academe simply, and added, 'I take it your father, Wind Jackal, has instructed you in the rudiments of skysailing.'

'Yes,' said Quint, a little confused. 'Yes, he has.'

'Good,' said Linius. 'For there is a similarity between skysailing and the operating of the cages. These days, of course, the trainee Knights Academic use training ships in Undertown, but once upon a time they learnt the basics of sky-flight in the cages.'

Quint nodded, but did not comment. Since he had no intention of staying in Sanctaphrax a moment longer than necessary, he was unwilling to discuss the Knights' Academy. Linius did not seem to notice his silence.

'I love Sanctaphrax by night,' he was saying, 'without

all the hustle and bustle of the daytime activity. The baskets, arriving and departing; the constant noise.' He turned to Quint. 'I mean, I know that we academics depend on the good creatures of Undertown for our survival but, oh my, how loud they can be! Squabbling, shouting, touting for trade. Every day, I long for midnight, when the last of them go back to their Undertown homes and Sanctaphrax returns to what it should always be – a place of peace, quiet and academic reflection . . .'

Just then, from a building to their left, came a piercing howl of surprise followed by a roar of scornful laughter. A chant rose up. '*Down the bung-hole! Down the bung-hole! Down the bung-hole!*'

Quint turned to Linius questioningly. The professor sighed.

'Some of us are perhaps better at academic reflection than others,' he said.

'Who are they?' asked Quint.

'Stormwatchers,' said Linius, raising his eyes impatiently. 'In the middle of one of their ridiculous initiation ceremonies by the sound of it.' He frowned. 'Stormwatchers can be as unpredictable as the weather conditions they record.'

As he and Quint continued on their way, the sounds of carousing faded away behind them. The silence returned; heavy, impenetrable. The Most High Academe might have loved it, but Quint did not. It felt eerie to him; unnatural – and perhaps because he found it hard to believe that the place he'd always seen thronging with people could be so empty, Quint started imagining faces in the shadows, eyes peeking out from every nook and cranny. When he looked closer, there was never anyone there – yet he couldn't shake off the feeling of being observed.

On the approach to the great landing now, with the wooden boards groaning beneath their feet, the professor steered Quint towards an ancient-looking cage which creaked gently in the breeze. It was suspended in mid-air from a winch near the end of the stage. The professor strode over to it, released the cotter-pin lock and brought the cage up on its chain with a rusty *clang* till it was at the same level as the landing-stage itself. Then he unlatched the barred door. It creaked open.

'After you,' he said.

Quint stared at the dangling contraption with some trepidation. Unlike the hanging-baskets which carried passengers up and down between Sanctaphrax and Undertown, the low-sky cage was ancient. With its spindly frame, its caged buoyant-rock and the tarnished funnels and pipes, it looked so fragile, so rickety . . .

'It's safer than it looks,' Linius assured him as he climbed into his seat in the cage. Inside, he lit both his own lantern and the lamp hanging from the frame by his head before turning back to Quint. 'But then, as I said, there's always an element of danger in cage-riding – especially with ice in the air.'

Quint swallowed. Above his head, a snowbird soared across the sky, mewling like a babe-in-arms. With his teeth clenched, and trying hard to be brave, Quint gripped the frame of the door and stepped into the cage. It swung wildly to and fro. The professor leant across him and secured the door.

'Right, then,' he said. 'This is the up-down whatchamacallit and these are the lever things . . .'

'The weight-levers,' said Quint, nodding knowingly. 'They're simpler than those on the helm of the *Galerider*, but if it's anything like a sky ship then they should maintain our angle, speed and balance.'

The professor was impressed. 'So, do you think you can handle it?'

Quint leant forwards and pulled one of the levers towards him, then pushed a second one back. The cage responded by tilting first this way, then that. He nodded appreciatively. 'The weights have been well-tuned,' he said. 'Shall we go?'

'At once,' said Linius Pallitax. 'Before it gets any colder.' He patted the pocket of his gown. 'It's time I discovered how accurately I have translated that barkscroll you brought me. The Old Woodscript can be tricky at times. I just hope I haven't made too many mistakes...' He paused and an expression of utter weariness passed across his face. 'Sky willing it will prove accurate enough. Come, Quint. Let us descend.'

As the winch turned, the chain chinked and the cage sank down below the landing-stage, a hulking great figure with a deep scar down one side of his face stepped out of the shadows. It was Bagswill, a flat-head goblin guard who had been observing the Most High Academe and his new young apprentice with growing interest ever since they'd arrived.

As the low-sky cage disappeared from view, Bagswill pulled a length of thick twine from his side pocket. This was his remembering-rope. In his head, he went over everything he had seen and heard. Linius Pallitax. The apprentice. He noted the time, the place, the weather . . . and with each detail he committed to memory, so he tied a knot in the remembering-rope. Later on, the knots would help him recall everything that had taken place. The information would be sold to the highest bidder.

At first, with the length of chain so short, there was little Quint could do to steer the cage. As it descended, however, and the unwinding winch-chain above them grew longer, the buoyant-rock came into its own and Quint was able to make use of the intricate controls. With nimble fingers he responded to Linius's instructions to *go lower*, or *further to the right*, or *closer to the rock* with no difficulty at all.

'Admirable, Quint!' he exclaimed. 'Sky above, lad, it would have taken me half an hour to perform that little manoeuvre.'

'It's just a matter of developing the touch,' said Quint modestly. 'Leastways, that's what my father says.' He turned to the professor. 'I don't suppose he has sent word since dropping me off in Sanctaphrax, has he?' he said.

'Your father?' said Linius Pallitax absentmindedly, as the cage swung round and the pitted surface of the floating rock loomed up before him. 'No. No, he hasn't. And I don't expect . . .'

All at once, he lunged forwards and wrenched at the brake-lever. The low-sky cage came to a juddering halt, and keeled over ominously to one side. Quint clung on to the bars for dear life.

'What did you do *that* for?' he yelled, forgetting for a moment whom he was talking to. His hands darted feverishly over the levers – raising this one, lowering that – until the cage was upright and stable once more. 'I'm sorry, Professor, but this cage is old and delicate. It must be treated gently.' He paused. 'Shall we continue?'

Linius shook his head. 'This is as far as we go,' he said.

Quint was confused. The cage was hanging beside the great rock itself.

Just this week at the Fountain House school, Quint had been learning all about the sky around Sanctaphrax. It was, for academic purposes, divided into three areas. *Low Sky* was the area which lay between Sanctaphrax and Undertown; the cages were used to study it. *High Sky* was the area above the top of the floating rock; the tall towers of the sky-scholars probed this expanse. And then there was the sky around the rock itself, neither low nor high. He wasn't sure who studied here.

'This is *Middle Sky*, isn't it?' he said.

'Indeed it is,' said Linius. 'And Middle Sky is an area of especial interest, my lad, if my esteemed colleagues did but know it. Oh, I know it's not fashionable these days, but here in Middle Sky, the air flows through this immense rock of ours.' The professor had a faraway look in his eyes. 'There are great mysteries to be answered here,' he said. 'The old earth-scholars knew that.' He pointed to a semi-circular patch to his right, darker than the rest of the pitted surface. 'Can you steer the cage closer to that?'

'I'll try,' said Quint.

He raised the winch-chain and realigned the weight-levers. The cage swung gently several strides to the right. As the patch of darkness got closer, Quint saw that there was a small hole in the side of the rock. When they were parallel with it, the professor abruptly reached through the bars and grabbed hold of a jutting outcrop of rock beside the hole and, with expert hands, used it to secure the cage with a tolley-rope. Clearly he'd done this many times before. He turned to Quint.

'Right,' he said, climbing from his seat and unhooking the lantern. 'There is something I must now do. Alone. You will wait for me until I return. You will not move from here. Is that clear?'

'Yes,' said Quint, 'but . . .'

'There is no time for questions now,' the professor said, opening the door of the cage and scrambling out onto a ledge of rock at the entrance to what Quint could now see was a tunnel running into the great rock itself. 'I shall be back as quickly as possible.' With that, he ducked down and disappeared into the inky blackness.

Quint watched the yellow light and listened to the professor's scurrying feet and tapping stave as he hurried along the tunnel. The light faded and vanished. A moment later, the sound of footsteps was also gone.

If it hadn't been for the bell chiming the hour at the top of the Great Hall, Quint would have had no idea of the time. As it was, shortly after the professor had disappeared, a single muffled chime echoed through the air. It was one hour. By the time it chimed two Quint had had enough.

For a start, he was bitterly cold. As forecasted by the cloudwatchers, the temperature had dropped and a light, granular snow had begun to fall. Despite his cape, Quint was chilled to the bone. He tried flapping his arms around, hugging himself, kicking his legs up and down – but no amount of movement in the restricted space of the sky cage could warm his body or stop his teeth from chattering. And as he trembled, tiny vibrations amplified themselves through the cage and up the chain until the whole lot rippled with movement. Quint peered down below him uneasily.

Having grown up on a sky pirate ship he was used to heights, but this was different. On board the *Galerider* he had always had complete faith in the flight-rock which, ninety-nine times out of a hundred, would maintain lift in even the most serious emergency. The buoyant-rock of the low-sky cage, on the other hand, seemed to be little more than a steering aid – certainly it was nowhere near large enough to keep the cage air-borne. That task was left to the chain – and a very ancient chain it was! The way it clanked and creaked as the cage swayed was making Quint increasingly anxious.

'Don't break,' he muttered miserably. 'D . . . don't even c . . . c . . . consid . . . der it!' he stuttered, with cold and with fear. To take his mind off the old rusty chain to which he'd entrusted himself, he tried thinking about his old life . . .

He imagined his father, Wind Jackal, sinking a glass of woodgrog and turning in for the night. He remembered his own hammock – how soft it was, how warm . . .

'I'm so cold!' he grumbled.

He turned his attention to the pitted rockface in front of him. It was the first time he'd been this close. In essence, the great floating rock was exactly the same as the flight-rocks which kept the fleets of sky ships aloft, and even the small buoyant-rock of the cage. Except for its immense size.

Wilken Wordspool's lesson at the Fountain House school came back to him. What was it he'd said? Ah, yes. The outer rock was not as solid as it seemed, but was hollow, translucent. At its centre was the hard rock. Red. Glowing . . . What had Wordspool called it? Quint frowned.

'*Heartrock,*' he murmured. That was it. Solid, permanent, and home to the treasury – the safest, most secret place in all of Sanctaphrax. Around it was . . . Quint shivered as the word came to him. There was the *stonecomb*.

The stonecomb – a vast network of cavities like woodbee honeycomb – surrounded the heartrock. Alive, growing all the time, ever-changing, it was this stonecomb that gave the rock its buoyancy. But it was a terrible place, the old sky-scholar had warned the class. A place of terrors. A maze that changed behind you each time you took a step forward. *Sky-scholars don't go there*, Wilken had intoned solemnly.

And why would one want to? Quint had thought at the time. Yet, here he was, freezing cold and staring glumly at an entrance into what must be the dreaded stonecomb. Was he mad? He stamped his feet. The chain gave an ominous clang. More to the point, was the Most High Academe mad?

'If only I could go back to bed,' he whispered, his thick breath pouring from his lips. But the professor had been clear in his instructions. Quint was to wait for him to return. He was not to move.

The Great Hall bell chimed three hours.

The snow had by now stopped falling. Quint's hands and feet were numb. His temples throbbed. If it hadn't been for the burning lamp, he might have frozen solid. His thoughts had wandered so far, he was no longer thinking of anything at all. It was as if – like some of the hibernating creatures from the least hospitable depths of the Deepwoods – his body and mind had been switched off.

Quint didn't notice the bell chime four hours. He didn't register the flickering light in the tunnel, or hear the sound of approaching footsteps. It was only when the professor appeared before him, kicking the drifted snow away from the ledge as he emerged, that Quint stirred. He blinked once, twice. His long cold wait was finally over.

'Professor,' he said. 'Am I glad to see you. I was beginning to worry that . . .' He paused. Even by the flickering shadowy light cast by his failing lamp, it was clear that something was wrong. Ashen-faced and trembling, Linius looked dazed, drained. 'Professor?' Quint asked gently.

'Over . . . it's all over,' Linius Pallitax rasped. His voice, like his face, seemed to have aged during the time he'd been gone.

Quint unlatched the door and helped the professor back inside the cage. As the light from the cage-lamp fell across his face, Quint gasped and recoiled with horror. Linius's mouth was pinched, his expression desperate and his skin bore the waxy pallor of the dead. His eyes – usually so animated – stared straight ahead, dull and

unseeing. They registered
nothing – neither his surroundings,
nor Quint's helpless
concern.

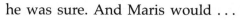

Quint knew he had
to get the professor
back to the Palace of
Shadows as quickly as
possible and get help.
Tweezel would know
what to do. Welma would
have potions and medicines,
he was sure. And Maris would . . .
Quint winced. Maris! What would Maris say? He could
only hope that she did not blame him, Quint, for her
father's condition.

Quint tried to think clearly. He must move fast, but
carefully. He knew he could not simply turn the winch
handle once the hook and tolley-ropes had been
released. It could jam or even sever the chain. No, before
he went up, he would have to go down further, to dis-
lodge any frozen blockage around the pulley wheels.
With the buoyant-rock ice cold and straining to rise, that
would be difficult.

'You can do it,' he muttered to himself through
clenched teeth as he slipped the knots of the tolley-rope.
'*We* can do it,' he added, as he used the rope to lash the
professor into his seat – just in case. Linius Pallitax neither
struggled nor spoke. 'That's it,' said Quint. 'Now, if I can
just untie us and at the same time . . .'

All at once, the low-sky cage gave a violent lurch as it tried to soar upwards. The professor clung on tightly. Quint spun round and lowered the entire fore-set of levers with a sweep of his arm. It was a brutal way to treat the delicate balancing mechanism – but it worked. Instead of rising, the cage fell sharply as it swung back away from the rock face. A flurry of snow and a clatter of ice tumbled down around them.

Quint wanted to yell for joy, but he fought to remain calm. He *had* to concentrate. With the winding-winch now free, he seized the pulley-wheel and turned it and turned it, as fast as he could. The cage rose. The rock receded. The landing-stage drew closer . . .

If Quint had been too cold before, now he was too hot. However, he waited until he had untied the professor and secured the low-sky cage to its moorings before wiping the sweat from his eyes.

'Come on, then, Professor,' he said, helping Linius from the cage and onto the relatively solid ground of Sanctaphrax. He pushed the traumatized professor's almost rigid arm over his own shoulder and supported his weight, and the pair of them made their way back along the wooden boards of the landing-stage. 'Not far to go,' Quint whispered. 'Soon be there.'

But what could possibly have happened down there in the stonecomb to leave the professor in such a terrible state?

Quint wasn't the only one wondering what was wrong with Linius Pallitax, the Most High Academe of Sanctaphrax. For, as the pair of them stumbled past,

Bagswill once again stepped out of the shadows. 'The Most High Academe in obvious distress,' he murmured, and tied a knot in the remembering-rope. 'Pale. Dazed. Assisted by apprentice . . .'

He tied another knot, and looked up to see Linius leaning heavily against the young apprentice. A smile spread across his heavy features.

'Investigate apprentice!'

·CHAPTER SEVEN·

THE FOUNTAIN HOUSE

In the event, neither Maris nor Welma appeared when Quint and the professor made it back to the Palace of Shadows. Only Tweezel – whose acute hearing woke him up the moment they stepped into the hallway – came down to greet them.

'Oh, master,' he trilled when he clapped eyes on Linius. His antennae waved wildly. 'You look dreadful! What in Sky's name has happened to you this time?'

Quint frowned. 'You mean this has happened before?'

'I've never seen him looking *this* bad,' said Tweezel. 'But, yes.' He nodded his huge, angular head. 'Yes, he has returned from his night-time jaunts in a sorry state on more than one occasion.' He tutted. 'Accursed sky cages,' he complained. 'He's going to kill himself one of these nights. I keep telling him to take a low-cage puller with him but he won't listen . . .'

Quint said nothing. Perhaps it was better if Tweezel

thought that the professor's condition was in some way connected to the sky cage. It spared him all sorts of awkward questions, like why an apprentice had allowed his professor to go into the stonecomb, of all places, on his own – and then stood for hours in the freezing night without going in to look for him.

The spindlebug tutted sympathetically as he inspected the professor's trembling body. 'Curious,' he observed, and turned back to Quint. 'What do you know about this?'

'Nothing,' said Quint, truthfully enough. 'I . . .'

Linius stirred. 'Over,' he murmured. 'And it's all my fault . . .'

'Aye, well,' said Tweezel, turning to the professor. 'I'll have to get one of my most efficacious cordials out of the larder. Hyleberry perhaps. Or healwort . . . And then get him to bed. He looks totally exhausted.' The spindle-bug's eyes narrowed. 'As do you, Quint.'

'I am,' said Quint. 'Shattered!' He rubbed his eyes. 'What *is* the time?'

'Approaching five hours,' said Tweezel.

Quint groaned. 'And school at six,' he said wearily.

'Look, I'll take care of the master now,' said the spindlebug considerately. 'You go and grab yourself a bit of shut-eye. After all, one hour's sleep is better than none.'

'True,' said Quint wearily. What with the night in the Great Library and the night in the low-sky cage, snatched naps were all the sleep he was getting. He turned to go. As he did so, the spindlebug reached out and grasped him by the shoulder.

'By the way,' he said, 'not a word of this to anyone outside the Palace of Shadows. Is that understood?'

Quint nodded. He'd been in Sanctaphrax long enough by now to know the importance of minding what one said. Rumours, however unfounded, could and often did prove perilous – even fatal. As Welma had so neatly put it, *One loose tongue can still many a beating heart.*

'My lips shall remain sealed,' he promised.

Still fully dressed, Quint collapsed onto his bed and fell into a deep yet troubled sleep the moment his head touched the pillow. Time and again, he dreamt he was falling – from the top of the Central Viaduct; from the ladder-ways high up in the vaulted ceiling of the Great Library; off bridges, out of baskets, from the low-sky cage – arms flailing, legs pedalling. Yet not once did he land. Every time, just before the moment of impact, the dream would shift to a new location as if, even in his sleep, Quint knew that once he struck the ground, his heart would stop.

It was during the fall from the West Landing that Quint realized – as dreamers sometimes do – that he was in the middle of a recurring nightmare. He'd been peering into the shadows, convinced that someone was there, when all of a sudden and without any warning a white-collar woodwolf had sprung at him. Its yellow eyes glinted. Its yellow teeth sparked.

'No,' he groaned as he stepped back, lost his footing

and began the long, tumbled fall to the ground far, far below him. 'It's not happening,' he gasped. 'Wake up, Quint. Wake up!'

He opened his eyes.

A grey light was streaming through the unshuttered windows. The bell at the top of the Great Hall was chiming. Quint looked round. It was seven hours, and he was late for school. Wilken Wordspool would be furious.

'Oh, Maris!' he exclaimed, as he leapt out of bed. 'Why didn't you wake me?'

Having quickly splashed his face with water from the wash-bowl and run his fingers through his hair, Quint dashed off. He skidded down the flights of stairs, across the marble hallway and out through the front door. To his surprise, the weather had changed completely. The temperature had risen, and the snowfall had given way to torrential rain.

Collar up and head down, Quint barrelled past the Faculty of Moisture and on towards the school building. And as he rounded the Patriot's Plinth, there it was standing before him: the Fountain House.

Quint gasped in amazement. It was the first time since he'd arrived in Sanctaphrax that he had seen the Fountain House in all its glory. Now, at last, he could see why all the other apprentice-students in his class called it the Holey Bucket, for in the heavy downpour that was exactly what it looked like – a huge bucket full of holes out of which flowed streams of water.

'It's incredible,' he murmured.

THE FOUNTAIN HOUSE

At the very top of the building was a huge bowl-shaped structure which all but sheltered the entire dome below it. It was in this bowl that the rain collected. If the rainfall was light, the bowl served as a makeshift bird-bath to the white ravens that lived in the Stone Gardens. When the rainfall was heavy, as it was today, the bowl filled and a valve in its base sprang open. Then the collected water would flow down inside the dome itself, along a series of pipes and out through gushing spouts which sent mighty cascades of water thundering down into the ornamental moat, complete with its collection of pink and green birdfish, which surrounded the building. It was truly a magnificent sight.

Quint made a dash for the front entrance and burst in. A portly grey shryke sat at a huge carved stone table. Her long talons drummed on its polished surface with brittle clicks. Her eyes narrowed.

'Student?' she demanded.

'Yes, I . . .'

'Name?' She picked up a pen and smoothed out a yellowing scroll before her.

'Quint, and I . . .'

'Class?'

'Wilken Wordspool, but . . .'

The shryke made a note on the register and looked up. 'You are late, Quint,' she said. 'Professor Wordspool does not like students who are late.'

'I know, but . . .'

'You'd better save your excuses for him,' she said and

the talons on her feathered hand resumed their rhythmic tapping.

Quint nodded glumly. He turned and made his way across the entrance hall. The vaulted ceiling echoed with the sound of gushing water. It was like being in the middle of a waterfall.

As he passed the dark varnished doors of the Lower School classrooms, Quint heard children's voices coming from inside. They were reciting cloud formations in expressionless sing-song voices – *'cursive low, cursive flat, anvil wide, anvil rising . . .'*

'Pay attention, Peawilt!' shouted Professor Lemuella Vandavancx, her strident voice ringing throughout the building.

Quint sighed wearily as he climbed the central circular staircase to the Upper School. The landing there was panelled, and decorated with paintings of ancient professors. Unlike the Portrait Gallery where, for several decades, no paintings of the Most High Academes had been completed, here the tradition had continued unbroken. The oldest, high up in the shadows, were Quint's favourites. They looked impossibly wise with their long wide beards and simple black caps; High Librarians every one.

The most recent paintings were down at eye-level. The individuals they depicted looked an unpleasant bunch: fussy and over-dressed, with sly faces that stared back at Quint mockingly. Sky-scholars! Professor Barnum Trapcott. Professor Spleenewash. And there, smug and prim, was Professor Wilken Wordspool himself. Quint stopped momentarily beside the portrait. It was a good likeness – the ferret-eyes, the pointed nose tilted up as if sensing a bad smell, the thin sarcastic mouth . . .

Quint looked back and forth to check that the coast was clear. There was no-one about. He took a piece of black chalk from his pocket, leaned forwards and, meeting the portrait's stare, drew a small arrow pointing into Wordspool's left ear. Then, with a flourish, he wrote OPEN SKY.

He stepped back to admire his handiwork.

Tap, tap, tap, tap . . .

Someone was coming! Quint rushed across to the heavy ironwood doors and knocked three times.

'Enter!' came a thin, reedy voice.

Quint took a deep breath and pushed the doors open.

The room he entered was as high as it was narrow. Ledges rose up on three sides, on which bored students slumped, their heads lolling, their legs dangling, while around their necks hung trays upon which scrolls, inkpots and pens sat untouched. They looked like sleeping puff-puff birds, roosting in a lullabee grove. The air in the room was stale and stifling.

At a high lectern, suspended on silver chains hanging from the tall ceiling, sat a fussy little individual in ornate robes and a tasselled cap. It was Professor Wordspool. Eyebrows raised, he peered over the top of his half-moon spectacles at the latecomer.

'Master Quint,' he said, with a little sniff. 'So good of you to spare some of your precious time for our humble little gathering.' He gave a short, high-pitched laugh.

'Yes, Professor Wordspool,' said Quint, feeling his cheeks redden.

The other students gazed down at him with dull, uninterested eyes. Nothing, it seemed, could rouse them from the numbing torpor of the class.

What was it this morning? Quint wondered as he made his way up the wooden ladder to the upper ledge. Mist-tracing?

Rain-grading? He sighed. Before he'd started at the school, Quint had imagined that he would be spending his days immersed in fascinating studies. Instead, every lesson was filled with the constant repetition of text that Wordspool would recite from the ancient *Great Tome of Skylore*.

When Quint reached the top of the ladder, several heavy-set youths in costly robes moved aside for him grumpily. A bottle of ink slipped from a tray and fell with a dull thud to the greasy floor below.

Cloudcraft! Of course, thought Quint. Today it was cloudcraft: endless lists of measurements to be memorized and repeated, and accompanied by just the right nods of the head, movements of the hand, low bows and eye-blinks. What *was* the point?

'The point of cloudcraft – when you're quite ready, Master Quint!' said Wordspool, his thin, reedy voice piercing the classroom's thick gloom, 'is not *what* is said but *how* it is said. A wattle cloud rising at three strides by quarter sight, obscurity grade high, for instance, must always be stressed with the third finger and an oblique nod, like so.'

The professor waved a bony finger past his left ear and wagged his head sharply to one side, like a demented shryke pecking at an ironwood trunk.

Quint looked across at the girls' ledges and tried to catch Maris's eye. He still wanted to know why she hadn't woken him. Had she simply forgotten? Or was she angry with him? Did she *know* he had been out with her father last night? It was impossible to tell. Blud Oakcross – a fat mobgnome student – was snoring gently next to him. Quesling Winnix, he noticed, was passing notes to Lod Quernmore and grinning nastily, while Ambris Ambrix looked as though she'd been cry-ing. Maris turned her head and stared at him. Her face was expressionless. Quint turned back to the professor.

'. . . storm rain at three and a half, semi-log at branch range building to good.'

His finger jabbed at his right ear, his right eye winked meaningfully. Quint thought of the portrait outside and smiled.

'Open sky,' he murmured.

'Master Quint?' Wordspool was looking straight at him with a nasty glint in his eyes. 'You wish to share something with us?'

'N . . . no, Professor,' said Quint, staring down at his desk tray and fidgeting with a quill.

'No?' said Wordspool, his voice higher and thinner than ever. 'No? Come, come, Master Quint. An exalted sky pirate like you? *Open sky*, you said.'

'Yes, sir,' said Quint miserably.

'I am attempting to teach the finer points of cloudcraft and you interrupt me, Master Quint, with talk of open sky! Open sky, Master Quint!'

'I . . . I . . .' said Quint, stumbling to find the words.

'Open sky, indeed! We are sky-scholars here, Master Quint. Sky-scholars study the sky from the glorious spires of our beautiful city. We study *High* Sky, Master Quint, while those of us less – how shall I put it? – less *gifted*, study Low Sky or Middle Sky. But open sky, Master Quint. Open sky! The audacity of it all. The presumption. Only in death do we turn to open sky.'

'But . . .' Quint began, only to be airily dismissed by a wave of the professor's hand. He turned to the others in the room.

'We do not study open sky because it is *out there*, while *we* are *here*! The sky comes to us, my dear students, never forget that.' The professor was shaking with excitement, the tassels on his cap fluttering uncontrollably. 'I fear, Master Quint, that you are fit only for the lowest of Low Sky study. Why, you might as well find a low-sky cage right now. I obviously have nothing to teach you!'

'But, sir,' said Quint, 'I didn't mean . . .'

'Get out,' squeaked Wordspool, his voice high, almost hysterical. 'Get *out*!'

'Professor Wordspool!' All heads turned. Maris stood, eyes blazing down at Wordspool from the high ledge. 'Professor Wordspool, you forget yourself!' she said coldly.

There were titters and shooshes from behind her.

'My father has let it be known that all study – high and low, sky and ... earth–' There were gasps of astonishment. 'Sky *and* earth,' Maris repeated, 'is to be welcomed in Sanctaphrax. Your outburst would sadden him, Professor, should he ...' Maris paused for effect, 'should he ever get to hear of it.'

Wordspool was speechless. His knuckles were white as his grip tightened on the lectern. 'Why, why, why ...' he blustered, 'why should he get to hear of it, my dear young student?'

'Master Quint can be trusted to be discreet, Professor.' Maris smiled across at Quint. 'If *you* can.'

Wordspool was sweating.

'Of course, of course. I was hasty, Master Quint. Hasty. When I said "get out" I meant in fact . . . *errm* . . . I meant . . . Class dismissed!'

A cheer went up from the ledges as the students scrambled down the ladders and made for the heavy ironwood doors. Only two of the apprentice-students did not join in the riotous exodus: Quint and Maris. They turned towards each other and their eyes met. Maris raised an eyebrow and jerked her head towards the door. Quint nodded. The pair of them climbed to their feet.

Outside, there were cries of laughter as a crowd gathered round the professor's portrait. 'Open sky!' the chant went up. 'Open sky! Open sky!'

'Thanks,' said Quint simply.

'What for?' said Maris, with icy calmness.

'For coming to my aid,' he said. 'When Wordspool was picking on me.'

'That's all right,' said Maris. 'Anyway, I didn't do it for you,' she added hurriedly. 'I was defending my father's honour.'

'I know that,' said Quint. 'Nevertheless, you helped me out, too.'

Maris nodded. 'I did, didn't I?' She turned to him. 'We must talk, Quint,' she said.

'Talk?' said Quint. 'What about?'

'I think you know,' said Maris pointedly. Her voice was harsh.

Quint swallowed nervously. 'All right,' he said. 'But not here.'

They – along with several others – were standing under cover at the bottom of the Fountain House, waiting for the rain to ease off. The birdfish were splashing about in the moat at their feet, twittering for food. The rain was heavier than ever.

'You want to walk back in that?' said Maris.

'If you want to talk about what I think you want to talk about,' Quint replied, 'then we'll have to.'

He glanced round at the others meaningfully. Maris looked over her shoulders too. 'All right, then,' she said. 'Let's go back to the palace.'

The pair of them went down the steps and across one of the bridges which spanned the moat. Anyone watching them, huddled together against the rain, would have assumed they were close friends. Yet as he hurried after Maris, Quint was still confused. Did Maris hold him to blame for her father's condition?

As they reached the Patriot's Plinth, Maris abruptly spun round, unable to contain herself any longer. 'I hate you!' she shouted, hammering on his chest. 'Hate you! Hate you! Hate you!'

Quint froze, refusing to retaliate. Maris's blows became weaker and weaker until her arms fell limply to her side and her fists unclenched. Tears welled in her eyes and mingled with the raindrops on her cheeks. She looked up. Quint stared back.

'How could you have let it happen?' she said, her voice low and quavering.

Quint turned away. 'You saw your father this morning, I take it,' he said.

Maris nodded. 'It was the worst I've ever seen him,' she said. 'Pale. Grey. Trembling. He could barely speak . . .! And then Tweezel told me that you had been with him.' She sniffed, and pushed the lank wet hair from her face. 'That was why I didn't bother to have you woken when you failed to appear for breakfast. I wanted to get you in trouble . . .'

'I'm sorry,' Quint admitted. 'It was one of those tasks . . .'

Maris saw the confusion in those indigo-dark eyes of his and swallowed. 'I'm sorry, too,' she said. 'I love him. I want to look after him. And instead, he chooses some . . . some apprentice to confide in, to share his work with.' Her eyes blazed. 'An apprentice who brings him back to Sanctaphrax half-dead! I mean, what *did* happen down there in Low Sky? And don't try and pretend you didn't go down in one of the sky cages. I *know* where he goes at night!'

Quint shook his head. 'I don't know what happened to him,' he said.

'Don't know?' Maris thundered incredulously. Quint looked round furtively in case any passers-by were listening. With the rain still lash-ing down, however, the streets were deserted. 'What do you mean you don't know?' she went on. 'You were both in the same low-sky cage, weren't you? How could you *not* know?'

'He . . . he wasn't in the cage the whole time,' said Quint quietly.

Maris's jaw dropped. 'He wasn't?' she said. 'Did you go all the way down to the bottom? Did something happen in Undertown?'

Quint shook his head.

'Then, where?' Maris demanded.

Quint frowned. 'He told me not to breathe a word of this to anyone,' he said, 'so you mustn't tell . . .'

'Sky above, Quint!' Maris shouted indignantly. 'I was born and raised in Sanctaphrax. You've hardly been here any time at all and yet you presume to tell me about the dangers of watching what one says . . .'

'I promised Linius Pallitax,' Quint butted in irritably. 'The Most High Academe. Your *father* . . .'

Maris looked at him. Her anger melted away and her eyes brimmed with tears. 'Forgive me, Quint,' she said. 'I'm just so worried about him.' She hesitated. 'Please, tell me what you know. Tell me everything.'

'Whatever happened to your father,' said Quint, his voice lowered, 'took place inside the great floating rock of Sanctaphrax. There was a hole in the side – the entrance to a tunnel which went deep into the stonecomb. He disappeared into it for half the night. When he returned, he was in the state you witnessed this morning.'

'The stonecomb,' Maris repeated quietly. 'But why?'

'The professor didn't say,' said Quint. 'Though I think it had something to do with the barkscroll I fetched him from the Great Library.' He shrugged. 'What about the Treasury Chamber?' he suggested. 'Isn't that somewhere inside the great rock? Perhaps he went there.'

But Maris was shaking her head. 'There is only one entrance to the Treasury Chamber,' she said, 'and that's here in Sanctaphrax.' She frowned. 'What in Sky's name could possibly have been important enough to make him risk entering the terrible stonecomb?'

Quint shuddered. 'Is it really as dangerous as they say?'

Maris shrugged. 'I've heard many stories,' she said.

'Stories?' said Quint.

'Stories of those who, when the rock shifted, lost their way and got trapped for ever in the honeycomb of twisting tunnels. Stories of blind, translucent creatures that haunt the shadowy depths waiting to prey on those who venture inside the rock. And stories of glisters.'

'Glisters?' said Quint. 'What are they?'

'No-one is really sure. Apparently, they inhabit the deepest, darkest parts of the rock, living off whatever wind-borne morsels filter through. And they glow. Occasionally, some will come up to the surface.'

'They will?' said Quint.

'Yes,' said Maris, 'though they're impossible to see straight on. But sometimes you kind of catch glimpses of them – sudden darting flashes of light out of the corner of your eye . . .'

'Yes,' said Quint excitedly. 'Yes, I've seen them. In the Palace of Shadows. And the Great Library.'

Maris nodded. 'For some reason they seem to favour the older buildings . . .'

'Could these *glisters* have attacked your father?'

'I don't know,' said Maris, 'but if the tales the treasury-guards recount are true, then it's certainly possible.' She shuddered. 'I would hate to go down into the stonecomb.'

Quint nodded. 'And yet, although he must have known all the dangers himself, your father decided to go there.'

'Yes,' said Maris thoughtfully. 'He must have had a very good reason.' She turned to Quint. 'Promise me that you will keep me informed of any future tasks he sets you,' she said.

'I promise,' he said.

'And I'll tell you if he lets anything slip when we're talking,' she said. 'He's up to something – something dangerous – that much is clear. We must find out what it is, for his sake.' She paused, and took hold of both of Quint's hands. 'If he takes you down in the low-sky cage again, you must follow him into the stonecomb,' she said. 'And please, Quint, look after him. I'm begging you.'

Trying hard to conceal his own unease, Quint smiled. 'I'll do my best,' he said. He paused. 'If it's any consolation, when your father came back to the cage, he did say that it – whatever that might mean – was *over*. I . . . *What is that?*' he asked, as a roar of jubilant voices filled the air. He looked round. 'It's coming from over there,' he said, pointing back towards the Loftus Tower.

All at once, the puzzled expression on Maris's face melted away. 'Of course,' she muttered. 'It's Treasury Day.' She smiled bravely. 'Come on, Quint. You'll enjoy this.'

·CHAPTER EIGHT·

THE TREASURY CHAMBER

Treasury Day occurred annually on the first day of the second moon when in its third quarter. It was a significant day in the Sanctaphrax calendar since it marked the time when the academics of sky-scholarship over-ruled those of earth-studies and first introduced stormphrax to the new Treasury Chamber deep down in the heart of the floating rock.

The earth-studies librarians had fiercely resisted the move, claiming not only that it broke the Third Law of Buoyancy but that it also wasn't even necessary. The answer to the buoyant rock's problem, they claimed, lay in the study of the rock and its properties, not in the crude solution of weighting it down with stormphrax.

The sky-scholars on the other hand maintained that if they did not do just that, Sanctaphrax would break from its moorings and be lost for ever. In the event the debate never reached a final vote, for the sky-scholars – convinced that they were correct and terrified of becoming lost in open sky – enlisted the help of a band of flat-head goblins to carry out their plans.

At first light on that fateful day, the flat-heads broke in and forcibly removed the earth-studies scholars from their Great Laboratory. By noon – for the first time in the history of Sanctaphrax – the sky-scholars were in complete control of the floating rock. They had a chest of stormphrax carried down the tunnels to the newly-created Treasury and, having determined the exact centre of the chamber, aligned it carefully. A company of guards was left to ensure that no-one tried to sabotage what they had done – a company later to become the much-feared Treasury Guard.

All this happened many many years ago, with all the protagonists now long since dead and consigned to history books and civic records. Yet certain aspects of that special day remain, enshrined in tradition, rituals – and even in the language. A cry of *Trust the skies!* for instance, took on the meaning of 'Good luck!' while *'Librarian's loss!'* meant the opposite, both in Sanctaphrax and, later on, in Undertown. *Treasury Day*, as it had become known, was a holiday marked by many with message-sending and gift-swapping, and was celebrated in the refectory with a seven-course banquet.

More relevantly, it was also the day when the Treasury Guard and Chamber were ceremoniously inspected by the so-called Next-Most High Academe. From early morning, crowds would gather outside the entrance to the treasury tunnel – festooned for the occasion with flags and bunting – to watch and cheer on the spectacle.

'An excellent turn-out this year,' said the Professor of Light from the stately prowlgrin-drawn carriage which – at precisely three hours – was rolling into the Mosaic Quadrangle.

'Excellent indeed,' said the Professor of Darkness as he pulled up the sleeves of his fur robes and waved back regally to the cheering onlookers. 'And perfect weather for it, too, now that those rainclouds have cleared.'

The carriage continued across the intricate tiled mosaic and on towards the pyramid-shaped entrance. The spectators fell back excitedly as it clattered towards them. Seven strides from the doorway, the prowlgrin halted and the two professors stepped down onto the red and gold carpet awaiting them.

From his viewpoint on the steps of the Great Hall, Quint was enthralled. He had never witnessed such pomp and splendour before. 'Look at the prowlgrin!' he said excitedly. 'Those look like real marsh-gems and mire-pearls on its bridle.'

'I'm sure they are,' said Maris.

'And the professors' robes!' said Quint. 'Can that really be genuine pine-ermine?'

'Of course,' said Maris. 'A white winter pelt for the Professor of Light, and a black summer coat for the Professor of Darkness.'

Quint nodded and fell silent – though not for long. 'I don't get all this *Next-Most* High Academe business,' he said. 'Why doesn't the Most High Academe perform this ritual himself? And why are there *two* of them?'

'You've so much to learn,' said Maris in a rather superior voice, 'but if you keep on chattering, you'll miss the ceremony. Hush, here they come now.'

'So-rry,' said Quint sullenly. 'I shan't say another word.'

'Good,' said Maris primly, patting her damp hair and straightening her steaming robes. 'It's Treasury Day and I have to keep up appearances.' She acknowledged a wave from the Sub-Professor of Mistsifting with a dignified nod. 'After all, I *am* the daughter of the Most High Academe . . .'

A stooped figure with a hooded cape and silver nose-piece who was standing on the step directly below them turned to face them. 'Forgive me for interrupting,' he said, his voice deep and gruff, 'but the lad does have a point. We accept what's going on so blindly these days. Perhaps one ought to question a little more.'

Maris snorted and turned away. Quint drew closer. 'Do *you* know any of the answers?' he asked the stranger.

'Some,' he said. 'For a start, the Next-Most High Academe was originally chosen because at the time the Great Laboratory became the Treasury Chamber, the Most High Academe was an earth-studies High Librarian. For this reason, a sky-scholar was selected to ensure that the new Treasury was adequately guarded. Nowadays, of course, the Most High Academe himself is a sky-scholar, and the role of the Next-Most High Academe little more than theatre.'

Down at the entrance to the treasury tunnel, the two professors were hammering, slowly and simultaneously, on the door with their staves. Once. Twice. Three times. As the loud, resonant thuds faded away, the quadrangle fell still. Then, out of the silence, came a muffled voice.

'Who goes there, by Sky?' it demanded.

'A friend of Sanctaphrax,' the two professors shouted back in unison.

There was a creak as the door swung open and a massive flat-head guard – with sword in one hand and studded cudgel in the other – stepped forwards to inspect them carefully.

'Who's that?' whispered Quint.

'Sigbord, the chief guard,' Maris whispered back.

The crowd remained still, scarcely daring even to breathe. Then the flat-head lowered his weapons and spoke up.

'Enter, friend!' he proclaimed, and a roar of approval echoed round the quadrangle.

The two professors disappeared inside, the door slammed shut behind them and the roaring of the crowd grew louder still. But Quint was puzzled.

'A *friend* of Sanctaphrax,' he repeated. 'That's what the greeting said. *Friend*, not *friends*. So, how come there are two of them? Is it because they're twins?'

'Oh, they're not twins, for all that they look so similar,' the stranger with the silver nose-piece growled. 'They met as young apprentices, drawn together by their shared interest in matters of luminescence. As time passed, they began to sound the same, even look the same . . .' He glanced towards the door. 'Like the subject they study, they're two sides of the same coin. It was impossible to appoint one of them to the post of Next-Most High Academe without appointing the other.'

'I see,' said Quint. By now, the crowd was beginning to disperse. Quint was about to depart himself when the stranger gripped him by the arm.

'Not that I am in any sense condoning the situation,' he hissed.

'I beg your pardon?' said Quint stiffly, as he tried to shake his arm free. The stranger tightened his hold.

'There are many,' he said, his eyes darting around him, 'who are suspicious of the influence the Professors of Light and Darkness have over the Most High Academe. After all, why has a mistsifter seen fit to take on advisers from another school? And why . . . ?'

'Come on, Quint,' Maris said sharply and suddenly, seizing him by the other arm. 'We should be getting back.' And with that, she dragged him away.

As they joined the crowds – now spilling out of the Mosaic Quadrangle and going their separate ways – Quint glanced round.

'What was the rush?'

Maris turned to him. 'He was starting rumours and spreading gossip, that's why I wanted to leave,' she replied. 'I've heard it all a hundred times before. The whispers. The intrigue. The lies. The question is, *what was he after?*'

As the door slammed shut behind them, the Professors of Light and Darkness relaxed. Since the rest of the annual ceremony would be performed out of sight of the excited spectators of Sanctaphrax, they had no need for any further pomp and ceremony. The Professor of Light removed his traditional white tricorn-hat and scratched his head.

'So, Sigbord,' he said, 'have you any fresh news on the matter we were speaking about yesterday?'

Sigbord was a large flat-head goblin, long-limbed and powerful; his many scars and intricate tattoos testified to a long career as a guard. He raised his lamp and turned.

'I have, sir,' he said, and looked round furtively. 'Two new developments. First,' he whispered, 'the mistsifters are up to something – and not just the apprentices. This one goes right up to the top. The Dean. The Sub-Dean. The Sub-Professor. One, two or possibly all three of them are involved.'

The Professor of Light shook his head. 'Linius should have noticed . . .'

'And would have,' the Professor of Darkness broke in, 'were he not so preoccupied. Poor fellow. He started out as Most High Academe so well – yet recently, he's been looking appalling . . .'

'He never sleeps. He never eats,' agreed the Professor of Light. 'And though I hate to say it of so old and valued a companion, he has been neglecting the duties of high office . . .'

'That's because he spends so much time down in the cages studying Low Sky,' said the Professor of Darkness hotly. 'I just don't understand it.'

'Neither do I,' said the Professor of Light. 'But as his two closest friends, we must persuade him to face up to his responsibilities.'

'Sirs, you must also warn him,' said Sigbord, and sighed. 'He will not listen to me.'

'Warn him?' they said in unison.

'That was my second piece of information,' Sigbord said urgently. 'Someone has been trying to bribe the cage-guards . . .'

At that moment, a grating sound came from the shadowy crevices of the tunnel, far to their right.

Sigbord drew his sword, cocked his head to one side and listened. He turned back to the professors.

'We must be discreet,' he hissed. 'Even here in the treasury tunnel, there are those who would not hesitate to make capital from an ill-chosen remark.'

The Professor of Darkness frowned. 'Are you suggesting that the treasury-guards are not now to be trusted?' he whispered.

Sigbord's voice dropped further. 'I'm afraid I am, sir. The Most High Academe's curious behaviour is affecting all of Sanctaphrax. Morale among the treasury-guards is lower than I have ever known it.'

They continued in silence, down the tunnel cut through the stonecomb and on to the heartrock at its centre. It was there – carved out of the solid rock – that the Treasury Chamber housed the sacred stormphrax. When it was first constructed, the tunnel had been completely straight, following the shortest route between the surface and the centre of the great Sanctaphrax rock. As time passed, however, this first tunnel within the stonecomb had begun to curve, to bend. That was the problem with tunnelling through rock which was still growing. What was more, as the porous rock continued to expand and shift, so the tunnel itself had threatened to close up as the ceiling lowered or the walls closed in; tunnel maintenance became a never-ending task.

'I swear this tunnel gets longer each year,' complained the Professor of Darkness.

The Professor of Light nodded. 'It's high time we had a new treasury tunnel built,' he said. 'Direct from the School of Light and Darkness.' He looked round. 'It would be difficult and costly, but well worth it.'

The shifting expanse of stonecomb was as porous as a ball of brittle-sponge. Filled with cracks and cavities which linked up to form a sprawling intricate warren of tunnels and holes, it hummed and hissed endlessly. Some of the tunnels were large enough for a person to proceed comfortably through the rock; others were too small even for the tiny spider-shrews – of which there were many – to squeeze into. It was a vast, confusing maze, everchanging, full of echoes and whispers, shadows and strange beings which glowed in the dark- ness. Some were ghostlike, some half-formed – and some predatory.

Ahead of them came the sound of muffled voices. At the same time, the stonecomb gave way to the hard, deep-red heartrock.

'Thank goodness for that,' said the Professor of Darkness as he continued down the long, straight passageway, running his fingers along the smooth solid rock. 'The stonecomb always gives me the jitters.' He chuckled. 'I'm far too unfit to outrun a glister!'

The voices ahead of them grew louder and, as they neared the end, a great studded door opened to their right and yellow light fanned out over the floor. A heavily-built flat-head guard stepped out and blocked the passage.

'Halt!' he ordered. 'Who comes this way?'

Sigbord stepped forward. 'It is I, Mogworm,' he said angrily. 'Have you forgotten what day it is?'

'No, sir ... I...' said Mogworm. His voice was gruff, and heavy with the rich, ponderous accent of the Deepwoods flat-heads. He looked at the professors and jutted his chin towards them. 'Who are these two?'

Sigbord sighed and turned to the professors. 'Excuse him,' he said. 'He's new to the guard.' He turned back to the goblin. 'Today is Treasury Day, Mogworm. The day of the year when the Next-Most High Academe ceremonially inspects the stormphrax.'

Mogworm looked down. 'How was I supposed to know?' he muttered.

'Because,' said Sigbord, 'I reminded you only this morning. Now step aside and let us pass.' Mogworm fell back, and as Sigbord strode past, he cuffed him around the head. 'Imbecile!' he growled, and turned to the professors. 'Like I said, he's new to the guard. Fresh out of the Deepwoods in fact. Strong in the arm, but soft in the head, that's his trouble. But he'll learn.'

He turned and continued down the corridor, past a huge carved door, half open. The professors hurried after him, their gowns flapping. As they passed the door, they glanced in to see a long, rounded chamber carved out of the solid rock.

This was the guard-room, home to a company of hand-picked flat-head goblins who divided their guard-duty into three shifts. Some guards were snoring in bunk-beds cut into the walls of the chamber, some were at a table playing cards, while

the others – of whom Mogworm was one – were on duty. Like Sigbord, all of them were fearsome specimens.

They reached the end of the corridor. Sigbord pulled a ring of keys from his belt, unlocked the door there and stood aside for the Professors of Light and Darkness to enter first.

'It never fails to impress me,' the Professor of Light whispered as he walked into the vast Treasury Chamber.

'Absolutely awe-inspiring,' the Professor of Darkness agreed.

Across the floor they went, their footsteps echoing round the great domed ceiling. Beneath their feet, carved into the rock itself, was an enormous circular design of calibrated triangles, concentric rings and a fanned circle of lightning bolts. It was identical in design to the Quadrangle Mosaic. The two professors stepped forward to where a chest – ludicrously small for the room that contained it – stood in the very centre of the floor.

'Douse your lamp,' the Professor of Darkness instructed the flat-head goblin.

Sigbord lowered the wick until the flame guttered and died. The Treasury was plunged into absolute darkness. The Professor of Light leaned forwards and raised the lid of the chest. Instantly, the entire chamber was lit up with the dazzling glow of the stormphrax it held. The two professors silently counted the shards of precious stormphrax. When they had finished, they bowed their heads.

'*Light in the darkness*,' the Professor of Light whispered, as the ritual decreed.

'*Darkness in the light*,' the Professor of Darkness murmured in response.

And with those words, the Treasury Day ceremony was complete.

The Professor of Darkness lowered the lid. Sigbord re-lit his lamp.

Outside in the tunnel, the door once again shut, the guard turned to the professors. 'Takes my breath away, that stormphrax. Every year. It really does. Never seen anything so beautiful.' He paused. 'Though what I don't understand is, how can such a small amount of that stormphrax stuff weight down this whole great floating rock of ours?'

The Professor of Light smiled. 'A thimbleful of stormphrax weighs more than a thousand ironwood trees . . .'

'When in absolute darkness,' added the Professor of Darkness.

'Precisely,' said the Professor of Light. 'It is a wonder of sky science, Sigbord. Just as hot rock sinks and cold rock rises . . .'

'And lufwood becomes buoyant when burned,' added the Professor of Darkness.

'But we must be ever-vigilant,' the Professor of Light said thoughtfully. 'Since the great floating rock is constantly growing, we shall need increasing amounts of stormphrax to hold it in place. The cloudwatchers yesterday confirmed that there has been a recent increase in sourmist particles coming in from the Edge.'

'A Great Storm is on its way,' said the Professor of Darkness.

'Precisely,' said the Professor of Light. 'Garlinius Gernix is about to be sent from the Knights' Academy to the Twilight Woods in search of fresh stormphrax.' He turned

to the goblin guard. 'Beautiful stormphrax, Sigbord,' he
said. 'The most precious substance in sky or earth, formed
only in the Twilight Woods from the lightning bolts of a
Great Storm . . .'

Sigbord scratched his head. 'It's all beyond me, Professor.
I leave such learned matters to you academics,' he said. 'I'm
just a simple guard.'

'*Pfff!* You are being too modest, Sigbord,' said the
Professor of Light. 'You are our eyes and ears.'

'Without you,' said the Professor of Darkness, 'we would
know neither about the treacherous mistsifters, nor about
the attempts to bribe the cage-guards.'

'But forewarned is forearmed, as the saying goes,' said
the Professor of Light. 'We will alert the Most High
Academe at the earliest opportunity. He must be told of the
great danger he is in.'

CHAPTER NINE

The Stonecomb

For the third time in as many nights, Quint's dreams were disturbed. It was at four hours when the soft *tap-tap-tap* on the door of his bed-chamber roused him from sleep. He rolled over and peered across the gloomy room.

'Who is it?' he mumbled sleepily.

The tapping grew louder, more insistent.

'I said, who is it?' Quint called back, louder.

'Quint, are you in there?' came an urgent voice.

'Is that you, Professor?' said Quint, sitting up. 'Come in.'

'Quint!' the professor barked. 'I must speak with you!'

'The door's not locked, Professor!'

'*Quint!*'

'Oh, for Sky's sake,' Quint muttered as he climbed out of bed and trotted to the door. 'I said, it's not . . . *unkkh*!'

As he reached for the handle, the door burst open and sent him sprawling to the floor. The Most High Academe appeared in the doorway, a lantern in his hand. His face

was drawn, yet flushed. His gleaming red-rimmed eyes looked feverishly round the room.

'Quint, this is urgent,' he said. 'I need you to come with me. Immediately.'

Quint nodded and climbed unsteadily to his feet. The door had dealt him a sharp blow to the side of his head. 'Just let me get my things on,' he said.

'Quite, quite,' came the distracted reply and, as Quint got ready, the professor hung his lantern on the wall and began pacing backwards and forwards across the room. 'I haven't been able to sleep all night,' he muttered agitatedly. 'I doubt I shall ever sleep again, unless . . . unless I give it one more try.' His words got faster, louder, more breathless. He paused and clutched his head in his hands.

Quint watched him uneasily out of the corner of his eye as he buckled his boots, toggled his jerkin and fastened his belt. The venerable professor was quite clearly at the end of his tether.

'Oh, forgive me for what I've done,' he trembled. 'For what I've unleashed . . .' Quint said nothing. He knew the words were not intended for him. The professor resumed his pacing back and forwards, back and forwards. 'It's so clever. So cunning. This is my last hope. Sky willing, I'll succeed this time. For if I fail . . .' He turned to Quint and focused on the youth's face, as if seeing him for the first time. 'I *must* succeed.'

'Professor?' said Quint.

The professor retrieved his lantern 'Come, lad,' he said. 'We have work to do.'

It was dark outside, very dark; that darkest hour of the night just before the dawn. Apart from the professor's tallow-lantern, there wasn't a light to be seen and, as he followed the professor along the West Landing – its lamps now all extinguished – Quint stared up at the sky.

It was the first time since his arrival in Sanctaphrax that the stars above had appeared as bright as they did from the deck of the *Galerider*. There, to the south, was the constellation of Borius the Spider. And there, Mitras the Great Banderbear. And further to the east was Darsh the Dragon, with the constant East Star currently forming the tip of its left wing.

Quint sighed. When the lights of Sanctaphrax and Undertown were ablaze, the stars were all but invisible. He had badly missed their reassuringly familiar shapes. Yet now, seeing them once again, he realized that he missed both his father and his life on board the sky pirate ship even more.

'Stop dawdling, Quint,' the professor snapped from the spindly cage. 'We haven't a minute to spare.'

Quint trotted to catch up. This was neither the time nor the place for homesickness. His father had left him with the Most High Academe, and it was to him that Quint now owed his loyalty – at least for the time being. 'I'm sorry, Professor, ' he said. 'It won't happen again.'

'I should hope not,' the professor muttered as he stepped inside the cage. He lit the lamp and turned back to Quint. 'If you get me down to the entrance to the tunnel as efficiently as you did last time, we'll say no more about it.'

Quint nodded, wishing he had had the time to tell Maris of this new expedition. He took up his position at the weight-levers. 'Release the winch-chain when I give the word, Profess . . . *aaaagh*!' he cried out as the rickety cage abruptly plummeted.

Struggling to remain upright, Quint applied the brake-pedal with his foot while feverishly pushing and pulling at the weight-levers. Nothing happened. Had the cage broken away from its moorings completely?

The chain rattled as it unwound; the framework creaked. Then, suddenly – with a loud grinding jangle – the low-sky cage gave an almighty lurch and began to slow down.

'Thank Sky,' Quint breathed. 'I thought we were in trouble then. This old-fashioned type of flight mechanism can be very unpredictable, Professor.'

Looking down from the West Landing, Bagswill, the flat-head guard, raised a fleshy hand and wiped away the beads of nervous sweat from his forehead.

That was a close one, and no mistake, he thought. Why, the old cage might do the job on its own without his help. And that would never do.

For Bagswill was ready and more than willing to tamper with the cage mechanism to bring about the tragic death of the Most High Academe – but the time had to be right. He had to have received payment for the task. Two hundred gold pieces he'd mentioned, and though the hooded character with the silver nose-piece had not exactly agreed, neither had he refused. It wouldn't do for the professor to die before Bagswill had concluded the deal. No, that wouldn't do at all. He would end up with nothing.

He peered down at the stationary cage, far far below him. It looked so fragile. Chuckling unpleasantly, he turned and strode away. He had important business to attend to.

With Quint back in full control, the descent had continued smoothly. Once again, the sky cage had come down just next to the entrance to the tunnel. Once again, the professor had used a tolley-rope to secure the cage to the jutting spur of rock. And once again, Quint had been left on his own as the professor scrambled onto the rocky ledge – stave in one hand and glowing tallow-lantern in the other – and disappeared into the tunnel entrance. This time, however, Quint did not stay in the sky cage.

As the oily yellow lantern-glow and the *tap-tap-tap* of the stave both faded away, he reached over and – a little uneasily – unhooked the cage-lamp. Then, having checked that the tolley-rope which bound the cage to the rock would not slip free in his absence, Quint opened the door and stepped gingerly across onto the rocky ledge.

A massive white raven which had been perched above the opening in the rock flapped up into the air. It wheeled round and, cawing furiously, divebombed the intruder.

Quint ducked down and hurried into the tunnel. He raised his lamp – and gasped. This was his first time inside the great rock itself, inside the stonecomb, and it was extraordinary. Like a massive woodwasp's nest, full of chambers and tunnels, it seemed to continue for ever. The wind murmured and groaned as it passed through, and the tunnels glowed. Quint shivered uneasily. The stonecomb seemed almost to be alive.

Wordspool's emphatic words came back to him once more. *Sky-scholars don't go there.*

And neither do sky pirates, thought Quint. At least they shouldn't. Yet here he was standing at the edge of the treacherous labyrinth of narrow tunnels, any one of which could squeeze him to death or seal him up for ever if his luck deserted him inside the constantly shifting rock. Heart in his mouth, Quint set off.

He hadn't gone more than a dozen strides when he
came to not one, but three narrow passages fanning out
in front of him. It was only the faint yellow lamplight
glowing from the left-hand one that told him which to
take. He hurried along it gratefully, but the incident was
unnerving. It brought home
to him just how easy it
would be to become
lost inside the shifting
stonecomb, and he
pulled a piece of black
chalk from his pocket
to mark his route.

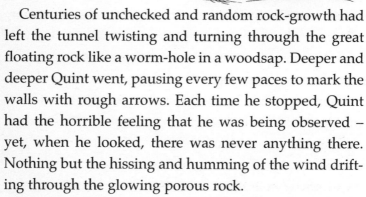

Centuries of unchecked and random rock-growth had
left the tunnel twisting and turning through the great
floating rock like a worm-hole in a woodsap. Deeper and
deeper Quint went, pausing every few paces to mark the
walls with rough arrows. Each time he stopped, Quint
had the horrible feeling that he was being observed –
yet, when he looked, there was never anything there.
Nothing but the hissing and humming of the wind drifting through the glowing porous rock.

Quint tried hard to keep up with the professor, mark-
ing the walls as quickly as he could and hurrying on. But
the tunnel was difficult to negotiate. The ceiling was
low; the floor was pitted and marked with countless pro-
trusions which tripped him up and grazed his shins;
while the walls were, in places, so close together that it
was only by squeezing sideways between the rough
surfaces that he was able to go on at all.

The professor, Quint realized, must have removed the worst obstructions on earlier trips, because every so often he would come to sections where the rock was scarred by recent pick-axe blows and the ground was strewn with rubble and dust.

All the while, the stonecomb echoed with curious groans and breathy murmurs. Could they really be caused by the wind alone? Quint found himself wondering, and his fingers trembled as he hastily scrawled another arrow on the uneven stonecomb wall.

It was at the end of a relatively clear stretch of tunnel that Quint caught a glimpse of the professor's flapping gown. He hesitated, fell back and held his breath. He didn't want Linius Pallitax to know that he was being followed. Above the constant hum and hiss of the rock came the sound of impatient cursing. The professor's gown had become snagged on a jagged spur of rock.

'Calm yourself, Linius,' Quint heard the professor mutter as he tore the material free. 'It'll be the worse for you if you arrive with your emotions in turmoil. Control yourself, or it will control you!'

Quint frowned. What could he mean? There was only one way to find out.

With shivers running up and down his spine, Quint scurried after the professor. The atmosphere in the tunnels grew warmer, stuffier. The humming grew louder while the hissing faded. The air glowed a deeper, darker red. All at once Quint rounded a bend to find that the professor had stopped in front of a stone door set into the solid rock, no more than a few strides away.

He fell back and waited silently.

The door was round in shape and seemed to have been constructed from the outer edge of the deep red heartrock itself. If it hadn't been for the innumerable creatures carved into its surface, the door would not have been visible at all.

The professor approached the door. He clasped the Great Seal of Office which hung round his neck and leant forwards towards the carved stone. As he did so, Quint's view was obscured by the professor's hunched shoulders. The next instant, there was a low, grinding noise followed by a soft click – and the door slid open to reveal a vast, dimly-lit cavern.

Craning his neck, Quint caught a glimpse of the curious sight within. There were countless gleaming flagons and glass spheres, all swaying at the ends of long, glowing stem-like tubes that protruded from the curved walls, and in the very centre of the chamber a huge glistening sphere, seemingly woven from light, hovered in mid-air.

'What in Sky's name . . . ?' Quint breathed, crouching down and edging forwards for a closer look.

And then he heard it: a low pitiful sound that sent shivers scampering up his spine, like the sobbing of an infant in pain. He shifted forwards for a closer look, but the professor was still blocking his view. Whatever was in there sounded small, vulnerable.

'Be still, you evil creature,' the professor snapped.

As if in response, the plaintive cries turned into a hysterical high-pitched wail. And through the obvious distress, Quint thought he could hear words. Pleading. Imploring.

'No more,' it howled. 'I beg you. No more . . .'

Quint scrambled upright and was about to take a step forwards when the door abruptly slammed shut. The unhappy voice was instantly silenced and Quint was left staring at the circular design on the rock once more. He crept towards the door and pressed his ear against it, but the rock was too dense and too thick for any but the most muffled of sounds to penetrate.

Quint turned away. The professor had something – or some*one* – locked up in this underground chamber. It was the last thing he'd expected and he shuddered uneasily, his head in a whirl. He had trusted Linius Pallitax, admired him even. Now he was unsure what to think.

What had the professor got imprisoned inside the chamber? And what terrible experiments could he have performed on this creature for it to cry out so desperately? And *what*, it occurred to him with a jolt, was he to tell Maris – that her father was a madman who tormented luckless creatures in an underground torture chamber?

One thing *was* certain. He had to get back to the low-sky cage before the professor. On no account must the Most High Academe discover, or even suspect, that he had followed him. Turning his back on the sealed chamber, Quint set off back along the corridor, vowing to return as soon as he could.

He took turning after turning, sweating with a mixture of exertion and nerves. The rock hummed all round him as he followed the black arrows down the endless tunnels until . . .

'Oh, Gloamglozer!' he cursed as the familiar carved door in the rockface loomed up in front of him. 'How did *that* happen?'

Somehow, somewhere, he'd gone wrong and ended up back where he'd started. It was his own fault, he told himself angrily. He'd been so wrapped up in his thoughts of what was going on inside the chamber that he hadn't been paying proper attention to the trail he was following.

He set off once more. This time he would have to concentrate. The Most High Academe could appear at any moment. He could not afford to mess up twice.

Quint's heart began to race as he discovered *how* he'd gone wrong. Although he thought he'd marked the entire route from the entrance of the tunnel to the door of the chamber with small black chalk arrows, in his haste and nervousness, he'd drawn some so haphazardly that they hardly looked like arrows at all, while others were so faint that he could barely make them out. Moreover, in places the stonecomb was covered with marks of its own; dark stains, blots and blotches, black sooty smudges . . .

Which marks had *he* made? he wondered. Which were there before?

Worst of all, however, was the sudden realization that the rock itself had moved. Some of the narrow passages had become narrower still, while in places the low ceiling now forced him to stoop. Panic rose in his throat. Those groans he kept hearing – they weren't the wind, but rather the sound of the porous stonecomb growing, shifting, twisting out of shape. And if the walls were moving, then what hope was there of following the trail of arrows?

'Which way do I go?' he whispered, his voice low and tremulous as he came to a fork in the tunnel with identical black smudges apparently singling out *both* of them as the correct way to proceed. 'I can only have drawn one of you,' he groaned, 'but which one?'

He reached across, rubbed his index-finger over the first of the smudges and checked the tip. It was covered with a light powdering of black chalk.

This way, then, he thought, turning to the tunnel on the left – but then he tried the second mark as well, just to be sure. He inspected his hand. Like the index-finger, his middle-finger was now coated in the same black chalky substance.

'*No!*' he cried out, and the explosion of fear and frustration echoed down the intricate catacomb of tubes, tunnels and galleries all round him – *No No No No* – before fading away, only to be replaced a moment later by a different sound entirely.

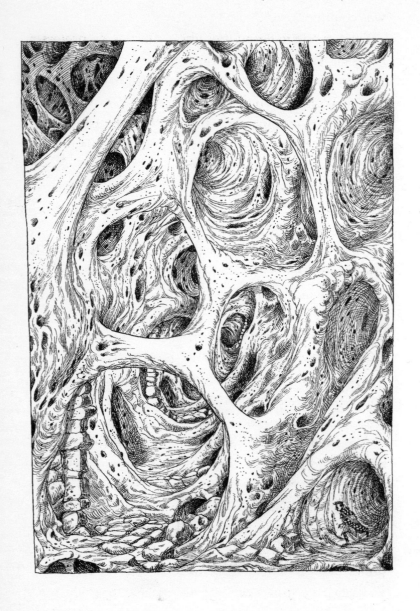

It was the sound of scratching and scurrying. And it was coming closer.

For a moment, Quint thought it must be the professor, hurrying back to the sky cage. But only for a moment. The noise wasn't coming from behind him at all, but from one of the two tunnels in front of him. Which one though? The echoing acoustics were so confusing.

He stepped into the first tunnel, cocked his head to one side and listened. He frowned. It was impossible to be sure. He stepped back and was just about to inspect the left-hand tunnel when he saw a light approaching from the other end.

Quint's heart missed a beat. Bright crimson and pulsing rhythmically, the light was speeding down the tunnel towards him. The sniffing and snuffling grew louder and louder.

Without a second thought, Quint turned tail and dashed down the right-hand tunnel. The scurrying quickened and the air echoed with slobbery snuffling and leathery flapping. The creature – whatever it was – was giving chase.

Glancing back over his shoulder, Quint stumbled, fell and gashed his right knee on a jagged rock where he landed. Thankfully, the lamp did not go out. The noises got closer still. The light behind him intensified.

Heart in his mouth Quint scrambled to his feet and, despite the searing pain in his knee, dashed off once more.

'Faster,' he urged himself, as he squeezed through a long, narrow stretch of tunnel and hobbled on. 'Faster!'

Behind him, the creature had paused. Quint heard sniffing, followed by loud slurping. He shuddered with disgust. It had found the place where he cut his knee.

'Whiii-whiii-whiiiiii!'

The excited high-pitched squeal resounded down the tunnel, filling Quint with absolute terror. Not only had the creature tasted his blood, but it had also liked it!

Quint tore his scarf from his neck and, wincing with pain, tied it tightly round his knee to staunch the blood. He had to stop the trail of tell-tale red drops that he was leaving behind him, leading the creature on.

Straightening up again, he limped off as fast as he could. His blood thudded in his temples. His heart hammered in his chest. All around him, above the sound of the humming rock, came the hissing of the wind once more. It was only now that it had returned that Quint realized it had been absent before. Something else was different too. The atmosphere was freshening, cooling. It could mean only one thing: he must be nearing the outer surface of the great rock.

'Sky protect me,' Quint murmured. 'May I be heading towards the entrance I came in through and not some dead-end.'

A moment later, he saw it.

At first, his brain refused to accept what his eyes were telling him. He leant forwards and fingered the scrap of tattered material clinging to the jagged piece of rock. There was no doubt. This was where the professor had snagged his robes. He *was* following the right path. It was the first piece of good news Quint had had since entering the terrible dark, claustrophobic system of tunnels. What was more, behind him the throbbing red light and the disgusting slurping noises both seemed to be fading away. Had he given the creature the slip?

The next moment he saw the light glowing ahead of him – and froze. Of course he hadn't! How could he even have considered it? Somehow, the fearsome creature had managed to get ahead of him. Staring fearfully at the light, he stepped slowly backwards. Noises behind him stopped him in his tracks. Flapping, snuffling, groaning . . . He spun round to see a second light, brighter than before. There must be two of them!

'Trapped,' Quint breathed. His palms were clammy; his scalp prickled.

Should he go forwards? Should he go back? The flapping grew louder. He *had* to go forwards.

Brow furrowed, Quint drew his knife, raised his lamp and continued. He remembered the lessons his father, Wind Jackal, had given him in self-defence. In such a situation, attack was the best, if not the *only*, means of defence. At the first sign of movement, he would lunge and stab.

Quint approached a narrow bend in the tunnel. He hesitated and listened before going any further. Behind him, the snuffling was getting louder again. The creature was so close. With his heart pounding and his muscles tensed, Quint edged forwards. The light seemed brighter than ever. He took a deep breath, turned the corner and . . .

'Thank Sky!' he murmured.

The light was neither crimson nor pulsing. It was the intense pinky-blue brightness of the new morning. Almost sobbing with relief and delight, Quint limped those last few strides towards the shining circle and stepped out onto the ledge. At last, he was free of the terrifying stonecomb.

Perched on top of the cage was the white raven. As Quint leaned across to open the cage door, it let out a raucous screech, hopped closer and jabbed at him with its vicious beak. Quint was gripped by a blinding rage.

'Do you think I'm afraid of *you* – after I've been chased by . . . by bloodthirsty monsters?' he roared. He swung a fist at the bird, which screeched again, its yellow eyes gleaming. 'Do you?' he shouted, swinging at the bird a second time. 'Well, *do* you?'

With a noisy clapping of its wings, the great bird launched itself into the air and soared off, squawking with indignation as it went. Quint opened the cage door and was about to step back inside when he heard a noise coming from the tunnel.

He looked round, and gasped. 'Professor!' he cried.

'But what . . . what's happened to you *now*?'

As he helped the professor into the sky cage, Quint's gaze fell on the gold medallion of high office which hung round the Most High Academe's neck. The bright sunlight glinted on it, throwing the famous design of lightning bolts into sharp relief. A thoughtful look played over his face.

'Quint . . .' the stricken professor groaned.

The apprentice dragged himself from his reveries. 'Sorry, Professor,' he said. 'Hold tight, now. We'll have you back in no time.'

·CHAPTER TEN·

PLOTTING AND PLANNING

'He *what*?' Maris cried.

Quint looked round him anxiously. A couple of apprentice windtouchers approaching the wind-tower had paused and were staring back. Quint took Maris by the hand and led her round behind the tower. 'Keep your voice down,' he hissed. 'The last thing we want to do is draw attention to ourselves now.'

'I'm sorry,' said Maris. She sounded a little guilty. 'But . . . I can't believe . . .'

'I'm just telling you what I saw and heard,' said Quint. 'He's got a creature locked up down there.'

Maris shook her head. 'What *sort* of creature?' she asked. 'A pet, like Digit? Or a guard-animal? Or . . .'

'It spoke,' Quint broke in.

Maris gasped. 'Spoke?' she whispered. 'Just repeated words? Like a loribus or a mimic-bird, maybe?'

Quint shook his head. 'It pleaded,' he said. 'It *reasoned*.'

'An intelligent creature, then,' Maris sighed. 'Some kind of minor goblin or troll perhaps . . . And certainly a vicious one, judging by Father's wounds. I'm frightened, Quint. He was nearly killed.'

'I know,' said Quint, as he pictured Linius Pallitax emerging from the tunnel. He had been limping badly, blood all down his robes. Then, as he had raised his head, Quint had cried out as he saw the professor's ear, hanging on by a thread as though something had tried to slice it off completely. For a creature that had sounded so abject, so pitiful, so weak, it had certainly put up a ferocious fight.

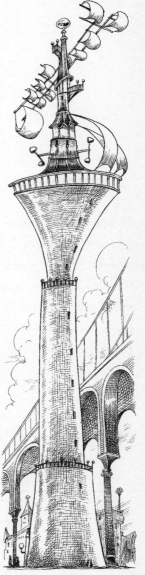

The professor's words came back to Quint; words he hadn't taken quite seriously enough when he first heard them. 'Your father called it an *evil* creature,' he said softly.

'I should think it must be, to cut him so badly,' said Maris hotly. 'And yet . . .' She fell still. Quint waited expectantly for her to continue.

The only noise was the soft *flupp flupp* of the turning sails far above their heads as their great nets billowed repeatedly, in and out;

although the air was almost still, the windtouchers' great wind-tower responded to the slightest of breezes.

'Yet what?' said Quint.

Maris looked up. 'I don't know,' she said. 'I was just imagining how *I* might behave if I'd been locked up against my will.'

Quint nodded sympathetically. He knew how hard it must be for Maris to conceive that her father might be in the wrong. It was heartening to see that she was not beyond putting herself in the place of the captive creature.

'We must go down there,' she said abruptly. 'You must take me there, Quint. I must see for myself what's going on. And if we find that . . .' She hesitated. 'If my father has . . .' She stopped, her voice choking up in her throat.

'We'll do the right thing,' said Quint earnestly. 'I . . .' All at once, there was a sharp grating noise above him. He looked up to see the same two windtouchers pulling their heads back inside an upstairs window in an effort not to be seen. 'We're being spied on, Maris,' he hissed. 'Let's get out of here.'

As usual, rumours and gossip, whispered plots and lies filled the Viaduct Steps, so that the air above them hissed like the pressurized steam which was currently spurting from the sourmist vats on the roof of the opulent College of Cloud. Like the steam, the words were heated, poisonous; sometimes opaque, sometimes crystal clear – and indicated that something dramatic was about to take place. In open sky, a Great Storm was imminent. In Sanctaphrax – if even half the rumours were true – an even greater storm was about to break.

The west side of the eighteenth staircase was more crowded than usual. As well as the habitual sprinkling of ranters and ravers with their conspiracy theories and apocalyptic warnings, there were other, less frequent visitors who were holding court on the marble steps. They were the fortune-tellers, the soothsayers, the prognosticators.

These sad individuals were said to be the last of the once-proud earth-scholars, now little more than carnival performers, their knowledge of the Deepwoods reduced to myth and superstition. The sky-scholars despised them, but tolerated them as evidence of how inferior earth-studies was. Each of the shabby soothsayers was armed with the tools of his or her trade: gyle-stones, tilder entrails, tripweed roots. One – a gangly, wall-eyed individual with grizzled jowls – had amassed a particularly sizeable crowd around him.

'The bones cannot lie,' he bellowed, his voice breaking with excitement as he waved the bleached oozefish skeletons at those standing closest to him. 'I have seen death and despair in the Palace of Shadows. I have seen the Most High Academe ringed with blue flames and dancing with the dead.' His voice grew hushed. 'I have seen our own floating city – beloved Sanctaphrax – being swallowed up . . .' His voice grew louder. 'Chewed to pieces . . .' And louder still. 'And spat out by a fiend . . .' He was shouting now. 'A fiend unleashed by ignorance and ambition. A fiend no prison bars can contain. A fiend so fearsome that none will escape its terrible wrath.'

The crowd gasped as one. Fortune-tellers were seldom as gory as this character.

'And how will we know this fiend?' someone shouted.

'With great difficulty,' came the reply. 'For it is a shapeshifter. It will speak with a familiar voice and bear the face of a nearest and dearest. It is a deceiver. A seducer. The most terrible creature in all of the Edge . . .'

'Sounds like the gloamglozer!' a high-pitched voice came from the back of the crowd, and a ripple of laughter went round.

Though feared by young'uns throughout the Edge, whose mothers, fathers and nannies would tell them bloodcurdling tales about the treacherous creature, among adults it was only the more primitive Deepwoods tribes and gatherings who believed in the gloamglozer. Those who had left the Deepwoods for Sanctaphrax and Undertown had abandoned not only their families and villages, but also their superstitions; while those born in the floating city or the urban sprawl below it had never considered that the stories of the evil creature might be anything more than ancient myths and legends.

The fortune-teller brandished his fishbones furiously. 'You can scoff!' he roared.

'Thank you kindly, sire,' someone shouted back sarcastically, and the laughter became louder.

Undaunted, the fortune-teller turned slowly round and surveyed the crowd darkly. With his eyes pointing in different directions at the same time, it was impossible to tell where his gaze fell. A hush descended.

'So you don't believe in the gloamglozer, eh?' he said, his voice an icy whisper.

No-one spoke. No-one moved.

'I know of those who didn't believe in flesh-eating trees either, yet that didn't stop them succumbing to the fearful bloodoak. Your lack of belief, my friends, is the gloamglozer's strength.' His voice became louder, sharper. 'Mark my words and mark them well,' he said, 'the gloamglozer is coming! The earth shall take its revenge on the sky. For so is it written in the bones!'

A derisory laugh went up.

'What do you take us for?' a voice called out.

'Deepwoods young'uns,' another shouted, and the crowd began to disperse.

Rumours of impending doom and gloom were nothing new on the Viaduct Steps. Before the fortune-teller with the oozefish bones had even arrived on the scene, feverish gambling was already taking place up and down the eighteenth staircase on the East Side. Despite their scepticism, news of these latest prognostications soon led to a fresh bout of wagers and bets. The tally-touts were besieged.

'Ten gold pieces say the Palace of Shadows will be struck by lightning,' said a tall apprentice raintaster in a fur-lined gown.

'*Fifteen* gold pieces says the Most High Academe will be gone by the next full moon,' said his companion.

The tally-touts noted the wagers and exchanged the gold coins for slips of paper bearing a record of both the bet and its odds. Further up the steps, the odds were shortening on whether the gloamglozer existed. A week, a day – even an hour earlier, you could have placed a bet at a thousand to one that the creature was no more than the stuff of fairy-tales and nightmares. But now the rumours had firmed up, the gossip had turned to gospel truth, and already there were several who were claiming that friends of friends had witnessed the terrible creature first-hand.

Further along the Viaduct Steps, an unusual cluster of academics had assembled on the seventeenth staircase. Situated beneath the middle of the viaduct, these steps – both East and West – were considered neutral ground, a kind of no-man's-land where academics from different schools and different places in the intricate hierarchy of Sanctaphrax could meet with one another anonymously.

Although they had all arrived without the character-istic robes of their particular schools, those who knew their faces would have spotted a dozen or so sub-deans from the ninth staircase on the East Side deep in con-versation with a group of fresh-faced mistsifter apprentices and sub-acolytes. Everyone, it seemed, was trying to talk at the same time.

'But aren't the proposals a little extreme?' someone asked.

'A drastic situation calls for drastic measures,' came the reply.

'The behaviour of the Most High Academe has been reprehensible. Intolerable. Unacceptable . . .'

'And now he must go!'

'And since he won't leave of his own free will . . .'

'Those who will not jump must be pushed . . .'

Moving unnoticed through the increasingly agitated crowd was a tall robed individual, his hood down low over his head. As he turned to his companion, the light glinted on his protruding silver nose-piece. 'You see how easy it is to set rumours rolling, Bagswill,' he whispered. 'To plot, to scheme, to sow dissent . . .'

The flat-head guard, also dressed in a long cape with his hood up, nodded enthusiastically. 'It's all going better than I had imagined,' he whispered back. 'But what of the deed itself?'

'It's all set,' came the reply. The pair of them looked round furtively. 'When the Most High Academe uses his cage tonight, he will find the chains cut . . .'

Still deep in whispered conversation, Quint and Maris continued slowly along the bank of the central canal which led from the wind-tower. The water – driven by a great wheel which, in turn, was powered by the sails on the wind-tower itself – coursed along the narrow channel and into the pipes which would deliver it to all but the very oldest and most rundown buildings in Sanctaphrax. As she listened to Quint, Maris found a small piece of sky-crystal in her pocket and absent-mindedly tossed it into the foaming stream.

She turned away. 'It sounds horrible,' she said.

'It was,' said Quint. 'Snuffling, snorting, slurping – and there was this glow. Red, it was, Maris. *Blood*-red!'

Maris shuddered. 'As if the stonecomb wasn't treacherous enough already,' she said, 'now you're telling me that it's full of . . . of . . . well, *what* exactly?'

'I don't know,' said Quint, shaking his head. 'I've never seen or heard anything like it before. But I'll tell you what – I count myself lucky to have escaped with my life.' Maris smiled weakly. Quint turned to her. 'Maris,' he said, 'are you *sure* you still want to go down there?'

'*What?*' said Maris, her eyes blazing.

'I . . . I just wondered,' said Quint. 'I mean, what with the rickety sky cage and the perilous stonecomb, not to mention the great blood-red whatever-it-is down there . . . it's still not too late to change your mind.'

Maris snorted. 'Change my mind?' she said. 'Of course I'm not going to change my mind. Wild prowl-grins couldn't keep me away.' And with that, she turned and hurried off. 'Meet me on the West Landing an hour after sunset,' her voice floated back.

Quint stood there watching Maris's busy little body bustling away into the distance, a look of bemusement playing around his lips. He didn't think he would ever be able to make her out.

·CHAPTER ELEVEN·

FREEFALL

Maris stood in the dark corridor in front of her
father's locked bedroom door. Her eyes were red
and her legs were trembling. Her knuckles were grazed
and throbbing from all the knocking.

It was bad enough that she was about to do something
behind her father's back. But going off without kissing
him goodbye somehow made her behaviour even worse.
It seemed like a betrayal. But she had to know the secret
of the underground chamber, however terrible it was.
And Quint would help her.

She felt a pang of jealousy. Why *had* her father turned
to this son of a sky pirate to run his errands for him
rather than entrusting her, his daughter, with his secrets?
She shook her head. This was no time for such negative
emotions. Whatever the reason, it wasn't Quint's fault.
In fact she should be grateful to him for the information
he had provided – not angry.

Maris turned her attention back to the door. She really
did want to see her father before leaving; she wanted

him to know that she loved him, that she was proud to be the daughter of the Most High Academe, no matter what. If only he would let her in!

'Open up!' she shrieked, and hammered on the door louder than ever. 'For the love of Sky, let me . . .'

There was a metallic click as a key turned in the lock. The door opened and Welma's rubbery features appeared in the gap. 'Mistress Maris!' she said sharply. 'What is all this nonsense about?'

'I want to see my father.'

'Your father is resting,' Welma said, a little more softly. 'He gave me strict instructions not to let anyone in.'

'But . . .'

'Maris, the Most High Academe has recently undergone some dreadful ordeal,' she explained. 'He won't even talk about it . . .'

'He'd talk to me, though,' said Maris. 'I know he would. He . . .'

Welma slipped out and closed the door behind her. 'My little sugar-dumpling,' she said, stroking Maris's cheek affectionately. 'He especially said that I was not to let you in yet.'

'Oh,' Maris gasped. A lump formed in her throat. 'Doesn't he . . . doesn't he love me any more?' she whispered. Tears welled up in the corners of her eyes.

'Love you? Of course he loves you, you daft thing. *That's* why he doesn't want you to see him the way he is now. His face is all scratched and bruised, and there's a horrible gash to his ear . . .' Her brow creased up. 'Come to that, Maris, you don't look too good yourself. Your nose is red and your eyes are all bloodshot and puffy.' She pulled a large spotted handkerchief from the pocket of her apron. 'Here,' she said.

Maris took the handkerchief, wiped her eyes and blew her nose. 'I'm sorry,' she said. 'I'm being silly. Besides, Father's probably tired now.'

'Sleeping like a baby,' Welma confirmed.

Maris smiled bravely. 'Thank you for looking after him,' she said. 'I know he couldn't be in better hands. Just tell him from me, tell him . . .' She leant forwards and planted a kiss at the end of her old nanny's rubbery nose. 'Tell him I love him, no matter what,' she said.

'Of course I will,' said the old nurse.

As Welma watched her young charge walk off down the corridor, she felt a pang of guilt. She had never liked lying to Maris. Yet, with the best will in the world, Welma could not have described the true state the Most High Academe was in. The great blood-soaked bandage which swaddled his head was bad enough, but even if she had wanted to – which she didn't – she had not words enough to describe the haunting terror in his unblinking eyes.

For Linius Pallitax was not asleep, as Welma had claimed. He was sitting up in bed – rigid, taut, coiled, staring with abject horror at something he alone could see.

*

'She's late,' Quint murmured.

An hour after sunset, she'd said. The sun had disappeared down below the horizon at five after seven
hours, yet the bell at the top of the Great Hall was about
to chime nine. Quint looked for her anxiously up and
down the West Landing.

'Where are you, Maris?' he muttered.

With the onset of darkness, the temperature had
swiftly dropped and it was bitterly cold once more.
Quint stamped his feet and swung his arms in an effort
to keep warm. Back and forth he paced, back and
forth . . .

Although he'd tried to avoid eye-contact, Quint knew
that he was arousing the suspicions of one of the
landing-guards – a hulking great flat-head with a deep,
menacing scar that passed through his brow and down
his left cheek. Finally, the guard came across to him.

'You've been
hanging about
here for nearly
two hours
now,' he
said. He
pressed his
face into
Quint's.
'Who are
you?' he
demanded.

'I . . . I'm an apprentice,' Quint explained, his breath coming in little clouds. 'The apprentice of the Most High Academe,' he added, in the hope that the mention of such an eminent academic would encourage the guard to leave him in peace.

It did.

But Quint couldn't help but notice the look of interest which flashed across the guard's face as he'd turned to go. He chewed into his lower lip uneasily, knowing that he'd been a fool to say so much. In Sanctaphrax, it was unwise to volunteer *any* information. After all, what would the guard do with this piece of news? Who might he tell?

Quint looked round to see where the guard was heading – but the flat-head had already disappeared into the swathes of dark, wispy mist. The landing was busy with much coming and going, yet Quint was unable to see him anywhere. He did, however, spot one familiar face.

'I remember you,' he murmured. It was the character with the silver nose-piece whom he'd met on the Viaduct Steps. Quint was on the point of saying *hello* – and apologizing for his rapid departure – when something made him pause. There was something deeply suspicious about how often the man glanced furtively around him. Was he looking for someone? Or trying to avoid someone looking for *him*? Quint didn't wait around to find out. He raised his hood and took refuge between a couple of the local traders' wooden stalls.

The bell chimed nine hours. 'That's it,' said Quint to himself. 'Something must have happened. I'm not waiting here a moment longer.' And with his hood still raised, he turned and walked slapbang into someone wrapped up in a great cape hurrying from the opposite direction.

'Sorry,' said Quint, 'I . . .' He paused and looked at the heavy cape in front of him. It was familiar. 'Professor?' he said softly.

A sleeved arm was raised, the hood was opened and a pair of startled green eyes stared out. 'Quint,' came a muffled voice.

It was Maris.

'You!' Quint shouted. 'Where have you been?'

'I . . . I was . . .' Maris began. The lantern she was holding trembled in her hand; her face crumpled. 'Don't be angry with me.'

Quint frowned. It was unusual to see Maris looking so distressed. 'I've been waiting here for ages,' he said, more gently.

'I'm sorry, Quint,' said Maris quietly. 'I went to see my father. I wanted to . . .'

Quint pulled her back into the shadows between the two stalls. What with the flat-head guard and the suspicious character with the silver nose-piece both hanging about, he and Maris would have to be careful.

'How *is* your father?' Quint whispered. 'He was in such a bad way this morning.'

'Sleeping,' Maris replied. 'I . . . I didn't want to disturb him.'

Quint nodded. The three-quarter moon glinted on the crystals of salt which streaked her cheek. She'd clearly been crying.

'Come on, then,' he said softly. 'Let's go and see for ourselves what he has discovered.' As Quint reached forwards to take her by the arm his hand closed round something cold and hard. 'What's that?' he hissed.

Maris lifted the voluminous folds of her father's cape to reveal a thick iron pikestaff with a vicious-looking hook that she had concealed there. Quint's eyebrows shot upwards with surprise.

'Just in case,' Maris said in a low voice. 'After all, we both saw what the creature did to my father. For whatever reason.'

Quint said nothing. This was another side to Maris he hadn't seen before: fierce, determined, almost ruthless, but behind it, somewhere in those green eyes, fear. Quint couldn't help but admire her bravery. He gripped the handle of the knife at his side. 'Just in case,' he repeated.

Keeping to the shadows, Quint and Maris scurried back along the West Landing. A cold spiral-wind had got up, sending the wisps of mist dancing over the boards and chilling the night-air still further. Along the length of the landing, the oil-lamps swung from their hooks, the haloes around them brightening and dimming, the flames inside flickering, flaring, and sometimes blowing out.

The closer they got to the far end of the landing, the

larger the thronging crowd about them. Shouts and cries echoed round the crisp night-air. 'Mind your backs!' and 'Going down!' and 'Step right this way!' as the basket-pullers ferried a constant stream of merchants, servants, guards and academics up and down between Sanctaphrax and Undertown. Not one among them seemed to notice the two youngsters picking their way between them and moving on towards the low-sky cage berths – yet the uncomfortable feeling that they were being watched persisted.

'Stand back,' said Quint. He uncleated the tolley-rope, brought the cage down and opened the door for Maris. As she clambered inside, the cage swung wildly.

Maris let out a small cry and clung on to the bars. 'I don't like this,' she said.

'You'll soon get used to it,' said Quint. 'It always takes you earthlubbers time to get your sky-legs. Of course,' he added cockily, 'I've spent so many years sky-borne that I can keep my balance in the wildest of storms.'

'Yes, well, while I am getting my so-called *sky-legs*, I may as well light the lamps.' She glared at Quint. 'Or would *you* rather?'

Quint smiled weakly. The palm of his hand, though healed now, throbbed painfully with the memory of the unpleasant incident in the balcony-chamber. 'Sorry,' he said. He paused. 'I wasn't trying to be mean. It's just that I love the feeling of skysailing so much, it's hard to imagine being someone who doesn't. After all, if we weren't meant to fly, we'd never have been given flight-rocks!'

Maris shuddered miserably. 'Let's just get this over with, shall we?' she said.

'Right,' said Quint. He rubbed his ice-cold hands together vigorously to get the circulation going, and seized the bone-handled weight-levers. 'Now, Maris,' he said, 'when I give the word I want you to release the winch-chain.'

'D . . . do you mean this?' she said, stammering with both fear and cold. She pointed to a flat, rusted lever at the centre of the coil of chain.

'That's the one,' said Quint. 'Pull it down . . . Now.'

With a little grunt of exertion, Maris shifted the stiff lever downwards. The cage gave a lurch and, from above her head, there came a soft chinking sound as the chain unwound, link by link. She sat down. The slow descent had begun.

Maris hung up her lantern and prepared to light the cage-lamp. Quint adjusted the weight-levers. Like every other good sky-sailor, he did not look at what he was doing. *Trust your fingers, not your eyes*; that was the advice his grandfather had given his father, and Wind Jackal had given him.

It was good advice. Anyone could sail badly, but it was only when you had developed the 'touch' that you could truly be said to have conquered the sky. Besides, if Quint *had* been looking at the weight-levers, he wouldn't have seen the two individuals emerging together from the shadows on to the landing stage. Looking up, Maris noticed them, too.

'Ugh,' she shuddered. 'There's that creepy individual with the silver nose-piece. From the Viaduct Steps . . .'

'I know,' said Quint. 'And the other one is a landing-guard. He spoke to me earlier.' He paused. 'They seem to know one another.'

As the cage dropped down lower, the pair of them disappeared from view.

'The guard's name is Bagswill,' said Maris. 'I recognized his tattoos. And the scar. He used to serve in the Palace of Shadows,' she added, 'before Father had him dismissed . . .'

'Dismissed?' said Quint. 'What for?'

'The usual,' Maris sighed. 'Intrigue. Double-dealing. Lining his own pocket . . . Didn't you see him tucking some bag or pouch inside his jerkin just then. It wouldn't surprise me in the least if the two of them weren't up to something . . .'

She fell still. The wind whistled through the bars of the cage as it continued downwards; the chain went *chink chink chink*.

'Unless it was just a coincidence,' said Quint at last, 'the pair of them being together.'

Maris shrugged. 'Maybe,' she said. 'I hope so. But then, if I know Sanctaphrax . . .'

CLUNK!

A loud, metallic noise vibrated down the chain and through the cage. Something was wrong.

Maris turned to Quint. 'What was tha . . .? *Aargh!*' she screamed as the cage abruptly plummeted down through the air.

'The chain!' Quint cried out. 'It's broken!'

Jangling like a traitor's bag of gold pieces, the chain slipped unimpeded through the winch-wheel. Faster and faster the cage fell. Maris pulled herself out of her seat and clutched at the bars. Quint gripped the weight-levers and trod down again and again on the brake-pedal.

The ice-cold wind howled up through the cage, freezing its two terrified passengers to the bone – and, at the same time, chilling the buoyant-rock to its core. Suddenly Quint's fingers detected a change of speed. He could feel it in the weight-levers.

'We're slowing down!' he exclaimed. 'The cold wind's making the rock more buoyant.' He looked round desperately. 'But we haven't got more than a few seconds,' he said, his hands leaping over the levers, raising and lowering them as quickly as his fingers would go. 'Maris!' he shouted. 'Can you see an opening in the rock? Somewhere below us . . .'

Maris seized her lantern and shone it towards the pitted surface of the rock. 'No . . .' she said. 'No, I . . . Yes!'

'Where?' shouted Quint.

'To . . . to our left.'

'To our left,' Quint repeated, frantically realigning the weight-levers. 'How many degrees?'

'D . . . degrees?' said Maris.

'Imagine it's a clock,' said Quint impatiently. 'How many minutes before twelve?'

'Five,' said Maris. 'A bit less perhaps . . .'

'Between twenty-five and thirty degrees,' Quint muttered grimly. He lowered the outer weights further. The cage continued to fall – but slower now and at a marked angle. The rock loomed closer. The entrance to the tunnel was coming up to meet them. He locked the weight-levers, scrambled over to the door and threw it open.

'What are you doing?' cried Maris.

'We've got to get out of here while we still can,' he said. 'Come on, Maris. Get ready to jump.'

'Jump?' Maris gasped. The panic in her voice was unmistakable. 'I . . . I can't . . .'

'You must!' said Quint.

The sky cage dropped lower. The hole in the rock came closer.

'See that ledge,' Quint said. 'We're going to jump onto it.'

'No, Quint,' Maris groaned, 'it's . . .'

But Quint was no longer listening. He seized her hand and dragged her towards the opening of the cage.

'NO!' cried Maris.

All at once the end of the cage's heavy chain, which had been falling so much faster than the cage itself, abruptly dropped below them – knocking the cage out of kilter  and dislodging the buoyant-rock from its casing. Now they were in freefall.

'Quint!' Maris screamed, and grabbed hold of his arm desperately.

'Jump!' shouted Quint. *'Now!'*

The pair of them leapt from the plummeting cage. Maris screamed as she flew off into the void, Quint holding her tightly. The next moment, the two of them – still clinging on to one another for dear life – landed on the rocky ledge and collapsed together in a heap. The lantern in Maris's hand smashed against the stone, guttered and went out.

From behind them came a creak and a crack and the entire low-sky cage tumbled away below them. Moments later, there was a loud *crash* and a wail echoed up through the air. Then silence. Maris climbed up shakily and helped Quint to his feet.

'We made it,' Quint said.

Maris swallowed nervously as she looked down over the steep side of the great floating rock. The curve made it impossible to see the ground directly below them, so she couldn't see the remains of the sky cage – but she knew they were there: twisted, broken, smashed to smithereens, as their bodies would have been if they had not managed to escape.

'*You* made it,' she said softly. 'You saved my life, Quint.' Her face darkened. 'The chain didn't just break. Someone cut it. It must have been that stranger and the guard. Quint, they tried to kill us!'

Quint shook his head. 'It wasn't *us* they were trying to kill,' he said. 'It's your father they're after. And with that cape of his you're wearing, they probably think they got him.'

The pair of them peered up. Far, far above their heads – no larger than a couple of woodants – were two figures silhouetted against the lamplight of the West Landing, staring down from the balustrade.

'There they are,' said Quint bitterly. 'Our would-be assassins.'

'Then, let's give them what they want,' Maris said, removing the hooked pikestaff from her sleeve, pulling her father's great cape from her shoulders, rolling it into a ball and tossing it over the side. Quint's followed close behind. 'For the time being, at least, they'll think they've succeeded.' She turned back to Quint, a big grin playing round her lips – only to find him staring back at her, his face a picture of gloom. 'Cheer up! They failed. We're still alive.'

Quint snorted. 'In case you hadn't noticed,' he said, 'we're stuck on the side of a floating rock, hundreds of strides above the ground. We can't jump. We can't climb up or down. We haven't got parawings. What are we going to do? You tell me that.'

Maris stared at him levelly. 'We're going to do what we came here to do,' she said, her green eyes flashing fiercely.

·CHAPTER TWELVE·

GLISTERS

'Maris, please hold my lantern still,' said Quint, trying hard to keep the irritation from his voice. He was checking the wall for the black chalk arrows and Maris wasn't making this task any easier. 'I can't see properly.'

'Why don't *you* hold it, then?' snapped Maris. Quint flinched. There was the old arrogance in her tone, the cold anger he'd heard in the Palace of Shadows, at the Fountain House . . . 'Oh, but then I forgot,' she added. 'You have that little problem with fire, don't you?'

Quint turned away, and swallowed hard. He examined the wall more closely. Not only were they in danger of losing their way, but now they were beginning to squabble.

'It's this way,' he said at last, pointing down the tunnel. He picked up the hooked pikestaff Maris had brought with her and set off.

Things had been very different the first time Quint entered the stonecomb tunnel. On that occasion he'd followed the professor, unaware of where he was heading. Now *he* was the one leading the way, the one

responsible for not getting both him and Maris lost in the endless labyrinth of shifting tunnels. At first, they'd tried to proceed with Maris at the front and Quint following. But it hadn't worked out. Maris, who could see clearly, was unsure what she was searching for, while Quint, who – since he'd put them there – knew exactly what the marks looked like, could barely see a thing. As the tunnel was too narrow for them to walk two abreast, they'd swapped places.

It worked far better with Quint leading and Maris following close behind, the lantern raised up above Quint's left shoulder – although having the hot, bright flame so close to his face coloured his thoughts with an intense unease. He bit his lip and peered into the strange, eerie gloom ahead. Reddish and faintly glowing, the air flickered with little flashes of light far in the distance.

'Sorry,' said Maris, close to his ear.

'Me, too,' said Quint. 'We've got enough to worry about without falling out with each other.'

'Being in the stonecomb, you mean?' said Maris.

Quint nodded. 'It's the most unpleasant place I've ever been,' he said. 'The endless maze of tunnels. The constant shifting of the rock . . .' He shuddered. 'We'd better keep moving.'

It wasn't only the stonecomb that concerned Quint, but also the creatures which the terrible place offered refuge to. Being pursued through the tunnels on his previous visit was still all too fresh in his memory. The pulsing crimson light. The flapping and snuffling and groaning – and the way whatever it was had cried out with such obvious relish when it tasted his blood.

He hesitated. They had come to a fork in the corridor and Quint needed to concentrate to make sure that they went the right way. As he scoured the walls carefully, an icy shiver ran the length of his spine. He was sure he was being watched.

'Is that it?' asked Maris, pointing to a small, ill-formed arrow on the wall at one of the entrances.

'Yes,' said Quint uncertainly. 'Yes, it's this way. Come on.'

They continued down the left-hand tunnel in silence. All round them, the atmosphere changed as they penetrated deeper and deeper into the rock. The hissing grew softer, the humming grew louder, the temperature rose. Both Maris and Quint were soon wiping their brows and loosening their clothes, and their discomfort wasn't helped by the fact that the path they were following was climbing. Quint suddenly stopped. Maris bumped into him and the lantern swung wildly.

'What is it?' she said.

'This isn't right,' said Quint.

'Not right?' she said, the cold anger returning to her voice. 'But I thought we were following the track that you'd marked.'

'We were,' said Quint, trying to stay calm. 'The thing is, when I was following your father, the tunnel we took was flat. This tunnel is . . .'

'Going upwards,' said Maris. She sighed.

'We must have taken a wrong turning,' said Quint. 'We'll have to go back.'

'Oh, great,' said Maris in a flat voice. She was no longer angry – just weary. 'You mean we're lost.' Suddenly her energy seemed gone. She slumped to the tunnel floor. The lantern by her side dimmed as its reserve of tilder-oil ran low.

'We mustn't give up,' said Quint. He reached down and, with an immense effort, forced himself to pick up the lantern. His hands shook; the fiery light flickered. 'Come on, Maris,' he said. 'If I can make myself carry this lantern, then you can make yourself carry on.'

Maris said nothing, her face now buried in her hands.

'Maris, please!' said Quint. 'I need you. I can't do this on my own.'

He held out his hand. Slowly Maris looked up. There were tears in her eyes, but also that look which Quint was beginning to know so well, the stubbornness and courage just below the surface. She smiled, took his out-stretched hand and let herself be pulled up.

'Sorry,' she said once more.

She reached out and took the lantern from his hand. As she did so, the flame sputtered and died, and they were enveloped by the oppressive gloom. Quint peered about him. Although it was not pitch-black in the tunnel, the faintly glowing stonecomb barely produced enough light to see by.

'The arrows will be even more difficult to find now,' he said.

'I was right, then,' said Maris despondently. 'We *are* lost.'

The words echoed sibilantly and faded away. Down the tunnels, little flashing lights glinted in the gloom – now ice-blue, now poison-green.

Quint could see Maris before him, silhouetted against the dull glow. Her head was down again, her shoulders slumped. He gripped her by the arm. 'We're going to be all right, Maris,' he said reassuringly. 'You'll see.'

Out of the corner of his eye, the clusters of flickering, floating lights turned to pastel pinks and yellows.

'But how, Quint?' Maris demanded. 'How? It's too dark to find the arrows now. You said so yourself.'

'*Difficult*, I said,' he told her. 'Not impossible. And if we can't see well enough, then ... then, we'll *feel* our way along. So long as we keep going in the same direction, we'll be fine.'

'Feel our way along *where*?' said Maris. 'We don't know which way anything is. Oh, Quint, this is *hopeless*!'

Her cry of despair boomed along the dark tunnel. Grains of sand trickled down to the floor, hissing softly as they landed. The flickering lights suddenly glinted brighter than ever. They flashed and sparked – on, off, on, off . . .

'Did you see that?' Quint whispered urgently. 'What are they?'

Maris nodded uneasily. She clutched at his jerkin and clung on tight. 'I think they're glisters,' she whispered. 'Though I've never seen so many together before.' She swallowed nervously. 'I don't like it.'

'It's almost as though they reacted to what you said,' said Quint. He paused. 'Do you think glisters could do that?'

'I . . . I'm not sure,' said Maris. 'Maybe.' She pulled away from him and peered back into the gloomy darkness warily. The hovering lights darted this way and that. Low, groans resounded ominously from deeper in the tunnel. 'Welma would say they could,' she said at last.

'She would?' said Quint.

'Oh, yes,' said Maris, her eyes looking round anxiously. 'She's convinced they know how we're feeling – that they react to our moods. For instance, she says that the glisters which are attracted to the Viaduct Steps for the annual *March of Fools* are warm-coloured, glowing creatures – quite different from the sparking, flashing ones that gather in the Stone Gardens during a funeral.' She shivered. 'Mind you, not everyone can see them as well as Welma.' She paused. '*She* reckons *none* of them are to be trusted.'

The lights sparked and flashed.

'There,' said Quint. 'It happened again. Whenever you speak, they go all sparky! Whereas when *I* speak . . .' He frowned thoughtfully. 'From the glimpses you do get, they're really quite beautiful. I wonder what they actually look li—'

'No, Quint,' Maris interrupted him sternly. 'They say you should never try to look at a glister directly.'

Quint started back in alarm. 'Why not?' he said.

Maris shrugged. 'It's supposed to bring bad luck,' she said darkly.

The strange lights, which had been glowing orange and red a moment earlier, abruptly flashed brightly. Some of them started advancing along the tunnel; others filtered through the porous rock and hovered just out of direct view. A soft moaning echoed from the shadowy depths.

Quint and Maris ducked their heads and kept on along the tunnel. They had to keep moving. Quint glanced back over his shoulder.

209

'But w . . . what *are* they exactly?' he said.

Maris shrugged. 'There are many tales,' she said. 'Some say they are the lost souls of those academics who died away from Sanctaphrax, far from the white ravens who would have picked their bones clean and sent their souls soaring up to open sky.'

'The souls of dead academics,' Quint murmured, the hairs on the back of his neck standing on end.

'Some say they are Deepwoods demons,' Maris went on, 'nameless ones, from the darkest reaches of the forest. Others, that they are the spirits of the stonecomb itself . . .'

Quint trembled. The lights flashed menacingly. The ominous groans grew louder.

'But then, who knows?' said Maris, a defiant edge coming into her voice as she fumbled her way behind him along the tunnel. 'Every story told in Sanctaphrax is embellished and exaggerated. Why should these be any different?'

The lights softened and fell back. The air seemed to sigh. Quint reached back for Maris's hand and squeezed it tightly. 'You're very brave, you know,' he said simply.

Maris squeezed back. 'It's not easy,' she admitted, looking round into the oppressive darkness of the stonecomb. 'I hate it so much down here.'

'I know,' said Quint. He paused, furious with himself for getting them lost in the labyrinthine tunnels. 'We'll soon come to that junction where we went wrong, I know we will,' he said at last. 'Then we can decide which way we want to go – either back to the tunnel entrance or on to the chamber.'

'Oh, on to the chamber,' said Maris. 'Definitely! We can't go back now, not having come so far. Besides, if my father . . .' She broke off mid-sentence. 'Quint, look!' she exclaimed.

'What?' he cried.

'There,' said Maris. 'On the wall by your elbow.'

The tunnel echoed with the rising sound of moaning and groaning. The lights glimmered. Quint turned and his heart leapt as he saw what she was pointing at. This time there could be no doubt that it was one of the black chalk arrows he had made.

'Thank Sky!' he exclaimed. 'I knew we'd find it.'

They headed off in the direction the arrow was pointing towards. The tunnel was wider here and it was possible to walk two abreast. Quint was holding the hooked pikestaff. Maris clutched the lantern, just in case, in the chamber, there were reserves of tilder-oil that they could use to help them find their way back. For the first time since they'd entered the maze of tunnels, they were both feeling optimistic about the task that lay ahead.

'Soon be there,' said Quint.

'Good,' said Maris. 'Now that we've come this far, I'm not going back until I've found out what's in that mysterious chamber.'

'Me, neither,' said Quint. 'I . . .'

'*Ouch!*'

Quint stopped in his tracks and turned to see Maris rubbing the side of her head gingerly. 'Are you OK?' he said.

'I'm fine,' she said. 'I just banged my head on that bit of jutting rock there.'

Quint winced. 'Let me take a look,' he said.

'It's nothing,' said Maris. 'Really.'

Her hair was glistening with something wet and sticky. Quint was gripped by a sudden, intoxicating fear. 'Maris!' he gasped. 'Maris, you're bleeding!'

His voice echoed. The tunnels groaned. Far in the distance, the lights flashed and sparked.

'Am I?' said Maris, unconcerned. She looked at her fingers. 'So I am,' she said. 'Still, it's only a graze . . .'

'No, Maris,' said Quint, his voice low with dread as he remembered the last time he was in the stonecomb. 'You don't understand. That creature I told you about . . . the huge, red creature . . . it follows the smell of blood . . .'

Already, above the gloomy moans and groans, he could hear a sniffing, snuffling sound. And it was getting closer! In a terrible blind panic, he grabbed Maris's arm.

'It's coming after us!' he screamed. 'Quick, Maris. We've got to get out of here now, while we still can!'

Together, they hurried along the dark corridor. Behind them the flapping and snorting grew louder. This was serious. Something was after them. Something that meant them harm.

'Faster!' he urged. 'Faster! Before . . .'

'*Whiii-whiii-whiiiiii!*'

Quint's heart missed a beat as the terrible high-pitched squealing filled the tunnel. It sounded exactly the same as before. The creature had found Maris's blood – and liked it as much as it had liked his own! He shivered violently as the slavering and slurping grew more frenzied.

'WHIII-WHIIIIII!'

All at once, there was a rushing, roaring noise close behind them and, for a moment, the tunnel became as bright as day. Quint stumbled, tripped and fell heavily to the ground. The air above his head turned warm and stale. It crackled and howled. It fizzed and sparked.

Then it fell still. Quint looked round anxiously.

The tunnel was once again bathed in the shadowy reddish glow. The creature had gone. And so had Maris!

'Quint!' he heard her screaming, her voice echoing back down the long tunnel.

Quint leapt to his feet. The terrible beast had just tasted blood – Maris's blood – and now it had Maris! Quint gripped the hooked pikestaff grimly. His dark eyes blazed. 'I'm coming!' he shouted back.

He dashed along the corridor as fast as he could. All around him now, the air was sparking and flashing. Ahead of him he could see the deep-red glow of the retreating creature.

'*Quint!*' Maris cried out. She sounded terrified, desperate, close to the end of her tether.

'Remember how brave you are!' Quint yelled back.

The light faded abruptly. Quint kept on till he arrived at a fork in the tunnel. He paused. He cocked his head to one side. From the right-hand tunnel came the faint sound of snuffling and snorting.

'*There* you are,' Quint muttered through clenched teeth, a burning rage suddenly gripping him. 'I'll get you if it's the last thing I do.'

He ducked his head and hurried into the low, narrow tunnel. The rock hummed and glowed.

'Quint!' Maris's voice floated back. The snuffling and snorting grew louder. The air flickered. Far ahead, the red glow came back into view.

Quint sped up, in hot pursuit of the creature which, only the previous day, had been pursuing him. He fumbled and stumbled his way along the cramped tunnel as fast as he could, determined to lose neither sight nor sound of his quarry. He would never forgive himself if anything happened to Maris.

All at once, the light disappeared again. The creature

must have turned a corner. Quint scurried to the end of the stretch of tunnel, paused, cocked his head to one side – and dashed off once more after the receding sounds.

'Hang on, Maris!' he yelled. 'I'll get to you!'

He grazed his knuckles on the rough walls, he tripped on the irregular rock below his feet and knocked his head painfully against the low ceiling – but he kept on, the anger burning in his chest as he tracked the snuffling, snorting beast which flapped on relentlessly with Maris. He was going as fast as he could – but all the while, the pair of them were getting farther and farther away.

'Come on,' Quint muttered. 'I mustn't lose them.'

Yet even as he urged himself on, Quint knew that his task was becoming harder with every passing second. The stonecomb was a terrible, treacherous maze. Tiny tunnels gave way to huge ones that suddenly branched into countless smaller passages which zigzagged off in all directions. Had he lost them already? He stopped. Which way should he go now?

'Maris!' he bellowed. 'MARIS!'

'Quint!'

The voice came from his left. It sounded weary, frail. He turned and ran towards it. The tunnel became wider and higher, and he sprinted along it, trying desperately to catch up.

'*Quint!*'

It was louder now. He *must* be getting closer. 'I'm coming, Maris!' he shouted back. 'Just hold on!'

At the far end of the tunnel, he skidded round the

corner – and stopped dead. His jaw dropped. The dimly glowing tunnel ahead was empty. There was no sight of the strange lights: no flickering, no flashing. And though he strained to hear, not a sound.

'But I was so sure,' he murmured, his voice low, trembling. 'Maris!' he called. 'MARIS!'

Apart from his own echoed cries, there was nothing. He shook his head and advanced slowly.

'She can't just have disappeared. She . . .'

And then he heard it: a soft, scratching sound. But where was it coming from? Not from in front of him, that much was certain. He turned round, retraced his footsteps and listened intently.

There it was again. Scratching. Scraping. And, unless his imagination was playing cruel tricks, a low slurping sound. His blood ran cold.

Cautiously, he rounded the bend and there, not a dozen strides ahead of him, was a crimson light fanning out from a low hole at the bottom of the tunnel wall like a pool of blood.

'Sky curse this place!' he shouted. 'I must have walked straight past it.'

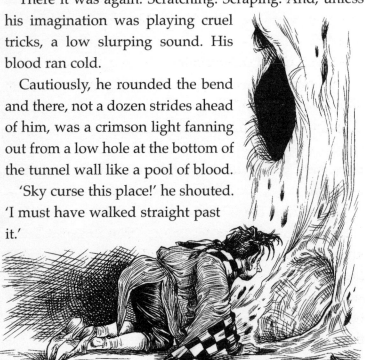

As his anger echoed round the tunnels, the scratches and slurps fell abruptly silent and the red light disappeared.

Puzzled, Quint walked over to the low hole, crouched down and peered in. His heart pounded loudly. Before him lay a long, narrow tunnel. If Maris had come this way then he had no choice but to continue on his hands and knees to find her. But what if she hadn't? What if it was a trap?

'Maris?' he called out, listening nervously for a reply as the echo faded away.

At first there was nothing. Quint waited silently. Still nothing. Then, just as he was about to continue his search elsewhere, the same scratching, slurping sounds resumed from the far end of the winding, tube-like tunnel.

'Maris?' Quint called again.

This time a weak, tremulous voice answered him. 'Qui . . . i . . . int,' it faltered. 'Help . . . m . . . *mffllmfff.'*

Quint's stomach sank as her cries were abruptly stifled. But she was still alive. That was the important thing. She was *still alive*! He felt for the hooked pikestaff.

'I'm coming, Maris,' he muttered grimly.

Heart hammering in his chest, Quint dropped to his knees and crawled into the tunnel. As the hole through the rock grew narrower, the walls squeezed in at his sides and forced his shoulders down. The rough rock beneath him frayed the knees of his trousers and grazed the palms of his hands.

'Can't be far now,' he muttered to himself encouragingly.

His body shook, his face glistened with cold sweat. All round him, the rock was edged with the bright red light which was once again streaming down the tunnel from somewhere up ahead. The scratching was intermittent now, and much less insistent, but the hideous slurping was low and regular.

'Oh, Maris,' Quint said. 'Be brave. I'm coming as fast as I can.'

He craned his neck to see ahead. And there it was – a bright circle of light in front of him. The end of the tunnel.

'Nearly there,' Quint murmured.

As he drove himself on those last few strides, head down and teeth clenched, the quality of the air changed. It became cooler, damper, and his ears picked up the empty, echoing resonance of a great hall. Again, with effort, Quint craned his neck to peer ahead.

He was even nearer to the end than he'd dared believe. Just in front of him a wedge-shaped heap of scree fanned out into an opening beyond. He found himself peering into what seemed to be some great cavern.

'Be on your guard,' he told himself. 'Keep your eyes peeled and your ears pricked.'

He edged himself forwards to the very end of the tunnel. All at once, the vile slobbering noises started up again, louder than ever.

'*No*,' he breathed, and tried to draw back – but his hand skidded on the slippery scree, his body lurched forwards and he slid helplessly down out of the tunnel in a noisy flurry of dust and fragments of rock.

The slurping stopped. The red light went out. Quint scrabbled to his feet and looked round him wildly.

He was indeed inside a cavern – a vast, egg-shaped chamber which was dark, chilling and filled with spectral lights and flitting shadows. The walls were pitted and rough to the touch, and – he noted with grow-ing panic – without any means of escape save for the narrow tunnel he had come in by.

'Sky protect me,' he murmured, his breath coming in jerky gasps.

Whatever had attacked Maris must be out there in the darkness somewhere. Watching. Listening. *Waiting* for him . . .

'Stay c . . . calm,' he told himself. But his heart was thumping fit to burst. How *could* he stay calm in this terrible place? Everything about it filled him with fear . . .

And then he heard it: the ominous wet snorting and snuffling so difficult to identify. It was coming from the oppressive shadowy darkness some way to his right. His heart missed a beat. He was shaking from head to foot.

All round him, the glimmering lights began to sparkle and flash from the rough, pitted wall and Quint could just make out countless tiny glisters which clung to its jutting ridges and jagged protuberances. Occasionally, one would detach itself and fly through the air, flickering in the corner of his eye as it passed.

A cold sweat bathed Quint's face. There were so many of them. With a shudder that racked his entire body, he realized where he must be – *inside a glister lair!*

The revolting noises grew louder. Quint shivered. He must find Maris before it was too late. Rallying all his dwindling courage, he stepped cautiously forward, towards the sound. The flashing lights bounced off the bumps and boulders strewn across the cavern floor. Quint's footsteps echoed round the cavern. He dropped to his knees and tried to move as silently as he could.

Had the creature heard him? Or smelled his blood? Did it still have Maris in its clutches, or had she managed to give it the slip in this vast cavern? Was she even now crouched down in some corner, scared and alone, waiting for him to rescue her?

Quint edged closer to the awful sound. Then, with a sickening jolt, he saw an indistinct dark shape ahead of him. He paused. The glisters flickered above him and Quint shivered with horror as the hunched figure of a massive creature came briefly into view.

'What the . . . ?' he whispered.

The creature flickered with light as if in response to Quint's voice – but did not turn.

It was awesome – a great formless blood-red beast

constantly shifting its shape like a sackful of fighting fromps. Now round, now long; now perfectly smooth, now a writhing mass of eyes and tentacles. And all the while, inside its glowing body – no matter what the shape – a chain of dull red lights coursed endlessly along its throbbing veins.

'It's dis-*gust*-ing,' Quint groaned, sickened by the sight of the repulsive, blood-red creature.

He turned away. He wanted to go. But where was Maris? He couldn't leave without her.

Quint looked round desperately, squinting into every crack and crevice for his missing friend. He stumbled forwards. His foot struck a bump on the cavern floor.

As the noise echoed throughout the cavern, the slurping sound stopped and, once more, the light inside the great creature went out. It was listening. A few moments later, the crimson light flickered into life again and the disgusting sounds began with renewed vigour. Rooted to the spot, Quint stared at the creature in horror.

And then he saw it! Sticking out from beneath the enormous formless creature was a foot.

'MARIS!' Quint bellowed, and dashed forwards – only to trip and fall heavily to the ground. He sat up nervously. It had felt as if someone had grabbed at his ankle.

All about him the chamber was lit up as the countless tiny glisters flashed and flickered in response to his own terrible fear. Suddenly Quint saw what had tripped him.

It was a corpse – a leathery mummified corpse with shrunken lips and sunken eyes, frozen at a moment of

absolute terror. He had stumbled against its left hand –
which had become detached from the rest of the body
and now lay in the dust some way off.

Quint gagged emptily. 'No, no!' he groaned as he
scuttled back, terrified, horrified, yet unable to tear his
eyes away from the appalling sight.

The corpse had once been a treasury-guard. Quint
recognized the tooled leather breastplate and spiked
helmet. But this was one flat-head goblin whose
immense strength and fighting prowess had failed to
save him. And if *he* had fallen victim to the monstrous
blood-red creature . . .

'Maris,' Quint whispered, bile rising in his throat.
'MARIS!'

Pikestaff raised high, he staggered forwards – stumbling for a second time. With his arms flailing wildly, he
managed not to fall – and looked down to see a second
corpse. Like the first, it had been frozen at the point of
death with its gruesome gurning head bent backwards
at an impossible angle and its arms and legs akimbo.

It was not alone.

All round him, as the glisters flashed and sparked brighter than ever, Quint now saw that the entire floor was littered with dead bodies – woodtrolls, slaughterers and mobgnomes, identifiable only by their amulets and their hair; academics, their gowns wrapped round their bones like funeral shrouds; and curious shrunken individuals, with limbs like driftwood and clothes that Quint had only seen in history books.

Ahead of him the great shapeless beast, now glowing a deep, violent red, rose up from the lifeless body of his friend. No wonder it was so immense, Quint realized shakily. How many centuries had it lurked down here, picking off the unwary, the reckless, the foolish? How many individuals had it drawn into its grisly lair, and sucked dry?

A slobbery wet slurp echoed round the chamber as the formidable creature withdrew long, glinting tentacles from Maris's eyes. Quint felt sick with fear. This was no game: no childish adventure with rules and truces. It was real. And frightening. Possibly Maris was dead already. Probably he would be next. Yet he couldn't turn back. He couldn't abandon her, even if it meant risking the same terrible fate.

With an animal-like scream of rage, Quint hurled himself forwards. The hooked pikestaff hissed through the air. Bones scattered before his feet.

'*Whiii-whiii-whiiiiii!*'

The ear-splitting screech echoed menacingly round the death-filled chamber as the furious creature turned to face him. Quint seemed to freeze in mid-air, his head pounding and his body quaking. There was a loud roaring noise and a rush of stale air.

Quint screwed his eyes shut. The pikestaff was knocked from his hand. The next instant, he found himself being tossed down onto his back.

The creature was on him in an instant, swallowing him up in its great, amorphous body. Quint was unable to move so much as a muscle. And as he lay there – immobile, silent, scared – he felt something burning hot probing at his face, trying to prise his eyelids apart.

He couldn't cry out; he could barely breathe. The screeching – within his head, and without – grew louder. His body felt racked and pummelled. Outside, and inside, the terrible light grew more and more and more intense until he felt his head would explode with blood-red light . . .

Then, nothing.

·CHAPTER THIRTEEN·

BUNGUS SEPTRILL

As consciousness slowly returned to him, Quint stirred. A dull pain grumbled at the base of his spine. He groaned softly and the sound echoed round the still, dark air. His head felt light, fuzzy, and curiously empty – as if his thoughts had all been stripped away.

Where am I? he wondered. *Who* am I? For a moment, it was a struggle even to remember his own name.

'Quint,' he whispered, the name rising to the surface of his mind like an oozefish in a dark Mire pool. 'Quint, I must be Quint.'

And yet he couldn't be sure. His mind was as blank and featureless as the Mire itself. Another thought swam upwards. It floated there just below the surface, indistinct yet menacing. He had encountered something in the darkness; something evil and formless – something impossible to grasp hold of, yet as pervasive as a foul Mire mistwraith.

Quint grimaced. It had attacked him. It had pinned him to the floor. Unable to move, he'd felt it probing, prising . . .

With a mounting sense of unease, Quint became aware that, even now, there was something close by. He could hear it rustling softly. He could smell the faintly acrid smell of rotting leaves. He held his breath, kept his eyes tightly shut and prayed feverishly that it would leave him alone. Then all at once he felt something papery brushing across his smarting eyelids.

'*Aargh!*' he screamed, and lashed out wildly.

There was a sharp *crack* and a cry of pain as his left fist struck flesh and bone.

Quint gasped. Whatever he'd hit, it was solid enough. His eyes snapped open and he found himself staring at a gangly old individual who was crouched down beside him, tenderly rubbing his jaw with gnarled fingers.

In the dim lantern-light, Quint saw his big, bushy moustache, his twitching beak-like nose and heavy brow. He was dressed in curious, papery clothes and had a small leather satchel slung over one shoulder. As he returned Quint's gaze, his eyes narrowed.

'A fine way to treat someone who just saved your life,' the stranger grumbled in a low voice, as dry as parchment.

'Saved my life?' Quint murmured questioningly.

'You've had a very lucky escape,' he said. 'If I hadn't come when I did . . .'

Quint gasped. 'There was a blood-red creature!' he cried as the terrible memory washed over him. 'It attacked me!'

'It was a glister,' said his rescuer.

Quint turned to him. 'A glister?' he said. 'But it can't have been. It was enormous.'

'I know,' the stranger replied, 'but it was a glister, nevertheless. A great rogue glister that haunts the stonecomb. It hunts the weak, the lost . . .'

'Maris!' Quint shouted. He pulled himself up and clutched hold of the stranger's crinkly coat. 'My friend, Maris,' he said, and winced as the dull ache in his back became a sharp stab of pain. 'She . . . she . . .'

'Don't move,' the old fellow told him, and pressed him gently, but firmly, back down to the ground. As he moved, his clothes rustled. The whiff of damp compost grew more intense.

'But . . .' Quint began.

'Your friend is alive,' the stranger said. 'Now, lie back.'

'She is?' Quint breathed. 'Thank Sky . . .'

'That's enough of that, my lad,' came a sharp rebuke.
'It's Earth, not Sky, you need to thank.' He leant back on
his heels and retrieved an open pot from behind him.
'Now let me just get some of this salve on your eyelids
where that great brute of a glister burned them,' he said.
'Close your eyes.'

Quint did as he was told, and this time he did not react
as the old, papery fingers rubbed in the soothing salve.

His eyelids stopped smarting and were flooded with a
wonderful coolness. The pungent smell of decomposing
vegetation grew stronger than ever.

More memories came back to Quint: a mere trickle at
first, then a stream, and finally a great wave which broke
over the ugly blank mire of his mind and set it awash
with thoughts. Maris. The Professor. The barkscroll, the
mission to the stonecomb, the mysterious chamber . . .
The pungent odour had brought them all back.
Suddenly, Quint knew exactly where he had smelled it
before – *and* heard the soft rustling noise.

'The library!' he exclaimed. 'You were the one who caught me when I was falling. You . . . you saved my life.'

The old fellow snorted. 'I seem to be making a habit of it,' he muttered. The fingers stopped rubbing Quint's eyelids. 'That should do you,' he said. 'Now roll over so I can take a look at your back.'

Once again, Quint did as he was told. He craned his neck backwards. 'Who are you?' he said.

'You won't have heard of me,' came the reply. 'My name is Bungus Septrill. I am the High Librarian, the custodian of earth-studies.' He sighed. 'Not that that means much these days.' He pressed firmly into the base of Quint's back with his spatula-like thumbs. 'Does that hurt?'

'No,' said Quint.

'And that?'

'No.'

'And . . .'

'*Aaaiiii!*' Quint yelped. 'Yes, that *really* hurt!' It felt as if a shard of ice had lodged itself in his back.

'*Mmm*,' he heard Bungus musing. 'A glister-wrench,' he said, 'and quite severe.'

'What does that mean?' asked Quint, alarmed. It sounded serious. Would it prove fatal?

Bungus shuffled round until he was crouched down at Quint's head. 'It means,' he said matter-of-factly, 'that we will have to try and make it better. Now, let me see.'

He reached round for the leather satchel and unfastened the clasp. Quint looked up and watched, half in fear, half in fascination, as Bungus removed a second small pot. From this, he extracted eight streaky, waxen-looking leaves, which he put in his mouth and chewed vigorously. Meanwhile, he returned to the bag, removed a large bandage and laid it out on the floor.

'Am I . . . am I going to die?' Quint asked weakly.

Bungus just smiled and, without a word, extracted the green pasty wad from his mouth and began smearing it down Quint's spine. 'Brindleweed-leaf poultice,' he said simply. 'Good for reducing inflammation and numbing deep pain.'

'It burns,' said Quint.

Bungus nodded. 'That's the poultice taking effect,' he said. He wiped his fingers on his robes, picked up the bandage and pressed it against Quint's back, sealing the poultice into position. The burning sensation turned to a glowing warmth that penetrated down and seemed to melt the terrible ice-spike in his spine. 'There,' said Bungus at last. 'Now stand up, and tell me how it feels.'

Quint picked himself up cautiously, nervous that the sharp pain would make him cry out again. But it was gone, completely gone – and as he stretched his cramped muscles even the remaining dull ache disappeared.

'Well?' said Bungus.

'It feels great,' he said. 'As good as new.'

'Brindleweed was once a common-enough remedy,' said Bungus. 'Though I dare say the so-called scholars of the sky, with all their new-fangled nonsense, know nothing of the herb's properties . . .'

But Quint was not listening. As his eyes had grown accustomed to the darkness of the great egg-shaped cavern, he'd seen his friend, sitting with her back propped up against the wall, eyes closed. She looked pale and tense.

'Maris,' he murmured, and hurried across to her. He knelt down and took her hands in his own. 'Maris, are you all right?'

Maris opened her eyes and nodded weakly, but said nothing. Her skin was clammy; her expression was glazed.

'She needs time,' said Bungus, coming up behind them. 'Like you, she's had a narrow escape, and

the glister had her for far longer. I've done what I can for her.' He patted the leather satchel. 'The study of the medicinal plants of the

Deepwoods is one of the oldest of all earth-studies. Mind you,' he added with a shake of his head, 'it was touch and go for a while. That rogue glister is a terrible, dangerous creature . . .'

'It caught me, Quint,' said Maris, her voice low and flat; every word an effort. 'Whatever I did, I couldn't seem to get free . . .'

'It tracked you,' said Quint. 'It smelled your blood and . . .' He noticed Bungus shaking his head slowly, and turned. 'It's true,' he said, 'and it wasn't the first time either. The same one chased me once when I cut myself.'

'The glister *was* tracking you, that much is true,' Bungus said. 'As I told you, it is a hunter. But it isn't the scent of blood it follows.'

'It isn't?' said Quint, confused. 'Then what?'

'Your fear,' said Bungus. 'It follows the scent of your fear.'

Quint shuddered as he recalled just how frightened he and Maris had been.

'Of course, fear is not the only emotion that draws a glister's attention,' Bungus went on. 'There is also rage, frustration, envy . . . All glisters, whatever their size, are sensitive to emotions.'

Quint nodded vigorously. 'We noticed that, didn't we, Maris?'

'It came after me,' Maris murmured weakly. 'I couldn't lose it.'

Quint turned to Bungus. 'Every time we spoke, the glisters seemed to react differently. Sometimes glowing. Sometimes sparking and flashing.'

'The stronger the emotion, the brighter the light,' Bungus said. 'Though it is fear which causes them to blaze brightest of all.' He paused. 'For it is fear which makes them hungry.'

'Hungry,' Quint repeated, dread in his voice.

'They feed on fear,' said Bungus, and shook his head. 'Though normally glisters are like . . . like woodgnats feeding on a hammelhorn. They do no harm. The prickles at the back of a neck or a shiver down a spine are enough to satisfy them. As an earth-scholar I have studied glisters down here in the stonecomb since I was a junior librarian, and believe me when I tell you . . .' he glanced round at the mummified corpses littering the cavern, 'the rogue glister is like no other glister that has ever . . .'

'It was horrible,' Maris moaned, more animated now. 'It chased me. It caught me. I couldn't struggle. I couldn't move. I couldn't stop it prising my eyelids apart and forcing itself inside my head. And it hurt, Quint! It hurt so much.' She fell silent and turned to Bungus, tears welling up in the corners of her eyes. 'If you hadn't arrived when you did!'

'But I did arrive,' said Bungus softly. He stooped down and took hold of her hands. 'You're safe now.'

Quint frowned uneasily. 'How *did* you find us?' he said. 'Were you following us, too?'

At the back of his mind lurked the suspicion that the High Librarian was perhaps in on the intrigue against the Most High Academe. If Bungus Septrill noticed the mistrustful tone to Quint's question, he did not show it.

'No, not you,' he said in his dry, papery voice. 'I was tracking the rogue glister itself.' He sighed. 'After the Great Library, the stonecomb is a second home to me – a refuge from the sky-scholars up there.' He gazed up into the blackness and brandished his fist. 'But for a long time now, I've been hearing rumours; talk of disappearances, of inexplicable noises and strange goings-on down here. You were followed, you say. Well, you weren't the first. It was the treasury-guards who initially reported sightings of a huge, blood-red glister. According to them, it not only fed on fear but, entering through the eyes, devoured every feeling, every memory, every thought – leaving its victims empty, dried out, without the instinct even to breathe. The sky-scholars dismissed the reports as Deepwoods superstition, but I knew better. And now, so do you.'

'How did you get it off me?' asked Quint. 'Did you kill it?'

'Kill it?' Bungus shook his head woefully. 'You clearly know nothing about glisters,' he said. 'What *do* they teach you in that school of yours?'

Quint suddenly found himself back in the Fountain House classroom chanting out cloud formations once again – *cursive low, cursive flat, anvil wide, anvil rising* . . . Mechanical. Pointless.

'A lot of superstitious nonsense is spoken about glisters,' Bungus was saying. 'About them being souls, spirits or the like. In fact, they are the seeds of open sky which blow in from beyond the Edge. This they have done since the beginning of time, sowing the land with life. They are the building blocks of existence itself, carried in on storm-force winds to Riverrise, where they come to earth and flow out into the Deepwoods along the Edgewater River, to blossom into every form and kind of life.'

He fell still, and Quint watched as his expression became thoughtful.

'At least,' he said, 'that is what happened before the great Sanctaphrax rock rose above the Edge. Since then, some sky seeds have inevitably been blown into the great rock itself and taken root in the stonecomb. Here, far from Riverrise, they develop into glisters – the spectral beings that flitter throughout the tunnels.'

Quint glanced round him. Thankfully, there were none to be seen.

'Of course, most of them are harmless,' Bungus went on. 'Occasionally, one will leave a small glister-burn if provoked, but I've never seen any others as huge and deadly as this one.' He paused. 'But whether large or small, you can't *kill* a glister, for the simple reason that they're not alive – at least, not as we understand it. They are the phantoms of things that have never lived. Those that stray outside the stonecomb soon dissolve into nothingness.' Bungus pulled a leather pouch from the pocket of his cape and untied the drawstring. 'Inside, I use this to ward them off.'

Maris and Quint peered inside.

'Sand?' said Quint. 'What use is that?'

'It isn't sand,' said Bungus. He reached into the pouch and drew out a pinch of grainy white powder. 'To earth-scholars, it is known as chine,' he said.

Quint looked closely at the tiny crystals glittering in the High Librarian's leathery palm.

'It is gathered from the edges of the lake at Riverrise,' Bungus explained.

'Riverrise,' Quint said, impressed. 'Even my father's sky ship, the *Galerider*, has never ventured that far into the Deepwoods. I wasn't even sure it actually existed.'

'Yet the Scholar Librarians visited Riverrise many times,' said Bungus. He smiled. 'I have often dreamt of travelling there myself, but like so much of earth-scholarship, the route to Riverrise is lost. More's the pity.' He looked down at his hand. 'What stormphrax is to sky-scholars, so chine is to us earth-scholars. It is the crystallized essence of the Edgewater. And to a glister,' he added, 'a crystal of chine is as corrosive as the strongest acid. If one comes threateningly close . . .' He raised his hand to his mouth and blew a single grain into the air. '*Pfff!* And it is gone.'

'I wish we'd had some earlier,' said Quint.

'Alas, I fear it'll take my entire supply of chine to deter the monstrous blood-red glister we encountered,' said Bungus, returning the leather pouch to his pocket. 'The pinch I caught it with will have weakened it – maybe for a few hours – but it *will* be back.' He helped Maris to her feet and picked up his lantern. 'Come now. We really should be leaving.'

Maris clasped his hand. She had still not fully re-
covered – either mentally or physically – from her
terrible ordeal.

'My father will reward you well for saving me,' she
murmured.

Bungus smiled and offered his arm as a support. 'Your
father?' he said. 'A sky-scholar, no doubt. You are very
kind, but no sky-scholar would risk his position to help
an old and decrepit earth-studies librarian like me.'

'My father most certainly would,' said Maris imperi-
ously. 'For he is the Most High Academe of Sanctaphrax
himself.'

Bungus stopped in his tracks. He turned to Maris, eyes
wide and mouth gaping. 'You are the daughter of Linius
Pallitax?' he said.

It was Maris's turn to be surprised. 'You know my
father?'

'Indeed I do,' Bungus confirmed. 'Or rather, I did.'

'But how is that possible?' said Maris, her eyes flashing. She grasped the old librarian by the sleeve. 'You
must tell me.'

'Earth alive!' Bungus exclaimed. 'How like him you
look. I can see it now . . .' He shook his head. 'Linius
used to visit the Great Library when he was a lad,' he
explained. 'He would sneak off from the Fountain
House, frustrated by the nit-picking tedium of the
lessons offered by those so-called teachers and keen to
discover more about the true and ancient wisdom contained in the hanging barkscrolls. Initially, I introduced
him to the rudiments of earth-studies. Later, once he had

got the hang of the library trees, he began to pursue his own interests independently.'

Quint nodded. 'That would explain how he knows so much about the place,' he said. 'He was able to tell me exactly where to go to retrieve the barkscroll he needed.'

'So that's what you were doing in my library,' said Bungus, thoughtfully. He looked up. 'I don't suppose you remember which barkscroll Linius was after?'

'I . . . didn't read it properly,' said Quint. 'It . . .'

'Then where exactly did you find it?' said Bungus. 'Do try to remember.' He fixed Quint with an intense stare. 'Which tree of knowledge did you climb?'

Quint racked his brains, fearing for a moment that his encounter with the rogue glister had erased that crucial part of his memory. But then, in his mind's eye, he suddenly saw the golden plaque. '*Aerial Creatures,*' he said.

Bungus nodded. 'Are you sure?'

'Yes,' said Quint, 'I had to climb right up to the top, following the "not" branches – *not bird, not reptile, not mammal* . . . The barkscroll was hanging from where two twigs crossed,' he said. '*Celestial* and . . . and . . . I just can't remember.'

Bungus's face darkened. 'What can my old pupil be up to?' he mused. 'Come to think of it, what is he doing allowing his daughter and apprentice to go wandering off through the stonecomb on their own?'

Maris and Quint caught each other's eye. Standing there in the empty lair of the blood-red glister, both of them suddenly felt very small, and very alone. Perhaps this strange ragged librarian with his papery clothes and powerful potions might actually be able to help. Quint squeezed Maris's hand in the darkness. She squeezed it back.

'Can we trust you?' said Maris.

'Trust me?' Bungus smiled. 'I may be an earth-scholar, but your father trusted me once.'

'Very well,' said Maris, suddenly very tired. 'Tell him, Quint.'

Quint nodded. He told him all about the Most High Academe's recent obsession with his work and how he, Quint, had been taken on to help him. He told him about the nightly trips down to the stonecomb and the terrible wounds the professor had sustained there. He described the shifty individual with the silver nose-piece, and the suspicious guard, and he explained about the sabotaging of the sky cage . . .

All the while Bungus listened in silence, head down and brow furrowed, his face betraying nothing of what he was thinking. It was only when Quint told him about what he had glimpsed and heard inside the chamber that he finally looked up.

'A great sphere of light?' he said. 'Sobbing cries?' The colour drained from his face. 'Can it be true?'

Maris trembled. Her encounter with the terrible rogue glister had left her feeling weak and light-headed. 'Can we just get out of here?' she whispered. 'Please.'

But Bungus made no reply. He gazed into the darkness. 'So long ago,' he breathed, almost to himself. 'So long ago as to be almost a legend . . . could my old pupil Linius really have discovered the lost Ancient Laboratory of the First Scholars?'

Quint frowned. 'But I thought the Great Laboratory was turned into the Treasury,' he said, remembering the brief history lesson he'd received from the individual on the Viaduct Steps.

Bungus shook his head. 'Once there were *two* laboratories,' he said. 'The Great Laboratory and the Ancient Laboratory. They each had very different purposes.

The Great Laboratory was the heart of earth-studies, a place where any new discoveries – be they animal, vegetable or mineral – were analysed and categorized ... Before it was seized by the sky-scholars and turned into the Treasury,' he added bitterly. 'Whereas the Ancient Laboratory ... Oh, Quint, lad,' he said, 'even back then when the rock was young, it was known as the *Ancient* Laboratory, because that is where the scholars of the origins of matter carried out their accursed work.'

He pulled a handkerchief from his pocket and patted away the cold sweat which beaded his forehead.

'What did they do?' said Quint.

Bungus shuddered. 'They were arrogant,' he said. 'They were vain. Understanding the world that already existed was not enough for them. They ...' His voice trailed off.

'What?' said Quint urgently.

'They wanted to unlock the most ancient mystery of all, the secret of life,' he said. 'They played at creation.'

Quint's jaw dropped. 'And ... and were they success-ful?' he asked.

'Nobody knows,' said Bungus. 'But obviously some-thing went badly wrong, for legend has it that the First Scholars shut the laboratory and blocked off the stonecomb leading to it. Soon after, the Great Schism between earth-studies and sky-scholarship took place, and both the laboratory and the experiments carried out there were forgotten.' Bungus sighed. 'From that day, it has remained a great mystery – yet from what you have told me, there is one person in Sanctaphrax who could know the answer. Linius Pallitax.'

Maris, who had been finding it increasingly difficult to concentrate, looked up as she heard her father's name being spoken. He'd done something dangerous, that much was clear, but she was confused. She could barely breathe. Her head was spinning and her legs had returned to jelly. She stood, rocking back and forwards on the balls of her feet, threatening to tumble to the floor at any moment.

'Maris,' said Bungus, stepping forward to support her. He turned to Quint. 'She went through far, far more with the glister than you did,' he said. 'Hanging on to life by a thread she was when I found her. It's amazing that she's still standing at all after such an attack. We must get her back to her father.'

Quint nodded.

'It's going to be fine, little one,' Bungus whispered to Maris. He pulled off his papery cape and wrapped it round Maris's shoulders. 'We're going now. Lean against me and put one foot in front of the other.' He set off once again, murmuring encouragingly as he went. 'That's the way. You can do it.' They soon came to the entrance of the tunnel. Bungus stopped and turned. 'I shall go first,' he said. 'Maris, I want you to follow me. Quint, bring up the rear. And make sure that she doesn't stop,' he added in a low whisper.

One after the other they climbed the scree slope, dropped to their hands and knees and entered the dark, narrow tunnel. Quint shuddered as he crawled into the blackness. With Maris in front of him, the light from Bungus's lantern was all but invisible. Chewing anxiously into his lower lip he inched his way along the tunnel.

It was cramped and claustrophobic, and when it narrowed and he had to squeeze through the unyielding rock that pressed in on all sides, his heart beat loudly. No-one who had been born and raised above ground would have felt comfortable in the confines of the stonecomb, but for Quint – used to flying

across the vastness of the sky – being locked inside the terrible rock was torture.

He tried to block his unease, to return to the reason he and Maris had first entered the stonecomb and concentrate only on what he now knew he must do: find the laboratory – the Ancient Laboratory – and discover what lay behind its locked door. And his heart thumped all the more furiously as he wondered exactly what might be there, imprisoned inside that strange, ancient place . . .

'*Unkkh!*' His head slammed into something solid in front of him. He looked

up, but could see nothing. His hands reached out to find a pair of feet and ankles directly in front of him. They were not moving.

'Maris!' he hissed. 'Maris, you have to keep going.'

There was no response.

'Maris!' he cried.

From farther along the tunnel he heard Bungus calling back to them. 'What's going on? Come on, we're nearly there.'

'Maris, don't give up now,' Quint urged her. 'You heard him. It's just a little further. Keep moving.'

'C . . . can't . . .' came the tremulous reply. 'S-so weak . . .'

'But you must!' said Quint and, in his desperation to escape the terrible tunnel, he shoved her hard.

Maris moved a little – then stopped again.

'Maris!' Quint shouted. 'For Sky's sake!' He felt as if the walls were closing in all round him.

'Grab hold of my belt,' Bungus called from up ahead. 'That's it. Now hang on tight and I'll pull you.'

In front of him, Quint felt Maris moving forwards. As she did so, Bungus's cape was tugged from her shoulders. Quint picked it up and squeezed hurriedly through the tunnel after her.

'Just a little further,' he could hear Bungus saying. 'That's it. That's the way . . .'

Hand after hand, Quint struggled on. His grazed knees chafed against the rough rock beneath him. All at once, he heard Bungus cry out.

'That's *it*!' his voice echoed. 'Well done, Mistress Maris!'

The next moment, Quint's own head popped out of the narrow opening and into the broader tunnel. Maris was sitting on the floor. Bungus was crouched down beside her, lamp raised, looking into her staring, unblinking eyes, one after the other, and whispering reassuringly.

'The difficult bit's over now, Mistress Maris,' he was telling her softly. 'We'll have you out of here in no time.'

She was in good hands, Quint realized. Bungus would take care of her and ensure she got back safely to Sanctaphrax and her father. As for himself, it was not yet time to return to the professor – even though, as he looked round, his former resolve began to waver. The maze of tunnels stretched out dauntingly in all directions, he had no lamp to help him find his way – and, worst of all, the blood-red glister was still out there somewhere. However, terrified as he was of a second encounter with the monstrous creature, his need to discover the laboratory was greater.

'Be brave,' he told himself. 'We set out on a quest to discover the secret laboratory. I can't give up now.' He squinted into the darkness. 'Anyway, the glow from the walls should just be enough for me to find my way. And as for the rogue glister it'll be weak at the moment. Bungus said so . . .'

He took a few steps along the tunnel. Good! The old librarian hadn't noticed him sneaking away. The light from his lamp disappeared but, as Quint's eyes grew accustomed to the deep dark glow of the rocks, he found he could see well enough – and there was bound to be a lamp in the laboratory when he found it. He hesitated. *If* he found it . . .

Quint was wondering whether he ought to return to Bungus and Maris after all when he saw something that made his heart jump. It was a small, black arrow chalked onto the wall just by his shoulder and point-ing further along the corridor.

'There's no mistaking that one,' he murmured. 'I'm back on track at last.'

His mind was made up. Without so much as a back-ward glance, Quint hurried off down the tunnel, the papery cape still clutched in his hand. A dozen strides further on, a second arrow confirmed he was still heading in the right direction.

'I'll find that Ancient Laboratory,' he told himself,

'and discover its mysterious secret.' He smiled to himself. 'I'm going to make you proud of me, Maris!'

In the distance, he heard a low, crackly voice. It was Bungus.

'I'll carry Maris,' he was saying. 'And you, Quint, stay close behind. You hear?' There was a pause. 'Quint? *Quint . . .?*'

·CHAPTER FOURTEEN·

UNWANTED VISITORS

Maris breathed in deeply, filling her lungs with the early-morning Sanctaphrax air and feeling it course through her entire body. It was cool, fresh, invigorating. Her head cleared, her muscles flexed, and the fear-filled lethargy which had held her in its grip down in the stonecomb finally melted away. She turned to Bungus.

'I'm worried about Quint,' she said.

'Linius's apprentice?' said Bungus.

Maris nodded. 'How did we manage to lose him?'

'I don't know,' said Bungus. 'One minute he was right behind us. The next minute he was gone.' He paused. 'He must have gone off to find the Ancient Laboratory.'

'On his own,' Maris said sadly.

Bungus took her hands in his own. 'I'm sure your friend will be fine,' he said. 'He struck me as the type of lad who's well able to take care of himself.'

'He is,' said Maris. 'But we were supposed to be checking out the laboratory together. I should be there with him now. Oh, I feel such a failure,' she groaned, and looked up into

Bungus's dark brown eyes. 'Will you take me back down into the stonecomb?' she asked eagerly. 'I feel so much better now. Will you, Bungus? Please . . .'

'Let's get you back to your father before we plan our next move,' said Bungus. He frowned thoughtfully. 'It's high time Linius and I had a heart to heart. I need to find out precisely what he's been doing down in that laboratory.'

Just then, the bell at the top of the Great Hall chimed.

'It's seven hours!' Maris exclaimed. 'I can hardly believe it. We were down in the stonecomb all night.'

'All the more reason to make haste now,' said Bungus. He released Maris's hands and raised the hood of his papery jerkin. 'Come,' he said, and scuttled off into the shadows of a side alley.

'Where are you going?' Maris called as she struggled to catch up. 'It's *this* way.'

'Not for me, it isn't,' said Bungus. 'I can't afford to be seen out on the main streets of Sanctaphrax.'

'Why not?' said Maris.

'Because I'm an earth-scholar,' Bungus replied irritably, 'and earth-scholars have no place in the modern Sanctaphrax – apart from the halfwits who rant and rave on the Viaduct Steps. If anyone caught me up here, I'd be expelled at once and banished for ever to a life in the slums of Undertown. That's why I have to remain hidden in the Great Library by day. No-one visits the place any more, so no-one knows I am there.'

Maris glanced round to make sure that they were not being watched or followed. Thankfully, few were out and about so early in the morning, and those there were paid them no attention.

'But surely my father . . .' Maris began.

'*Ssshh!*' Bungus hissed, darting into a dark alcove and pulling Maris in beside him. 'Guards,' he whispered.

The sound of heavy marching boots pounded through the air. Maris peeked out of the shadows to see a detachment of flat-head goblins passing the end of the alley.

'So far as your father's concerned,' Bungus continued in a low voice, 'I left Sanctaphrax years ago. He probably assumed I was expelled from the floating city during the last wave of purges.'

'But, as Most High Academe, he could have done something to help you,' said Maris.

'On the contrary,' said Bungus. 'If his association with an earth-scholar – and a librarian to boot – had ever come to light, it would have created a huge scandal. His own position would have become untenable. Indeed, the sky-scholars would never have elected him Most High Academe in the first place if they had known of his youthful studies in the Great Library.' He paused, and sighed. 'Oh, Mistress Maris, I had such high hopes for your father. I dreamt that, with his broad education, he might see the wisdom of healing the schism between earth-studies and sky-scholarship.'

'But he does,' said Maris. 'That's why he moved back to the Palace of Shadows. That's why . . .'

Bungus cut her short. 'I may be isolated in the Great Library,' he snapped, 'but not much happens in Sanctaphrax which passes me by.' He breathed out noisily. 'I know he started off as Most High Academe with fine intentions. He was going to reform this and reinstate that . . . but what happened? He got side-tracked, didn't he? He got distracted.'

Maris glanced back up the alleyway. The sound of the boots had grown faint and faded away. But Bungus made no move to continue.

'He's been so lost in this "great work" of his,' he said, his face twisting with contempt, 'that he's neglected everything else. His hopes, his dreams, his responsibilities . . .'

'His daughter,' Maris whispered softly.

'And these days Sanctaphrax is far too treacherous a place for a Most High Academe to allow his attention to stray, even for a moment,' he said. 'There are many who would not hesitate to leap at the chance of taking his place.'

Just then, Maris heard the sound of voices. She looked

round to see a pair of sub-apprentices – raintasters, by the look of the fur trim on their robes – entering the alley behind them.

'Someone's coming,' she whispered urgently. 'Let's go.'

Bungus nodded and readjusted his hood, then the pair of them scuttled on down the narrow passageway. When they reached the end, they checked furtively from side to side. Apart from some Undertowners, busy setting up stalls, there was no-one there. They scurried across the broad Central Avenue and disappeared into the shadows opposite.

Round the back of the College of Cloud they went, down a flight of stairs and beneath a low archway. The Palace of Shadows rose up in front of them. Maris looked up at the windows and groaned.

'The shutters to his bed-chamber are still closed,' she said gloomily. 'I hoped he'd be better by now.'

'He soon will be,' said Bungus, and he tapped the small bag of potions and poultices hanging from his shoulder.

'He was in a terrible state,' said Maris, shaking her head. 'Cut, bruised, babbling . . .'

'All the same, there isn't much I can't heal, cure or revive,' Bungus assured her. 'Come, Mistress Maris,' he said, as he set off up the palace steps for the front entrance. 'Let us make your father well – and let us also find out, once and for all, what mischief he has been dabbling in.'

Meanwhile, at the back of the magnificent Palace of Shadows, two other visitors were waiting expectantly by the kitchen door. The first was a powerfully-built flat-head goblin, heavily armed and clad in the helmet and breast-plate of a Sanctaphrax guard. Standing at his shoulder was a tall, slightly stooped figure, wearing a thick hooded cape from which a silver nose-piece protruded like the sharp beak of a white raven.

'Try again, Bagswill,' he said. 'And knock louder this time.'

The flat-head raised his arm and hammered on the door with a massive fist.

'All right, all right,' came a wheezy voice from inside. 'I'm hurrying as best I can.'

The flat-head turned and grinned unpleasantly.

'Here he comes,' he said.

'Yes,' said Seftus Leprix, and tapped his bulging pocket. 'And with a bit of luck this will prove more effective than cutting the chain of that sky cage.'

Bagswill grunted. 'I still don't understand what went wrong,' he said. 'I mean, they found his cloak in Undertown, so how did he manage to . . . ?'

There was the grinding sound of a bolt being drawn, followed by the click of a key turning in the lock. Leprix raised his finger to his silver nose-piece. 'That's enough, Bagswill,' he said. The door opened with a soft creak and clouds of steam billowed out. As the air cleared, an angular, almost transparent head appeared.

'Yes, yes?' he trilled impatiently. 'Do you not see which signal-banners are flying?' he said, pointing to the decorated lengths of material fluttering from one of the upper balconies. 'The Most High Academe is *not* to be disturbed.'

The guard smiled warmly. 'Tweezel,' he said. 'How good to see you again – and looking so well.'

The spindlebug frowned. 'Do I know you?' he asked.

Bagswill laughed. 'Do you know me?' he said. 'We met in the market-place yesterday.'

'We did?' said Tweezel.

The guard's face clouded over. 'Don't tell me you've forgotten,' he said, 'otherwise I fear my visit will be in vain.'

Tweezel clicked and trilled. 'Remind me,' he said. 'I've had a lot on my mind recently.'

'That's *precisely* what you said yesterday,' said Bagswill, and laughed again. 'I was looking to buy tilder sausages,' he added. 'You kindly pointed me in the right direction. It was good to see a friendly Deepwooder face.'

Tweezel looked more closely at the flat-head. His antennae quivered. 'I do remember,' he said at last. 'What can I do for you?'

'It's more a case of what *I* can do for *you*,' Bagswill replied. 'You know you were telling me about your master being under the weather and all. Well, one good turn deserves another. I think I've found the perfect answer to your problem.'

'You have?' said Tweezel.

'Indeed I have,' said Bagswill. 'Not half an hour after bidding you farewell, I ran into my old pal . . . Sef, here.'

'Pleased to make your acquaintance,' the silver-nosed

individual said and produced from the folds of his robes
a cut-glass bottle containing a thick, deep-green liquid.
He held it out. 'I bring you a bottle of sapwine and
hyleberry cordial,' he announced. 'The finest,
most efficacious pick-me-up in all of the
Deepwoods. I use it myself.'

Antennae trembling, the spindlebug
eyed the bottle with interest – but
made no move towards it. Behind
him, he heard a *tap-tap-tap* coming
from the main entrance.

'Take it,' said the hooded individual, stepping forwards.
'It'll work wonders. You mark my words.'

'It's very good of you,' said Tweezel, 'but I'm not sure
about giving the master something I haven't tested . . .'

'Just a little before he goes to bed,' Bagswill joined in.
'That's all it requires. You'll see the difference immediately,
Tweezel. Your master will be a new person.'

'All the same . . .' Tweezel began.

The tapping at the front-door became louder, more
insistent.

'I know, I know,' said Bagswill understandingly. 'You
have every reason to be cautious.' He looked round at his
companion. 'Didn't I tell you that he was loyal?' He turned
back to Tweezel. 'I dare say that master of yours has told
you that, as a sky-scholar, he has his own methods of getting himself well again.' He snorted. 'But you and I know
better, eh, Tweezel? We Deepwooders know the efficacy of
herbs and spices – of the *old* ways.'

The spindlebug's wedge-shaped head nodded slightly.

'Maybe I could give him just a wee drop,' he ventured.

'You do that,' said Bagswill. 'Hand over the sapwine-cordial, Sef.'

Tweezel took the bottle in his pincer-like claws and inspected it closely. At that moment the knocking at the front door became so loud that even the two visitors heard it.

'You'd best answer that,' said Bagswill.

'But the drink,' said Tweezel. 'What do I owe you for it?'

'Oh, there's no need to worry about that,' said Bagswill. 'Call it a gift, from one Deepwooder to another.'

'Very kind, I'm sure,' said Tweezel.

'Don't mention it,' said Bagswill. 'You just answer that door before you get into any trouble.' He winked conspiratorially. 'You don't have to tell me what it's like working for a demanding master.'

Tweezel withdrew his head.

'And you be sure to let me know how the master fares,' Bagswill called.

'Oh, I will,' the old spindlebug replied.

As the door clicked shut, Bagswill turned to his companion, a broad grin plastered across his face. 'Told you it'd work,' he said. 'That simple old fool swallowed my story, hook, line and sinker.'

'Yes, well done, Bagswill,' came the reply. 'Though I do wish you hadn't called me by name. ' "Sef", indeed. I just hope he doesn't work out my full name.'

'You worry too much,' said Bagswill. 'There's enough hover-worm venom in that cordial to poison a whole school of academics. Tasteless, odourless – and deadly. One sip,

and Linius Pallitax will blow up like an inflated trockblad-
der. It can't fail – unlike the chain idea of yours,' he added.
'By this time tomorrow, I will be Head Guard of
Sanctaphrax, while you, Seftus, will be its new Most High
Academe.'

The silver nose-piece trembled as its owner chuckled
with amusement. 'When you put it like *that*, Bagswill,' he
said. 'Come, let us away. There is still much we have to
prepare.'

'I'm coming, I'm coming,' the spindlebug wheezed as he
unbolted the front door and pulled it open.

He was confronted by Maris's furious face, tight-lipped
and blotchy. 'What in Sky's name kept you so long?' she
demanded. 'We've been waiting here ages.'

'Apologies, mistress,' said Tweezel. 'I was indisposed.'

'Well, it was very inconvenient,' said Maris, more huffy
now than angry. 'We have important business with my
father.'

The spindlebug turned his head and his gaze fell on the
figure in the shabby clothes standing next to Maris. He
looked him up and down with some disdain. 'And who
shall I say wishes to have an audience with the Most High
Academe?' he enquired stiffly.

'No-one, Tweezel,' said Maris, pushing past the be-
wildered servant, Bungus in tow. 'I'll introduce him to my
father myself.'

The spindlebug trilled indignantly. 'But, mistress,' he
protested, 'this is highly irregular. It's more than my job's
worth to allow you to . . .'

But Maris was already racing up the first flight of stairs with the mysterious hooded figure following close behind. Tweezel sighed. There was nothing he could do. These days, his joints were far too stiff for him to go chasing around the palace. And the young mistress was so wilful! By the time he reached the professor's bed-chamber she and that vagabond she had brought with her would no doubt already be perched on either side of his bed, chatting.

'That's the trouble with the youth of today,' he grumbled. 'No sense of protocol. No etiquette. No decorum . . .'

Still muttering to himself, he returned to the kitchen. It was time he took a close look at that sapwine-cordial . . .

As they reached the second landing, both Maris and Bungus could hear the sound of raised voices from the next storey. Maris turned to Bungus, her eyes wide with concern.

'Who can that be?' she said. 'And why are they arguing?'

'Let's go and find out,' said Bungus.

Together, they raced up the remaining stairs. The voices became clearer.

'How dare you do this?' boomed one.

'Do you not understand the gravity of the situation?' bellowed another.

'Sky strike you down if anything should happen to him!' blasted a third.

'You can rant and rave all you like,' came a fourth voice, more strident than the others yet studiedly calm.

'That's Welma,' Maris panted as she and Bungus ran down the long corridor. 'My old nurse.'

'I said "no", and I *mean* "no",' Welma's voice floated back. '*None* of you are going in.'

'Madam, do you know who I am?' one of them demanded.

'I don't care if you're the Professor of Darkness himself,' said Welma defiantly.

'But ... but I *am* the Professor of Darkness!' came the indignant reply.

'As I say,' Welma said dismissively, 'I don't care.'

There was a gasp, followed by three furious voices all shouting at once. Maris skidded round the corner of the corridor with Bungus – the hood of his papery jerkin down over his face – hot on her heels.

'Welma, what is going on?' she demanded.

'*There* you are, Maris,' said Welma. She was standing, barring the way to the Most High Academe's chamber door. 'Your bed hasn't been touched. Where have you *been* all night?'

'Never mind all that,' said the Professor of Darkness. 'The Most High Academe remains in great danger. There has already been one attempt on his life ...'

'And my spies have uncovered a second plot,' Sigbord, the Head Guard broke in. 'Bagswill the flat-head has been recruited by a second renegade – a shadowy figure hiding behind his ceremonial silver nose. It is my duty to protect the Most High Academe ...'

Welma raised her hands. 'As I keep saying,' she told them, 'he's safe and sound. And that's the way he'll stay so long as he remains in his bed, all tucked up and ...'

'But he *can't!*' the Professor of Light bellowed. 'How

many more times do I have to tell you, a Great Storm is imminent. He is to come with us!'

'The Inauguration of Garlinius Gernix must take place immediately,' added the Professor of Darkness. 'If it does not, then he will be unsuccessful in his quest for new stormphrax.'

A dismissive snort emanated from the folds of the brown hood, followed by, 'Stormphrax, indeed.' Maris kicked Bungus lightly on the leg and hissed at him to stay silent.

'And the ceremony must be performed by the Most High Academe. If it is not . . .'

Bungus spoke up again, louder this time. 'Strictly speaking, couldn't *you* do it?' he said, his voice muffled by the parchment-like material.

'I beg your pardon?' said the Professor of Darkness. He stared in disbelief at the gangly, shabbily dressed individual. 'Who are you, sir?' he demanded. 'Show your face!'

But Bungus had no intention of doing any such thing. These meddlesome academics must not discover who he was.

'As I understand it,' he went on, 'in your role as Next-Most High Academe you could perform the ceremony yourselves. Either individually. Or together.'

The Professors of Light and Darkness turned to one another, eyebrows raised. 'Could we?' they asked each other. 'Should we? Is it legal? Is it constitutional?'

Certainly it was worth considering, for the great floating rock upon which the city had been built was growing bigger by the day. If the amount of heavy stormphrax in the Treasury was not constantly increased, then Sanctaphrax was always at risk of breaking its moorings and sailing off into open sky. Reaching their decision at the self-same moment, the two professors seized one another by the arm, and marched away.

'First of all, we must consult the *Great Tome of Skylore*,' the Professor of Light was saying.

'Time is of the essence,' the Professor of Darkness reminded him. Their voices grew fainter. 'Perhaps it would be wiser to consult the great book *after* we have performed the ceremony.'

Bungus snorted for a second time. 'Avaricious old buzzards,' he muttered. 'The first whiff of power and they're onto it like a woodcat on a weezit!'

'At least they've gone,' said Maris. She turned to Sigbord. 'And since my father won't be leaving his room after all, he will have no need of your services either.'

The brawny Head Guard looked down at Maris and, for a moment, she was sure he was about to argue with her. But Sigbord bit his tongue. He had learned, and to his cost, that it was always as well to keep the daughter of the Most High Academe sweet.

'Go on, then,' said Welma. 'You heard what the young mistress said.'

Sigbord nodded curtly. 'I shall send a consignment of twelve guards to surround the palace and watch the doors,' he said.

'As you wish,' said Welma. 'Now, off you go!' And, flapping her hands at him, she ushered the guard away.

The moment Welma moved from the door, Maris leapt forwards and seized the handle. She turned it – half expecting it to be locked – but her luck held. The door swung open, creaking as it did so. Welma turned.

'Mistress Maris!' she shrieked angrily. 'What did we talk about earlier?'

But Maris was in no mood for further questions. Pulling Bungus into the bed-chamber behind her, she slammed the door shut and turned the key.

'Maris!' Welma shouted. 'Maris, open this door at once.'

'Shan't!' Maris shouted back. 'He's my father and I have a right to see him.'

Welma fell silent. Maris pressed her ear to the door. For a moment she heard nothing, then the sound of her old nurse's footsteps plodding away along the corridor.

Slowly, nervously, Maris turned round. Why had her father not spoken? Surely he couldn't have slept through all the noise everyone had been making. She peered into the gloom. Apart from a stubby candle flickering from the mantelpiece, the room was in complete darkness.

Taking the candle with her, Maris walked towards the bed. The light fell across her father's face. Maris gasped.

Propped up in bed, he looked even worse than she had imagined he would. He was pale and haggard. Tufts of hair stuck out from the blood-stained bandages which swathed his head. Worst of all, however, were his eyes. They stared ahead, unblinking, unseeing, yet still filled with the horror of what they had witnessed.

'Father!' Maris cried. She climbed up on to the bed and hugged him tightly, her cheek pressed to his bony chest. His body was rigid and cold; if it hadn't been for the heartbeat hammering away beside her ear, he might have been dead. 'Oh, Father, what has happened to you?'

Just then, there was a grating noise from the side of the chamber. Maris glanced round to see Bungus flinging open the shutters.

'All this appalling darkness and shadow,' he was muttering. 'Light is what Linius needs.'

A single shaft of dazzling early-morning sun burst into the room and streamed across the floor. It fell on the face of the stricken professor, who blinked, once, twice . . .

'Maris,' he said, his voice low and cracked.

Maris smiled. She knelt forwards and kissed him gently on the forehead. 'Hello,' she said.

Her father looked surprised. 'Why are you crying?' he asked.

'I'm not,' Maris sniffed.

Without saying a word, he raised a bony hand, lifted a tear from her cheek with the tip of his index finger and showed it to her. 'Tell me what's wrong,' he said softly.

'Oh, Father!' Maris wailed and hugged him again. 'I was so worried about you. All those cuts and scratches .. and your *ear*! What happened to you?'

'Hush, Maris,' he said, as he held her head and stroked her hair. 'It's all over now. I'm back. I'm safe. I . . .' He noticed the figure silhouetted against the window. 'Who in Sky's name is that?'

Maris pulled away and looked round. 'That's . . .' she began.

But Bungus silenced her with a finger to his lips. He walked to the bed, away from the blinding light, and lowered his hood. 'You tell me, Linius,' he said softly. 'Don't you remember your old friend?' He smiled. 'It's been a long time.'

Bursting with expectation, Maris looked at her father, then at Bungus – then at her father again. She watched the initial confusion turn to a look of recognition, then a broad, child-like grin spread out across his face.

'Bungus Septrill,' he said, shaking his head with dis-belief. 'Am I still dreaming? I never thought I'd live to see the day . . .'

'Greetings, Linius,' said Bungus, stepping forwards to shake his hand. 'I am no dream.'

'But I thought you had fled Sanctaphrax,' he said weakly. 'I was told . . .'

'You were told I'd returned to the Deepwoods,' Bungus said, 'to pursue my earth-studies unhindered.'

'Precisely that,' said Linius.

'Rumours started by myself,' he explained. 'I wanted no-one to know that the Great Library was still being tended.'

'You mean you've been hiding out in the Great Library all this time? But . . .' Linius paused, confused. 'But I've been there myself. Many times. I have never seen you.'

'I chose not to be seen,' said Bungus simply.

'But why?' said Linius. 'If only . . .' His voice trailed away.

'I couldn't risk it,' said Bungus, 'for both our sakes.'

'You're together now,' Maris butted in. 'That's what counts.' She turned to her father. 'Bungus is here to make you better again. He knows the healing secrets of the Deepwoods.'

'Does he now?' said Linius, his lips curling into a smile.

'It's true!' said Maris. 'After Quint and I were attacked by a giant glister, he . . .' She fell still, horribly aware of what she had just said. Her heart thumped. Her cheeks coloured.

'Glister?' gasped her father. He tried to sit up, but fell back, his face pinched with concern. 'Don't tell me you've been down in the stonecomb.'

Maris looked away, guiltily.

'You have, haven't you?' he said, gathering his strength. 'It's that apprentice. He put you up to it.' His eyes blazed. 'I'll have his hide for gaiters!' With great effort, he raised himself up on his elbows.

'It wasn't Quint's idea,' said Maris. 'It was mine. Please, Father, you're not well.'

'And there was me, thinking I could trust him,' her father continued without a break. 'You know, I've a good mind to get word to Wind Jackal to . . . to . . .'

'You're not listening,' said Maris. 'It was *my* idea to go down into the stonecomb. I was so desperate to find out what you've been doing. How you got injured . . . I *forced* him to take me.'

Linius fell back exhausted, his face ashen grey. 'And where is the little wretch now?' he breathed. 'Too ashamed to show his face, eh?'

'He . . . he's still down inside the floating rock,' Maris confessed.

The expression on Linius's face changed in an instant. He leant forwards. 'You left him there?' he said, his voice low with dread. 'Quint – my dear friend Wind Jackal's one and only son – alone in the terrible stonecomb? But why? If you went there together, why didn't you also return together?'

'I . . . I couldn't walk. Bungus was carrying me,' said Maris. 'Quint was following us . . .' She swallowed. 'And then he wasn't.'

Bungus stepped forwards. 'The foolhardy youth went off in search of the Ancient Laboratory.'

Linius's jaw dropped. He gripped Maris by both wrists.

'You know about the Ancient Laboratory?' he said.

'Of course they do, Linius, my old friend,' said Bungus. 'Why else do you think they were roaming about the stonecomb on their own?'

'But Quint is in great danger,' said Linius urgently. 'He mustn't set foot inside the laboratory! He mustn't even open the door . . .!' He buried his head in his hands and began rocking, back and forth. 'What have I done?' he groaned. 'What have I *done*?'

Bungus sat down on the side of the bed and pulled Linius's hands gently, but firmly, away from his face. He raised his head, and looked him straight in the eyes.

'Perhaps a broken-down earth-scholar can help an old friend,' he said. 'Tell me, Linius. Tell me everything.'

·CHAPTER FIFTEEN·

LINIUS'S STORY

L inius lay on the bed, his face turned towards the window and the dazzling beam of sunlight shining in his eyes. From the streets outside, there came sounds of the waking city: bell-chime and wheel-clatter; the buzz of conversation and hum of rhythmic chanting; and the white ravens, cawing raucously as they stretched their wings in the warmth of the rising sun. Linius sighed, rolled over and stared up at the ceiling.

'I started out with . . . with such good intentions,' he murmured. His eyes misted over. 'I wanted to do so much for Sanctaphrax.'

Bungus leaned forward and took the professor's left hand in his own. 'Tell me your story, Linius,' he said. 'I'm listening.'

Linius turned his head towards his old teacher and breathed out, long and deep. 'Oh, Bungus,' he said wearily. 'It seems like only yesterday that you shared with me the mysteries of the Great Library.' He smiled weakly. 'You showed me so much. Little did I know what it would all lead to . . .'

He closed his eyes, the same faint smile playing over his lips. Bungus squeezed his hand reassuringly. Linius looked up.

'Happy days,' he breathed wistfully. 'And yet I was so innocent then, Bungus; I was so naive. I assumed that Sanctaphrax was a benevolent place where all knowledge was good knowledge, and the duty of every academic was to add to the sum-total of that knowledge for the good of everyone.' His face creased up in disgust. 'Sky-scholars!' he said. 'I knew nothing then of the back-stabbing and double-dealing that went on among them: the treachery, the rivalry, the vying for position. Mistsifter against rain-taster, cloudwatcher against windtoucher . . . Sky above, the only thing that ever brought a temporary lull to their faction-fighting was the contempt and loathing they shared for earth-studies!' He wiped away the beads of sweat that had gathered on his forehead. 'And I hated it,' he said angrily. 'As an apprentice, as a lowly mistgrader, I hated it so much.' He sighed wearily. 'Even when I was forced to play the same game . . .'

Maris turned to Bungus. 'My father's too tired to go on just now,' she protested. 'He needs to rest.'

But Linius silenced her with a movement of his hand. 'It's all right, Maris,' he said, smiling bravely. 'I *want* to talk about it. I want to tell you both about the hopes and dreams I once nurtured.' He sighed again. 'And what hopes and dreams they were. I thought that, as Most High Academe, I would be able to reunite the battling academic factions for the common good. More than that,' he said, turning to Bungus, his eyes wide and earnest, 'I intended to bring earth-scholars back to Sanctaphrax. The schism between earth- and sky-scholarship had to be healed; the Great Library had to be re-opened. I knew we could not afford to lose such a wealth of information about the Edge.

'I told the assembled crowd of academics as much in my Inauguration Speech, but the fools were not listening to me. Or rather,' he added, 'they heard only what they wanted to hear. Even when I moved into the Palace of Shadows – both to show my independence from any and all of the Sanctaphrax schools, and to revive the tradition first started by the Ancient Scholars all those centuries ago – my motives were misunderstood.

'In fact, it seemed that each time I attempted to bring harmony to Sanctaphrax, I ended up causing greater discord. My own hopes were fast turning to despair.' He paused and shook his head. 'Yet for all that,' he added, his face brightening a little, 'I do not regret my decision to move into the Palace of Shadows one jot. How could I? For if I had not done so, I would never have met its curator, my faithful old retainer, Tweezel. And if I hadn't met him . . .'

Just then there was a light knock at the door, followed by the creaky sound of the handle being tested.

'Ignore it,' said Bungus. 'Keep on with the story.'

But before the Most High Academe could utter so much as a single word more, there was a soft click and the door swung open. Tweezel stood there, a tray

gripped firmly in his claws. Upon it was a plate of herb wafers, an empty glass and a jug of bright red cordial. The old spindlebug looked up.

'Did I hear my name?' he enquired.

The Most High Academe smiled. 'Yes, Tweezel, you did,' he said. 'Come in. Come in. I was about to describe our first meeting.' He turned to the others. 'As its long-time curator, Tweezel knows every inch of the Palace of Shadows. It was he who showed me the Blackwood Chamber.'

'The what?' said Maris. 'I thought *I* knew every inch of the palace too, and I've never heard of it.'

Linius looked up at Bungus. 'But I suspect *you* have,' he said.

'True,' said Bungus. 'Although before this moment I did not know whether it was real or mythical.'

'Oh, it's real enough,' said Linius. 'Is that not so, Tweezel?'

'Indeed it is,' Tweezel replied. 'The master loves the palace as much as I do. Over the years, I showed him all its secret nooks and crannies. But it is the Blackwood Chamber that has always fascinated him most.'

'What *is* it?' said Maris. 'Why is it so special?'

Linius's eyelids fluttered and then closed. '*You* tell her

its purpose, Bungus,' he whispered, 'for I am feeling weary.' He shivered. 'And a little feverish.'

'Then I have just the thing, master,' said Tweezel. He placed the tray down on the sideboard. 'Ferment of fruit-and-root cordial,' he said, 'made to a special Deepwoods recipe and guaranteed to perk you up in no time.' He poured some of the red liquid from the jug to the glass. It bubbled white and frothed up. 'And I've brought some wafers, too,' he added as he grasped both glass and plate. 'To help revive you.'

He turned and walked towards the bed. Linius opened his eyes and pulled himself up.

'Very thoughtful, Tweezel,' he said wheezily.

'Yes, very thoughtful indeed,' said Bungus stepping forwards and taking the refreshments off the spindlebug, 'but I think I have something a little more efficacious.'

'Upon my word!' said Tweezel indignantly.

'Oh, Bungus,' Linius smiled weakly. 'A remedy for everything in that little bag of yours. But I fear not even you can help me this time.'

Bungus paid neither of them any heed. He placed the glass and plate back on the tray and began rummaging in his satchel, muttering to himself all the time.

'Weary, feverish, overwrought . . .' He selected a phial of amber liquid and splashed twenty-four drops into a small bottle of pure water. The muttering started up again. 'Septic sores on fingers, scratches on cheek and an ear lesion. Skin-tone, pebble- to ash-grey. Eye-glint, down in the twenties – maybe lower . . .'

Maris watched, entranced. She noted how, with each

of his observations about her father's condition, Bungus would add to the liquid a pinch of powder from sachet after sachet that he pulled from the bag. Finally, he stoppered the bottle, shook it vigorously and held it up to the light. The liquid glittered and sparkled so brightly that it was as if, instead of herbs and powdered root, he had stirred in a spoonful of black-diamond dust.

He stepped towards the bed. 'Drink this, Linius,' he said.

The Most High Academe pulled a face. 'The cordial looked nicer,' he muttered.

'That cordial is without doubt the stuff that Deepwooders sell to gullible academics,' said Bungus, 'harmless enough, but completely useless. Whereas this . . .' He uncorked the fizzing bottle and held it out. 'This will heal you, Linius. In body and spirit, it will make you well – it will make you whole.'

Linius raised the bottle to his lips and took the minutest of sips, ready to spit it out if it tasted foul. But the concoction tasted good, very good. A contented smile spread over his face and he glugged the sweet herbal liquid down to the very bottom of the bottle. 'Excellent, Bungus,' he said. 'And do you know what? I can feel it working already.' He sat up, scratching gently at his ear through the bandages. 'It's itching,' he said.

'Which means it's healing,' said Bungus. 'And your eyes are clearer, too. Are you ready to continue with your story?'

'My story,' said Linius with a sigh. 'Ah, yes. My story. I can hardly bear to tell it, yet I fear I must . . .' He looked at Maris. 'I only hope my daughter will not think any the worse of me when that story is done.'

'There is nothing you could say, Father, that would make me love you less,' said Maris earnestly. 'I promise you.' She smiled. 'You were telling us about the Blackwood Chamber.'

Linius nodded seriously. 'Oh, Maris, my darling daughter, the Blackwood Chamber is one of the oldest treasures of the palace. The oldest and the most secret. Why, Tweezel didn't even tell me of its existence until he decided he could trust me. A detailed history of Sanctaphrax is cut into its wooden walls in the form of carvings. And such carvings! Countless wooden pictures, set in a raised, patterned framework. Ornate, intricate, exquisitely detailed . . .'

'And an absolute nightmare to dust,' Tweezel muttered as, abandoning the tray of refreshments, he made his way back across the floor and left the room. *He couldn't stand around chatting all day; he had important things to do. No-one noticed him go.*

'It is a marvel,' Linius went on eagerly. 'The carvings seem almost to be alive. Oh, and the stories they tell, Maris. *The Blessing of the Floating Rock*, for instance; *The Tale of Brother Ructus and the Banderbear. The Legend of the Naming Tower. The Great Sky-Dragon Siege* . . . And later, when I studied them more closely, I discovered that each scene was surrounded by swirling interlaced designs, like a tangle of Deepwood thorns. At first I thought they were mere decorative patterns, but nothing those ancient carvers created in that fabulous room was merely

decorative. Many visits to the Great Library and countless hours of study over dusty scrolls revealed them to
be the angular script of the Ancient Tongue. It was the
actual voice of those First Scholars – more ancient than
the oldest scroll in the Great Library – there, carved into
the walls.' His eyes gleamed with childlike enthusiasm.
'Absolutely fascinating,' he said excitedly. 'A celebration
of the genius of those who came before us.'

Maris smiled. She hadn't seen her father this animated
in so, so long.

'Think of it, Maris!' he exclaimed. 'The Blackwood
Chamber contains an almost complete record of the
history of Sanctaphrax, from the day the ancient

academics first secured the great floating rock in place with the Anchor Chain, down centuries of harmony and learning, through the Great Schism when the ancient academics split into earth- and sky-scholars, and on to the First Purges . . .' He paused for breath. 'And there it stops, halfway down the seventh wall. Presumably, the carvers – being *earth-studies* carvers – were cast out of Sanctaphrax.' He shook his head. 'It is all such a terrible shame . . .'

Outside, the bell at the top of the Great Hall chimed. Maris flinched nervously. Quint had been down in the stonecomb on his own now for far too long.

'And the Ancient Laboratory?' she prompted her father. 'Was that also recorded in the blackwood carvings?'

'Yes,' said Linius, his face lighting up once again. 'Yes, it was. The changing face of Sanctaphrax was recorded down the ages. The construction of buildings, the raising of the Central Viaduct, the tunnelling and excavating of the Treasury . . . I mean, the Great Laboratory,' he corrected himself as Bungus grumbled under his breath. 'And the digging of the Great West Tunnel,' he said, turning back to Maris. 'Accessible only by sky cage, the tunnel led to the second laboratory: the *Ancient* Laboratory.

'Well, you can imagine my excitement at stumbling across this lost centre of learning. Here was a place established by some of the finest minds Sanctaphrax has ever known, and I could hardly wait to see it for myself.' He frowned. 'Yet there were practical problems. From later

carvings, I knew that the laboratory had been abandoned and that the tunnel leading to it had been blocked
off. In the most recent carvings, neither the tunnel nor
the laboratory is marked at all.' He looked down guiltily.
'I suppose I should have given up there and then,' he
said. There was a pause. 'And yet I could not!'

'No,' said Maris, unable to keep a sharp edge from her
voice.

Linius looked at her sympathetically. 'Yes, I know
I neglected you,' her father said. 'And I'm sorry. I
neglected *all* my duties . . . But I couldn't help myself! It
was all far, far too fascinating to ignore. And the more I
discovered, the more I wanted . . . the more I *needed* to
discover. I am an academic, Maris, for my sins. You do
understand, don't you?'

'I . . . I suppose so,' said Maris reluctantly.

'I was this great explorer unravelling the forgotten
secrets of a whole lost world,' said Linius, his eyes burning with enthusiasm. 'At first, progress was slow. The
ancient script was difficult to read and, since it was in an
archaic dialect, even harder to translate. Time after time,
I had to visit the Great Library to uncover yet more
scrolls to help me with my difficult task . . .'

He paused again, and Maris watched him turn
towards the old librarian. Linius's face glowed with
gratitude.

'I owe so much to you, Bungus,' he said. 'It was you
who first showed me the old dictionaries and lexicons.
You who taught me the rudiments of the Ancient
Tongue. And you who instructed me in how to use the

library – which tree to climb to locate information, which branch to take . . .' He shook his head. 'If only I'd realized that you were there.'

'Yes, perhaps I should have made myself known, after all,' said Bungus. 'I could have knocked some sense into that head of yours and nipped this foolhardy nonsense in the bud . . .'

But Linius was shaking his head vigorously. 'Nothing could have stopped me by that stage,' he said. 'I was obsessed, Bungus. Intoxicated. Something incredible had taken place down in the Ancient Laboratory, of that I was convinced. I had no choice but to carry on until I had discovered for myself exactly what it was. Finally, after many long weeks, I had found out all I could from research. It was time for me to get first-hand knowledge of the Ancient Laboratory itself.'

'But I thought it had been sealed up,' said Maris.

'And so it was,' said Linius. 'Yet my curiosity was at fever pitch. I couldn't resist going to see for myself. That was the first time I went down in the sky cage.' He leaned forwards and his voice dropped conspiratorially. 'I had to be so careful,' he said. 'Quite apart from the difficulties I had manoeuvring the cage itself, I also needed to keep my destination concealed from my fellow academics. They considered it bad enough that their Most High Academe should sink to the levels of low-sky study, but if any of them had suspected I was dabbling in matters of earth-study . . .' He paused dramatically, and fixed Maris with an intense stare. 'My life would not have been worth living.'

Wide-eyed, Maris hung on her father's every word as he described his descent in the sky cage. It brought back memories of her own recent trip down to the stonecomb with Quint – and how terrified she'd been when the chain had been cut and the cage had sliced down through the cold night air.

'Because the great floating rock had grown since the tunnel was first built,' Linius continued, 'twisting itself out of shape as it did so, the entrance to the tunnel was no longer aligned with the sky cage drop. It took me more than an hour to swing over towards it – but not once did I consider giving up. Finally, I managed to secure my tolley-rope to a jutting spur of rock.'

Maris nodded. In her mind's eye, she could see Quint doing the selfsame thing.

'Besides,' he said, 'once *inside* the tunnel, it benefited me that the rock had changed in shape as it had grown. For although it meant I could not trust the old map I had brought with me, it also meant that when I came to the section that had been blocked off, it was blocked off no longer. The original rock-jam had shifted to create a narrow way through.

'It was a tight fit, and I snagged my robes several times as I squeezed my way between the jagged rocks – but in the end, I made it. And there in front of me, no more than a dozen strides away, stood the door I had seen depicted countless times already – on paper and parchment, in chalk, charcoal and sepia ink, and of course carved into the sacred blackwood.' He sighed. 'And yet seeing it in the flesh, so to speak, was quite different.' He hesitated, searching for the right words. 'It . . . it was the entrance to the Ancient Laboratory and I – Linius Pallitax, Most High Academe of Sanctaphrax – was the first academic to have clapped eyes on it since it had been abandoned centuries earlier.'

An icy shiver shot up and down Maris's spine. She knew *just* how he must have felt.

'I walked towards the great sculpted door with my heart in my mouth,' said Linius, his voice low and reverent. 'I reached out. I touched the stone. At that moment, it was as if a great electric charge surged through my body. My limbs tingled. My hair stood on end. I knew I was on the brink of a wondrous discovery.' He paused. 'But how to open the door? How to get inside?'

'You mean you needed a key?' said Maris. 'Was there nothing about one in the carvings or the scrolls?'

Linius turned to his daughter fondly. 'You have a good mind, Maris,' he said. 'Had you been older when I first started out, I would have involved you in my studies.'

Maris trembled with pleasure at hearing such praise. She had been wrong before. It was her age that had stopped her father confiding in her, not her gender. She smiled happily.

'I did come across a reference,' Linius was saying. 'But it was so cryptic. *The door shall open to golden lightning*, it said. I could make neither head nor tail of it. Only when I was standing in front of the door itself with my lamp raised did the carved stonework finally reveal its secret.'

'What was it?' Maris breathed.

'At the very centre of the stone door was a circular indentation. I recognized it at once,' he explained. 'Calibrated compass points with an outer circle of spikes and deep grooves of jagged lightning bolts. It was a concave impression of the Great Seal of High Office itself!'

Could that have been why he quizzed me about the mosaic I made him? Maris wondered. Did he think I was on to something?

'The Great Seal of High Office,' Linius repeated. 'That gold medallion with its zigzag bolts of lightning, which had been passed from Most High Academe to Most High Academe down the centuries, the Great Seal which now graced my own shoulders. I grasped it tightly and eased it into the indentation in the rock. It was a perfect fit –

but the door did not spring open as I'd hoped. I couldn't believe it. It *had* to work. Why else would the concave carving have been made in the first place? I thought that perhaps the mechanism had seized up, or the growing rock had twisted the door frame out of shape . . .'

He looked up, a grin on his face. 'Then, as I was trying to remove the medallion, I inadvertently twisted it to the right. The rock moved with it and, with a deep rumbling sound like faraway thunder, the door moved.'

Deep down in the treacherous stonecomb, Quint squinted along the gloomy tunnel. His eyes were as accustomed to the dull glow of the rock as they were going to get but it was still difficult to see where he was going. It was all he could do not to lose himself in the confusing labyrinth of tunnels. Every step he took became a commitment; every turn, a gamble.

'Maybe I should have gone back to the surface with Maris and Bungus,' he murmured, and was startled by the sibilant echoes that whispered back at him. *Marisss. Bungusssss . . .*

Quint sighed. The tunnel sighed with him.

'Still, I made my choice,' he said. 'It's too late for regrets now. I *have* to keep going. Before the glister regains its strength . . .'

With heavy feet, Quint stumbled on. It was a while since he had seen the last black-chalk arrow pointing the way and, as with every other time this had happened, he was becoming increasingly edgy. His palms sweated. His scalp itched. What if he *never* found it?

Then, suddenly, there it was – on the wall at Quint's side – the very moment after he had abandoned all hope of ever finding his way again. Unless . . . He stopped and traced his finger round the arrow. A smile plucked at the corners of his mouth. He was still on the right track.

'The Ancient Laboratory,' he murmured as he peered ahead into the darkness. He gripped the hooked pikestaff tightly. 'It can't be far now.'

'As I removed the Great Seal of High Office from the sunken indentation,' said Linius, 'the heavy carved door slid open. Though unused for hundreds of years, it glided smoothly and silently. I stepped forwards and went through the doorway. After so much striving, so much endeavour, I was finally inside the lost laboratory I had read so much about.

'I raised my lamp high into the air, and gasped. For the vast cavern I found myself in was like no other laboratory I had seen before or have seen since. It was spectacular . . .'

Maris listened closely as her father continued. She wanted to remember every single detail.

'I was in an immense, dome-shaped chamber which had been carved out of the solid heartrock. Huge, glass pipes, like great twisting roots, protruded into the chamber from all round the walls and across the ceiling, while others, even wider still, sprouted up from the floor. Some of the pipes were capped. Some hung free. Most, however, branched and fanned to form a great, convoluted network.

'At first, I thought it was like being inside a huge machine. Yet as I stood there, looking round, I was overwhelmed by the sense that this was a place which had once been alive. There was something organic about the configuration of the pipes – they were like veins or arteries, or some vast nervous system. I decided, there and then, that my aim would be to breathe life back into the great dormant chamber.

'I didn't stay long that first visit. But I was soon back, with tar-dip torches for the walls, and buckets and brooms – as well as all the scrolls and parchments about the laboratory that I'd managed to uncover so far.

'With the Ancient Laboratory now brightly lit, I cleaned and swept and polished until every inch gleamed like new. Oh, Maris, I can't tell you how exhilarating it all was, returning the place to its former glory . . .' He paused for breath. 'As I peeled away the layers of dirt, I discovered that the system of pipes – which I'd initially taken to be haphazard – had in fact been carefully planned. The pipes divided and sub-divided in a highly complex network through which its air-borne contents could be controlled and directed. And – as the scrolls confirmed – from the widest conduit to the narrowest filament, each and every one had been designed to perform a specific function.

'Some of the thinner tubes had glass spheres, sparkling like ripe fruit, attached to their ends. Others had glistening, gossamer-fine nets suspended between them, while in the centre of the laboratory a cluster of thick pipes reared up from the floor like three great wood-pythons; writhing, coiling, mouths gaping. Between them was a great central pipe into which all other pipes flowed, like tributaries into the Edgewater River.

'At the very centre of the laboratory was a raised platform, reached by a short flight of steps and surrounded by a wide array of levers, wheels and stops. Like everything else in the Ancient Laboratory, this intricate apparatus also had a purpose. All I had to do was discover what it was.'

He turned to his daughter. 'Oh, Maris, it was all so exciting! The time sped past so fast that I was barely aware when it was day and when it was night. Countless hours I'd spend in the Great Library, checking up on the function of a specific cluster of pipes, then hurry back to the laboratory to experiment for myself – only to discover something I hadn't noticed before that sent me scurrying back to the scrolls again. I was totally engrossed in it all, Maris. Too busy to perform my other academic functions, too excited to eat or drink – even sleep became an inconvenience I thought I could do without.'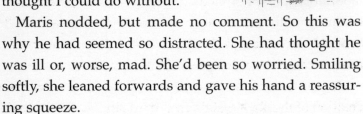

Maris nodded, but made no comment. So this was why he had seemed so distracted. She had thought he was ill or, worse, mad. She'd been so worried. Smiling softly, she leaned forwards and gave his hand a reassuring squeeze.

'My first major breakthrough came a couple of months later,' he continued excitedly. 'Closely following the instructions laid down in an ancient parchment I had found, I unscrewed the lids of the three capped pipes which emerged from the floor, and connected to them three free-hanging pipes which emerged from the ceiling

in a triangle formation, far above my head. Then, with trembling fingers, I seized the levers at the base of the three pipes and pulled them upwards, one after the other. With the first two, nothing happened, but as the third lever clicked into place, a sudden roaring sound came from deep within all three pipes.

'I jumped back nervously and hurried to the valve-platform. All round me, the mass of interconnected pipes had begun to creak, clatter, whistle and hiss with the air rushing through them. Initially, too, there were a lot of odd splutters and disconcerting bangs as the internal valves creaked into action and blockages were cleared. Soon, however, these random noises stopped, and all that could be heard was the pulsing sound of air being sucked in from outside and pumped round the laboratory paraphernalia.' Linius looked up, his face beaming with satisfaction. 'I'd done it,' he said. 'I'd brought the Ancient Laboratory back to life. Now it was time to carry out a few preliminary experiments.'

He sat forwards. 'The first I performed was the creation of the sky-crystals you like so much, Maris. Red, yellow, green, purple – they are formed in the net-like structures. Then, when I had mastered that, I turned my attention to a different part of the laboratory. I

made mood-salves – curious unguents, extracted from the weather, that collected in the glass spheres. The ancient academics once used them, albeit sparingly, in all their medicines. A hint of "greed", for instance, improved the appetite, while a little "anger"

was said to be a general cure-all.' He raised his eyebrows sheepishly. 'I, myself, developed rather a taste for "joy",' he admitted, and sighed. 'It was that which kept me going during the hard times.' He looked at Maris. 'For there were hard times, times when I wanted to give up and never visit either the Great Library or the Ancient Laboratory ever again. And yet . . .' He fell still.

'What, Father?' said Maris.

Linius frowned. 'There was one carving in the Blackwood Chamber which had intrigued me from the moment I stumbled upon it. It showed a First Scholar standing in the centre of the laboratory on the valve-platform, but I couldn't make out what he was doing because the carving – uniquely in the whole chamber – had been crudely disfigured. A chunk of blackwood had been hacked off where his hands rested on the controls, as if on purpose. But why? What was he doing, and what was the curious shape hovering above him?

'Of course I, too, had stood at that very spot, manipulating the valves in every configuration imaginable as I slowly learned how to operate the laboratory. Yet no matter how hard I tried, I was unable to concentrate the full power of the laboratory by opening the entire forest of tubes and inlet valves all at once and in the right sequence, so that everything flowed into the central root-pipe at the same instant. And so, the entity that they had managed to create eluded me.

'But I didn't give up. I undertook weeks of new research. Hour after hour I spent up on the platform, experimenting until my eyes blurred and my hands ached from shifting the valve-levers, turning the valve-wheels and pushing and pulling the valve-stops. Exhausted and frustrated, I was finally on the point of abandoning my task for good when, all at once, I  heard a tell-tale hiss of air. Scarcely daring to believe that I might be nearing my goal, I pushed the lever I was holding fully open. The hiss became a loud roar. Sparks began to course along the pipes. And then it happened!

'A great ball of charged particles appeared in mid-air above my head, held in position by the air streaming in from the end of the central root-pipe. It sparkled and pulsed. I'd done it! I'd created a lightning-orb. Like that First Scholar before me, *I* had managed to harness the electric charge of the sky!'

'The key to creating life itself,' Bungus murmured.

Linius turned to him. 'That's right,' he said. 'The creation of new life! And with the glisters that lived throughout the stonecomb, I also had the seeds of that new life. It was an opportunity beyond my wildest dreams and I buried myself deeper than ever in my work.'

Maris looked at her father proudly. What a genius he was! So clever. So determined. She glanced round at Bungus, expecting the expression on his face to confirm her own feelings – but the old librarian was not smiling. His mouth was pursed, his brow furrowed.

'Did you not realize what you were doing?' he said gravely. 'The creation of life is sacred, Linius. Tampering with such matters is sacrilege, a profanity. You should have left well alone.'

Linius's face grew long. 'Alas,' he said, 'I know that now. Yet all my life I have pursued mysteries. With so much knowledge in front of me, just waiting to be explored, how could I *not* have pursued it?'

Bungus snorted.

'Besides,' Linius went on, 'I was sure I could close the valves down the moment it became dangerous.' He looked away. 'I underestimated my own desire to succeed, for as the experiment progressed I became increasingly obsessed. Nothing else mattered. I *had* to create new life!'

'Linius, Linius,' said Bungus softly, 'this was the mistake the ancient academics also made. And it led to their downfall, as well you know.'

'I do,' said Linius, 'but by then, I believed I was better than those early scholars. I was beginning to see where their work had gone wrong. I was convinced that, by learning from their mistakes, I could complete the experiment they had started all those centuries ago.' He paused. 'You see, I had got the feel of the laboratory. It was like a living thing to me. Standing at the keyboard of valves, I felt like . . .'

'The Master of Creation,' said Bungus scornfully.

Linius hung his head. 'Yes,' he said simply. He shuddered, wrapped his arms tightly around him and raised his head to the ceiling. 'Oh, Sky above!' he wailed. 'If I had known then what I know now, I would have shut the door and turned my back on the laboratory once and for all. And yet I could not. It took until the other night before I was finally convinced – before I finally did what I should have done so long ago, and sealed the laboratory.'

He turned to Maris and took her hands in his own. 'It has taken many, many months,' he said, 'but finally I have seen the error of my foolish ways. It's over now. For ever.'

'Over?' said Maris. 'But don't you remember, Father? Even now, your apprentice, Quint, is down in the stonecomb, making his way to the Ancient Laboratory.'

'It's all right,' said Linius. 'He won't be able to get in. Only the bearer of the Great Seal of High Office can gain access.' He squeezed her hands. 'Be a good girl and fetch it for me.'

*

As he squeezed through the narrow gap in the rock, Quint knew that he had almost reached his destination. There was a scrap of torn material, still clinging to the spur of rock; hopefully Bungus's cape, which he was now wearing, was made of something stronger. Grunting with effort, he eased himself round the jagged spur and shuffled on further.

A moment later, the tunnel opened up once more as he reached the far side of the blockage. Ahead of him, bathed in the same dull red glow, was the door to the Ancient Laboratory.

'At last,' he whispered, 'I've found it.'

He stepped forwards and leaned the hooked pikestaff against the wall. Then he reached out slowly, laid his hands against the carved door and traced his fingers round the outlines of the sculpted creatures. He stroked their life-like fur; he tickled their ears. His touch fell on the circular indentation at their centre, and as he ran his fingertips around the outer circle, up and down the triangular jags, along the calibrations, his eyes glazed over.

He remembered what had happened to the professor the last time *he* had stepped inside the laboratory: the terrible wounds, the horror-filled stare.

'What monstrous creature lies behind this door?' he wondered out loud, and shivered with fearful anticipation. 'It still isn't too late to give up, Quint. You could just turn around and leave,' he told himself. 'No-one would think the worse of you. No-one need ever know . . .'

But even as he spoke the words, Quint knew that he could never pay them any heed. *He* would know if he turned and left – and he would never be able to forgive himself for such cowardice, no matter how long he lived. Besides, it *was* too late to give up. It had been too late ever since the moment when he had helped the stricken professor to bed the night before last, loosening his collar, unburdening him of the heavy chain around his neck . . .

Quint reached into his jerkin pocket and drew out the large, gold medallion. He breathed in deeply to calm himself . . . He raised the Great Seal, eased it into the indentation in the carved stonework and turned it to the left, to the right . . .

There was a soft click. The door slid open.

CHAPTER SIXTEEN

THE CREATURE

'Not there?' Linius collapsed back onto his pillow, his face pale and taut. 'Not there . . . But it must be there! Have another look, child.'

'I . . . I'm sorry, Father,' said Maris, 'but the case is empty.'

'No, no!' groaned the High Academe. 'It can't be. How could I have been so careless?'

'What is it?' Maris cried. She was frightened now. Her father looked so frail, so fragile, and so very small lying there in the great bed, shaking his head from side to side. 'Have you remembered where you left the Great Seal?'

Linius looked up at her miserably. 'I took the seal off,' he said. 'I was weak, half-delirious. I handed it to him and told him to put it in its case. Then I collapsed into bed. It never occurred to me that he would . . .'

'You don't mean. . .?' said Maris, as the truth dawned on her.

'Quint,' breathed her father. 'Quint has the Great Seal.'

'And the key to the Ancient Laboratory,' said Bungus quietly. 'I think you need to finish your story, Linius, old friend.'

Linius nodded weakly and cleared his throat. 'As I became more skilled with the levers and wheels up on the valve-platform, I often thought of the carving of that ancient scholar standing, just as I was, at the controls of the Ancient Laboratory. I went back to the Blackwood Chamber and tried to read the ancient script but it, like the carving itself, had been hacked about horribly. From what I could make out, however, this ancient scholar had succeeded both in isolating a glister in the laboratory *and* bringing it to life. This he did by re-creating the exact conditions of Riverrise during a Mother Storm. Given my own growing feeling for the minute workings of the laboratory, and the months I'd spent studying in the Great Library, I felt sure I could repeat his achievement.'

'Linius, Linius,' said Bungus, as if talking to a young child. 'Didn't you realize even then? There was a reason why the First Scholars abandoned the laboratory and mutilated all record of it in the blackwood carvings. Something went horribly wrong down there and they didn't want the catastrophe ever to be repeated.'

'Yes, Bungus,' said Linius, with an exhausted sigh, 'but with the power of the Ancient Laboratory at my fingertips – *my* fingertips, Bungus – it was just too great a temptation. I had the entire learnings of the Great

Library at my disposal. I was convinced I could succeed where they had failed. And I did succeed, Bungus. At first . . .'

Bungus shook his head. 'Of course, of course,' he muttered. 'It is all becoming clear to me now.'

'Is it?' said Maris. 'Then please tell me, because Father is really beginning to scare me, Bungus.'

'The First Scholar in the blackwood carving is in the act of giving a glister life,' he said. 'What happened next has been erased from history, but I think I now know.'

'What?' said Maris.

'He created the rogue glister,' said Bungus simply. 'Huge, monstrous, and very likely insane. Not life as we know it – life that begins at Riverrise – but an abomination that destroyed its creator and has haunted the stonecomb ever since!'

'No wonder they closed the laboratory,' said Maris, her blood running cold at the memory of the hideous creature.

'Aye, and sealed up the tunnel,' said Bungus. 'They probably hoped the glister would never escape.' He shook his head. 'They weren't counting on the tunnel itself shifting its shape over the centuries and giving it a way out.'

Maris shuddered. 'Please, Father,' she pleaded, 'tell me *you* didn't create a blood-red glister!'

'No, child,' said Linius. He trembled. 'Though as my unease grew, with each visit to the laboratory, I did sense something in the stonecomb. Something terrible, watching me, listening. A malevolent presence . . . Oh, Maris, I

thought I was so much cleverer than the First Scholars.'
He swallowed hard and tried to control himself. 'You
see, they had sucked a glister from the stonecomb into
the pipes and then, as a mighty electric-storm hit the
Sanctaphrax rock and passed through it, they diverted
the storm's power into the laboratory. They exposed the
glister to the full force of the lightning. That much you
can see in the carving.'

Linius shook his head and permitted himself a rueful
smile. 'Of *course* they created a monstrous glister – how
could they not have, exposing it to such indiscriminate
power? But I, Linius Pallitax, the greatest scholar in the
history of Sanctaphrax . . .' He gave a bitter laugh. 'I
knew better. When *I* sucked a glister into the pipes, I
waited. I studied the sky. I bided my time. I chose my
storm carefully, with all the skill of a sky-scholar, and
when it struck I was up on the valve-platform ready.

'You should have seen it,' he said excitedly. 'I diverted
the storm's power through every branch, every root of
the Ancient Laboratory; channelling, filtering, concen-
trating it with every flick of a valve-lever or turn of a
valve-wheel until the lightning orb – hovering in mid-air
– glowed brighter and brighter. Below it, in a sealed tube
which led up from the central root-pipe, was the glister.

'As I watched, the lightning-orb grew more dazzling,
more intense until, all at once, it began flashing with
bright blue tendrils of light. This was the moment I'd
been waiting for. I released some air from the root-pipe
into the tube to build up pressure, then opened the valve
at the other end. With a hiss and a *pop*, the glister burst

THE ANCIENT LABORATORY

from the tube. It flew up towards the sphere of light, penetrated its outer skin of crackling light and was held at the centre of the brightly pulsating lightning-orb.'

Linius fell back into his pillows, his eyes distant and unfocused. 'I shut down the valves an instant later,' he said. 'Then, as the ball of light faded and disappeared, my heart leapt. For there, at the very centre of the after-glow, was . . . was, my creation.'

As the door of the ancient underground chamber opened, Quint found himself staring into the curious laboratory with its tubes and pipes, its bell-jars and spheres. This time he stepped right in. The papery cape rustled as the door closed behind him. He sniffed the air and his nose crinkled up. It smelled musky in there: acrid, sour.

Quint stepped cautiously forwards. As he did so, he thought he heard a tiny, plaintive voice. But when he stopped to listen more closely, the voice disappeared.

'Is my imagination playing tricks?' he asked himself.

'Help me.'

There it was again. This time there could be no mistake.

'Please, help me.'

The voice seemed to be coming from behind him. Quint turned round, and there – crouching in the shad-ows on one of the glass pipes – was a wide-eyed, pitiful little creature, trembling like a wispen leaf. Quint felt his heart melt.

'It's all right,' he said softly.

The creature cocked its head to one side, and blinked

its large, doleful eyes. Quint took a step closer.

'So, little one,' he said, his voice low and lulling, 'what's your name? How did you get here?'

The frail-looking creature slumped down. Sobs racked its puny body. With a jolt, Quint noticed angry red welts scarring its back. He stood stock still, shock mingling with anger.

'Don't worry, little one,' he said, 'you're safe now.'

'There it was,' Linius breathed. 'A life created away from the sacred pool of Riverrise.'

'What did it look like?' asked Maris.

'Look like?' said Linius, the faraway expression returning to his eyes. 'It looked . . . it looked innocent. Yes, innocent – but so frail and flimsy as to be hardly there.' His eyelids fluttered. 'It had soft downy fur and clear, almost translucent skin on its paws and palms. Its little ears were floppy and its eyes – they were big, Maris, big and round and sparkling with intelligence . . . I reached out and cupped it in my hands – and it grasped hold of my little finger. Oh, Maris, it was so delicate, so vulnerable. I held it to my chest and felt its tiny heart hammering.' He looked up. 'Even though I was a scientist, a professor, a creature of logic, I . . .' He fell still. 'It was mine,' he said. 'I had created it, and I couldn't help but love it.'

Remembering the promise she had made her father at the start of his story, Maris tried to ignore the unpleasant pangs of loss and hurt that made her stomach clench. But it wasn't easy.

'Then a curious thing happened,' her father continued.

'Yes?' said Maris, hardly daring to breathe.

'I dropped it,' said Linius. 'My hands were shaking, and it was so light and insubstantial that it just slipped through my fingers. I caught it just in time, no damage done, but in the instant I fumbled to catch it, a sharp pang of fear ran through me, and when I held it to me safely back in my arms, I could have sworn it seemed bigger than it had been just a moment before.'

Down in the Ancient Laboratory, Quint took a step towards the terrified creature. 'I won't hurt you,' he whispered.

The creature paused and looked back. 'You won't?' it said. 'You're not like him then. *He* hurts me. He hurts me all the time . . .'

'W . . . what do you mean?' asked Quint nervously.

'He enjoys tormenting me,' the creature murmured weakly. 'Keeping me prisoner down here, with no-one to talk to . . .' It faltered. 'Then, when he gets angry, he punishes me.'

'Who?' said Quint. 'The professor?'

'He's not coming back, is he?' the creature wailed, and tears welled up in its large brown eyes. 'You haven't brought him, have you?' It shivered violently. 'He's so, *so* cruel.'

301

'The professor? Cruel?' said Quint.

But even as he spoke, Quint remembered the sound he'd heard when he first stumbled across the laboratory – that sobbing cry, like an infant in pain, which had turned into a high-pitched scream. *No more, I beg you*, it had pleaded.

The creature edged forwards and nuzzled its furry cheek against Quint's arm. 'You *will* save me,' it said softly, 'won't you?'

Quint stroked its shoulders and back. His ears were burning with indignation. All his worst fears about the professor's work had proven to be true. The laboratory  was little more than an elaborate torture chamber – and he, Quint, had been the unwitting accomplice to Linius's cruelty. He tickled the creature behind its ears.

'Yes, little one,' he said, 'I'll save you.'

*

'Then, one night, not long afterwards,' Linius went on. 'I was working at the lectern in the laboratory. It was late, but I was busy with some scrolls I'd retrieved from the Great Library, trying desperately to discover what this creature I'd conjured up could possibly be. Was it a waif? Or some sort of gnokgoblin? Or had I created something unique, something never seen before? I *had* to find out. I was so excited – and nervous.

'The creature, I remember, was skulking in a far corner of the laboratory, away from the light. Its large eyes never left me for an instant. Sometimes, when I looked up, our eyes would meet and I'd feel a twinge of unease deep inside – and the creature would flick out its tongue as if tasting the air.

'Eventually, exhausted, I fell asleep – only to be haunted by strange, disturbing dreams of storms and carvings and cackling laughter. Suddenly I awoke – minutes, maybe hours later. I couldn't tell. I was drenched in a cold sweat which chilled me to the core of my bones. And then I saw it.' Linius swallowed hard. 'I saw the creature in the shadows, clutching the scrolls from the lectern. It peered at each one in turn, almost as if it was reading them – though I knew that was imposs- ible. When it saw me, it stopped abruptly, flung them down and scuttled back into its corner.

'I walked over and began to gather up the scattered scrolls. Despite the chill in my bones, I felt light-headed and feverish. All at once, a searing pain darted through my fingers and up my arm. I glanced down and there beneath the pile of scrolls was a shard of glass – part of a shattered minor pipe – and blood dripping on to it from my hand where it had cut me. Fighting against a wave of nausea mixed with wild panic, I gathered up the scrolls and stumbled from the laboratory.' His voice lowered. 'I could have sworn that the last thing I heard as the heavy stone door eased shut was the lapping sound of the creature's tongue tasting the air.'

Maris's jaw dropped. Bungus took a sharp intake of breath. Neither of them spoke.

'And it didn't stop there,' Linius sighed. 'On my subsequent visits it would move glass jars and bottles so that I would knock them to the ground with my elbow, or else it would leave razor-sharp slivers of glass wedged in the controls up on the valve-platform to cut my fingers. It seemed to enjoy the sight of blood. A hundred different incidents there were, and with each one – no matter how hard I'd prepared myself not to react – I grew increasingly uneasy, fearful even. And every time I felt fear gnaw at me, the creature would respond, licking its thin lips greedily and staring at me through those large, unblinking eyes. It seemed to be feeding off my emotions, growing stronger and bolder with each day.' He sighed.

'Yet still I refused to accept that I'd made a mistake. I wanted to show the creature love and care and affection – so that those would be the feelings it would develop itself. Instead, the creature only seemed to respond to fear and pain.

'Sometimes, I admit, frustration got the better of me, and on one terrible evening, after I found it damaging a capillary tube – smashing it into those razor-sharp splinters it liked to torment me with – I'm afraid I lost my head. In a blind rage I lunged at the creature, cursing and swearing. "By Gloamglozer! I'll kill you, I'll kill you!" I roared. I grabbed it and lifted it above my head as if to dash it to the ground in my fury.

'I instantly regretted my actions. Why, the creature weighed virtually nothing at all. Although it had grown by several feet, it was no heavier than the first time I'd held it in my arms. It was as light and insubstantial as the glister from which it had come and I was overwhelmed with pity for my puny creation. I put it down gently. It looked up at me with those cold, staring eyes.

"Gloamglozer?" it said, in a small voice. "Gloamglozer. Gloamglozer."'

'Tears filled my eyes. "Poor creature," I whispered, "that you should have ended up with so foolish and arrogant a teacher. Perhaps it is apt that your first word should be a Deepwoods curse."

'"Gloamglozer!" it repeated, and slipped back into the shadows.'

Linius sat back in the bed, his face flushed with exertion. Then he turned to Maris. 'Could you pour me a glass of Tweezel's cordial?' he asked her. 'My throat's as dry as a bone.'

Maris did so and Linius grasped the glass eagerly, but as he raised it to his lips, it suddenly shattered in his anxious vice-like grip. The dark-red cordial poured down, staining the white sheets like blood.

'Careful, Father,' said Maris. 'Shall I fetch you another glass?'

'No,' said Bungus urgently. 'You must finish your story, Linius, for I fear time is running short.'

Linius nodded and cleared his throat. 'From that moment on, I knew that the tables had been turned,' he said unhappily. '*I* was the one now being watched. *I* was the one being experimented on.' He mopped his brow, which had broken out in countless beads of glistening sweat. 'I should have cut my losses and abandoned the experiment,' he went on. 'Yet I felt too responsible for the life I'd created. I'd gone wrong somewhere – with its education or its upbringing. Now I wanted to put matters right.

'I visited the Great Library increasingly often. If I could just find out exactly what type of creature it was, I thought I could do something to make amends.' He paused. 'Then I had my fall. It was stupid of me. I must have stepped out of the hanging-baskets onto the trunk-platforms a thousand times before – but on that particular occasion, I slipped and fell.'

Maris gasped. 'So *that* was how you injured your leg. You told me . . .'

'I know what I told you,' Linius interrupted. 'I didn't want you involved. That's why I sent for Wind Jackal's son. I needed someone I could trust to help me with those tasks I could no longer manage on my own. I sent him to the library . . .'

'You almost sent him to his death,' said Bungus accusingly. 'A mere novice, unversed in the use of the ropeways and hanging-baskets. Why, if I hadn't rescued him, he would have perished there and then.'

'Yes, yes,' said Linius hurriedly, 'but I was in a panic, Bungus. I'd witnessed something in the laboratory. Something bizarre. Something monstrous . . .'

Bungus fell still. Maris sat forwards. 'What was it, Father?' she said.

Linius shivered, and mopped his dripping brow once more. 'For several days after my attack on the creature, it refused to emerge from its corner. It built itself a kind of nest there, from an old cloak of mine, the lectern stool and numerous scraps of parchment which it gathered together around it. Half the time, I wouldn't have known it was there at all if it hadn't been for its voice . . .'

'It talked to you?' said Maris.

'If you could call it that,' said Linius with a shiver. 'It repeated everything I said in its small, whispering voice. I tell you, it sent shivers down my spine. So I stopped talking to myself – an irritating habit at the best of times, but now, when repeated back to me, positively alarming. But that didn't stop the creature. It simply began to recite everything I'd ever said in its presence, over and over again.' He shuddered. 'And that wasn't the worst part, oh, no . . .'

'What, Father?' said Maris anxiously.

'It was beginning to mimic my voice, practising over and over until it sounded exactly like me. I was getting frightened now. Just what *had* I created? So far as I was concerned, it hadn't come out of its lair in the shadows for days. But what did it get up to when I wasn't there? Was it safe to leave it unattended in the Ancient Laboratory any longer? Perhaps I should chain it up, or even – I shuddered at the thought – destroy it.' He paused. 'I decided to spy on it before I made up my mind what to do.

'So one evening, I pretended to leave as I usually did, inserting the seal in the door and waiting for it to slide open. Only this time, instead of walking out, I stepped to one side and crouched down behind a cluster of hanging-pipes as the door eased back shut, then waited. The creature in its lair seemed also to be waiting, listening for any sign that I was still there. Then a low cackle erupted from the corner. It made my blood run cold.

' "Linius, Linius, you old fool," came my voice. "What are you thinking of? By Sky, you'd forget your head if it wasn't screwed on."

'I put my eye to a gap in the tangle of pipes and tubes and peered into the shadows in the far corner of the laboratory. What I saw made my heart lurch into my throat. The creature emerged from its lair and moved towards the centre of the laboratory. It was wearing that old cloak of mine, the hood masking its features, and it had grown almost to my size. But that wasn't the most remarkable thing. It was something else which made me gasp and bite down hard on my lip.' He shook his head as he relived the terrible sight which met his eyes. 'The creature was hovering at least three feet off the ground. Then it threw back the hood of its cloak and, as I watched – open-mouthed, scarcely daring to breathe – the creature's wide eyes narrowed, its brow furrowed, its ears shortened, until . . .'

Linius's voice cracked with emotion.

'It's all right, Father,' said Maris, tears in her eyes. 'It's all right.'

'But it's *not* all right, Maris, my darling daughter. You see, the creature had changed itself into *me*!'

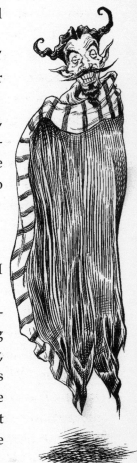

'A shape-shifter!' Bungus exclaimed. 'Oh, Linius, this is worse than I feared.'

'I hid for hours watching the creature hovering round the laboratory, changing into the various creatures it had seen in the scrolls it had read – but always returning to the shape it liked best. Me!'

'Finally, it seemed to tire and crept back to its bed in the shadows. And I crept out.

'Immediately I raced back to Sanctaphrax. I summoned my young apprentice. I knew precisely the scroll I needed him to fetch from the Great Library. It was filed far up in the high twigs of *Aerial Creatures* where *Celestial crosses* . . .'

'*Legendary*,' Bungus finished for him. 'You had created . . . a gloamglozer!'

Linius nodded. He looked crushed.

'I read the scroll Quint brought me,' he went on softly. 'It chilled my blood. Written in the ancient script I was now fluent in, it was full of folklore and superstition as one would expect and yet, the more I read, the more convinced I became that this was the creature I had created.

'The Gloamglozer – or Ancient Wanderer – is said to have been created aeons ago at Riverrise. It was an evil time, before the Mother Storm seeded the Edgelands with life as we know it. The gloamglozer was one of the ancient ones that dwelt in the air: one of the ghouls and demons that fought and fed off each other in the Age of Darkness. It lived on, long after the other nameless ones disappeared, because it was a shape-shifter, a beguiler, a seeker after lost souls. It was only with the Age of Light and the coming of Kobold the Wise that the terrible creature finally faded into the mists of the Edgelands – and into myth and folklore: a fireside fable to frighten children with.'

Tears ran down the High Academe's cheeks. 'And then, after countless centuries, I, Linius Pallitax, decided to play the great creator. I have brought life into being, far from the waters of Riverrise, in the arid centre of the Sanctaphrax rock. Is it any wonder I brought forth a demon from the very beginning of time?' He sniffed miserably. 'But at least now I knew what I must do. I had to return the abomination to the oblivion from whence it had come. And there was only one way to do that.'

'Chine,' said Bungus. 'From the banks of Riverrise.'

'Yes, my old friend,' said Linius. 'I gathered the last ampoule of chine confiscated from the exiled earth-scholars, and, for the first time, Quint took me down in the sky cage.'

'What went wrong?' said Maris. 'Did that evil thing do *this* to you?' She brushed a hand lightly over her father's bandages.

Linius shook his head. 'No, my child. This I did to myself. You see, unlike a flat-head goblin or a bander-bear, the gloamglozer has no physical strength to speak of. It is a creature of the air, a demon. It feeds on fear and despair, pain and death. It is a schemer and a trickster.' He took a sharp intake of breath. 'That is what makes it so deadly.'

'So what happened? Tell me, Father,' pleaded Maris.

'For his own safety, I left Quint behind in the sky cage and proceeded along the tunnel. Then, trembling with anticipation, I entered the laboratory. What appearance had my creation taken on this time? I wondered. I looked round, and there it was – crouched down in the corner.

'I shut the door and turned to face my tormentor. I was trying not to let the fear that had gripped me show in my voice, but the creature was not tricked even for a moment. I could hear its tongue flicking the air – in, out, in, out – tasting it, relishing it.

'It skulked in its lair as if sensing I meant it harm. I gripped the chine, easing the lid off the ampoule with my thumb whilst in my other hand I brandished the scroll Quint had fetched. "Look what I've brought you," I said. "Wouldn't you like to see? Don't you want to know what you are? Your true identity?"

'I heard a rustle from the shadows, and shook the scroll. "Here," I said. "It's all here. Come out and read it for yourself."

' "Give it to me," came the creature's voice. A hand reached out from the shadows.

' "Come closer," I coaxed. "Read it here by the light."

'The creature emerged and floated towards me. It resembled a gabtroll. It grasped at the parchment and I let it take it. It scanned the contents of the scroll, cackling and crooning as it did so. Then it paused. I watched as a finger traced the primitive outlandish drawing decorating the margin. It was a folk-drawing of the imagined true shape of a gloamglozer: horns, matted hair, long claws . . .

'All at once the creature began to change into the exact likeness of this evil beast. Moments later, hovering in front of me, there was the gloamglozer. Overcoming my horror, I swung my arm in a great arc. The chine rained down on the abomination.

'With a horrible scream it fled into the shadows. The terrible smell of burning flesh filled the air. I sat and waited. No sounds came from the lair. I prodded the shapeless bundle. It gave no sign of life. I sat there all night, despondent and brooding, going over and over what had happened. Finally, I left.

'Back in my bed-chamber, I awoke from dreams filled with monsters and demons. What if the gloamglozer wasn't dead? How could I be certain? I decided I would never have any peace until I returned to the laboratory to make sure. So Quint took me down a second time.

'The moment I entered the great underground chamber, I sensed that something was wrong. The huddled body beneath the cloak was gone, though the terrible smell of burnt flesh still lingered in the air. Then I heard it – a soft sobbing whimper coming from the far corner of the laboratory. But I wasn't fooled. I knew the creature was simply playing one more of its devious games. I shouted at it to be still. It responded by letting out a loud, defiant wail and demanded that I set it free.

'Suddenly, a cold shiver of fear pierced my spine and I looked up. There, above me, hovered the horribly disfigured gloamglozer. It screamed in a voice I recognized as my own. "By Gloamglozer! I'll kill you! I'll kill you!"

'I stumbled back and tripped over a thin wire stretched between two glass pillars at ankle height. A razor-sharp shard of glass flew down, gashing my scalp and almost severing my ear. Blood blinded me, but I managed to stumble to my feet. I brandished the empty ampoule at the hovering creature. Hissing with suppressed fury, it retreated – and I took my chance.

'I dashed for the door, pressed the Seal into place and leapt through the gap. As the door slammed behind me, I heard the gloamglozer's muffled screams of rage. It thrashed about inside the laboratory. It pounded at the door. It threatened and pleaded – but I was deaf to its entreaties.

'The gloamglozer had been imprisoned. I could only hope that, in time, its stone jail would become its coffin, and that the threat from the terrible monster would disappear for ever. I, for one, would never return to the Ancient Laboratory, and – by destroying all those clues which had led me to it – I intended to make sure that no-one else could either . . .' He clutched at Maris's hand. 'I didn't think that anyone would ever set foot in there again!'

'Please, please,' the creature said softly. 'Open the door and let me out of this . . . this torture chamber. Hurry, before he returns.'

'I'm trying,' said Quint, as he fumbled with the Great

Seal. He was finding it difficult to hold it in the stone indentation and turn at the same time. 'Can you give me a hand?' he suggested.

The creature made no reply. Quint turned, and gasped as he found himself looking into his own eyes. 'What the . . .?'

As the door slid open he stepped back nervously.

'By Gloamglozer!' the other Quint smiled. 'I'll kill you! I'll kill you!'

A glass pillar snapped above his head and crashed down. A scaly hand reached out for the Great Seal as it slipped from Quint's grasp. And everything went black.

CHAPTER SEVENTEEN

REVENGE

L inius sat up in bed, and hugged his knees to his chest. Having completed his story, he looked drained and haggard. The tears of remorse he'd shed had stopped, leaving his eyes red and his bony cheeks stained with glistening streaks.

'Oh, Father,' said Maris softly, and she leant forwards to comfort him.

But Linius pulled away. 'I don't deserve your sympathy after everything I've done,' he said. His eyes darted round feverishly. 'After what I have unleashed on the world . . .'

'This is no time for self-pity, old friend,' said Bungus. 'You have been reckless and foolhardy, that is true – but if we hurry, we can still avert a catastrophe. It is up to us to ensure that the gloamglozer remains contained in the Ancient Laboratory.'

'But what if Quint has already released it?' Linius moaned. 'Oh, I could never forgive myself if anything has happened to the lad. And neither could Wind Jackal,' he added softly. 'He entrusted the youth to my care.'

'Try to remain calm, Linius,' said Bungus. 'There is no point speculating about what *might* have happened.' He stood up from the bed. 'I shall return to the stonecomb at once.'

Linius looked up at the old librarian. 'You would do that for me?' he said.

'Of course, Linius,' said Bungus kindly. 'For you, and for Sanctaphrax.'

Linius nodded slowly. '*You* should have been Most High Academe,' he said, 'rather than me.' Suddenly, he threw back the bedclothes and swung his legs down onto the floor. 'But I can't allow you to go alone, Bungus. I must come with you.' He stood up. 'We . . .'

'Father!' Maris cried out, as Linius stumbled forwards and collapsed to the floor in a heap. She ran round the bed and crouched down beside him. 'You're still too weak,' she said.

'Yes, child,' he groaned pitifully. 'I am useless. Hopeless . . .'

'*Shush*,' she said gently. 'We'll have none of that. You've been through a lot . . .' She turned to Bungus. 'Can you give me a hand?'

Taking an arm each, the pair of them helped Linius up from the floor and placed him gently on the bed. He flopped back heavily against the pillows. His eyes closed.

Bungus leant over the High Academe and spoke softly but urgently. 'Linius? Can you hear me? Time is short.'

Linius's eyelids flickered.

'Linius, I need to know how to get to the Ancient Laboratory. The Librarians' Passage leads down from the Great Library into the heartrock, but . . .'

Linius opened his eyes and frowned. 'Librarians' Passage?' he said. 'What is that?'

'A vertical tunnel, old and secret,' said Bungus, 'constructed by earth-scholars many centuries ago.'

'I had no idea,' said Linius and shook his head. 'If I had, I would never have had to go down in that appalling sky cage.' He paused. 'This passageway – does it emerge in a broad horizontal tunnel?'

'Yes,' said Bungus eagerly. 'Yes it does.'

Linius nodded weakly. 'This is the Great West Tunnel,' he said, his voice barely a whisper. 'You must follow the direction where the air glows deepest red.' He paused a moment. 'As you continue, you will find that movements in the rock have caused the tunnel to split into various minor passageways at several points. At every junction, you must take the left-hand tunnel.'

'Always the left-hand tunnel,' said Bungus, nodding.

'At the final junction, the correct path looks like a dead-end,' Linius continued. 'But it isn't. You'll be able to squeeze through the fallen rocks. The laboratory door lies on the other side.' He opened his eyes and stared into the distance. 'Oh, I'm so weary. How I wish to sleep,' he moaned. 'Yet when I do, what dreams I am haunted by! Oh, Bungus, you can't imagine . . .'

Bungus said nothing. He reached into the leather satchel and removed a small phial of purple liquid. He unscrewed the top and handed it to Linius.

'Drink this,' he said softly. 'It will help you sleep.'

'But the dreams . . .' said Linius.

'It'll take care of the dreams too, old friend,' said Bungus. 'You have my word.'

'Drink it, Father,' said Maris. 'Everything will seem different when you wake up.'

Linius reached forwards. He wrapped his fingers round the glass phial, raised it to his lips and swallowed it in one gulp.

'It tastes good,' he said, and turned to the old librarian. 'Now, go, Bungus, as quickly as you can. Sky willing, you are not already too late.'

'Sky willing, Linius,' said Bungus. 'And Earth willing, too.' He turned away and strode towards the door.

Linius lay back against the pillows. His eyelids grew heavy. 'Oh, and Bungus,' he said drowsily. 'Promise me . . . you'll . . . take . . . care . . .' His voice faded away. Moments later, the room echoed with soft, rhythmic breathing.

Bungus smiled. 'Pleasant dreams, Linius,' he whispered. Then he turned to Maris. 'It has been an honour meeting you, Maris, daughter of Linius Pallitax,' he said. 'Maybe one day our paths will cross again. Fare you well.' He turned and opened the door.

'What?' Maris exclaimed. Her father sighed in his

sleep and rolled over – but did not wake up. Maris leapt from the bed and ran after Bungus. 'I'm coming with you,' she said.

'No, Maris, you must not,' said Bungus sternly. 'Have you heard nothing your father has just told us? Don't you realize the danger? And you are still weakened yourself . . .'

'I don't care!' Maris shouted. 'It was only because of me that Quint went down there in the first place. I can't just abandon him!'

'Mistress Maris,' came a trilling voice from behind her on the landing. 'Whatever is wrong?'

'It's Bungus,' said Maris indignantly. 'He's returning to the stonecomb – and he doesn't want to take me with him.'

The spindlebug's antennae quivered. 'I should think not,' he said. 'It's a terrible place . . .'

'Oh, you're as bad as he is!' Maris stormed. She turned to Bungus. 'Well, I *am* going,' she said defiantly. 'I *am* strong enough. And if you don't take me, I'll just follow you!'

Bungus's expression softened. 'You're a stubborn one, aren't you?' he said. 'Just like your father.' He sighed. 'Is there nothing I can say to make you change your mind?'

Maris shook her head.

'Come on, then,' said Bungus. 'But if you're coming with me, you'd better not slow me down,' he added gruffly.

There was a stiff breeze blowing when Maris and Bungus stepped out of the Palace of Shadows. It brought with it the smell of oil-pine incense and the sound of loud cheering voices. As the pair of them ran down the palace steps and through the narrow alleyways which led to the Western Avenue, both the intensity of the incense and the volume of the cheering increased.

'What's going on?' asked Maris.

'The Inauguration Ceremony, at a guess,' said Bungus. 'Didn't the Professors of Light and Darkness say a Great Storm was imminent?'

'Of course,' said Maris. 'With all this excitement, I'd quite forgotten. Garlinius Gernix is to set sail for the Twilight Woods in search of stormphrax. I've heard that he's one of the very best scholars ever to have gone through the Knights' Academy.' They continued to the end of the alley where it joined the avenue. 'Look,' she said, and pointed up to the top of the Central Viaduct. 'There he is now.'

Far above their heads, the newly-dubbed knight sat astride a powerful prowlgrin. As ceremony decreed, they were making their way solemnly across the viaduct from the Great Hall, where the Inauguration had taken place, to the Loftus Observatory, where a great storm-chasing sky ship, tethered to a ring at the top of its gleaming dome, awaited them. Garlinius was dressed in shining full armour.

'Gar-lin-ius! Gar-lin-ius!' the heaving crowd chanted up at them.

'Good luck, Garlinius!' a lone voice called out.

'Sky speed be with you!' cried another.

Bungus took Maris by the arm. 'Come,' he said. 'As an earth-scholar, I've learnt how to avoid the crowds. Let's double back and go by the side-alleys. It'll be quicker in the long run.'

Maris nodded, and trotted after the gangly librarian as he set off back the way they'd come. They hurried this way and that along the maze of alleyways and twittens, with Bungus leading and Maris following close on his heels. She was just beginning to wonder whether he knew the layout of the floating city quite as well as he claimed when, all at once, they emerged into a deserted square. Before them stood the Great Library.

'At last!' said Maris.

Inside the huge, deserted building, Bungus scurried about busily. 'Light, light, light,' he muttered as he unhooked two lanterns from the wall and lit them. 'Earth willing I have everything else I need already.' Then, without pausing, he climbed a ladder which led to a raised platform, returning a moment later with two heavy belts. A curved sword hung from one, a dagger from the other. 'Take this,' he said to Maris, handing her the belt with the dagger. You could need it.'

With trembling fingers, Maris put the belt around her waist and secured the buckle. The sheath of the knife pressed into the top of her leg as a constant reminder of the possible dangers which lay ahead.

'Are you still determined to come?' asked Bungus.

Maris nodded.

'Then, let us go.' Bungus crossed to the far side of the library, crouched down and lifted a trapdoor. He handed Maris one of the lanterns. 'After you,' he said.

Maris hesitated. As she stared down into the dark tunnel below her, she was flooded by memories of that awful place: the endless narrow tunnels, the parasitic glisters, the terrible blood-red monster that those ancient scholars had created . . .

'It's still not too late for you to return to your father,' said Bungus gently. 'You don't have to come with me.'

Maris turned to him. 'Yes, I do,' she said simply. Then, without saying another word, she raised the lantern before her and descended the narrow flight of wooden steps which led down to the entrance of the tunnel.

'That's it,' said Bungus encouragingly. 'I'm right behind you.'

As Maris reached the bottom of the stairs and felt the wooden planks beneath her feet give way to solid rock, her heart missed a beat. This was it. She was back inside the terrible stonecomb once more.

As they went deeper into the rock Maris realized how much she'd missed earlier that day when Bungus had carried her out. For a start, although it had seemed impossibly steep as she had clung on round his neck, she now discovered that the so-called *vertical* passage was in fact a series of short stretches which zigzagged downwards. In places, where ancient shifts in the rock had caused the walls of the tunnel to crumble, drystone buttresses had been cleverly constructed to prevent it collapsing completely. A long thick rope – shiny with centuries of passing hands – was secured to the walls as a makeshift banister. With the scree-like rubble beneath her feet, it made the descent safer, if no faster. The biggest surprise of all, however, was just how far they had to go.

'This tunnel goes on for ever,' she complained.

Bungus chuckled. 'It takes a lot longer going in the other direction,' he said. 'Particularly when you've got someone on your back.'

Maris shook her head. 'I don't know how you managed it,' she said.

'Years of lugging heavy tomes and crates of scrolls around the library,' said Bungus. 'Besides, you weren't the first individual I've had to rescue from . . .' He fell still.

Maris turned. 'What?' she asked uneasily.

'*Ssh*,' said Bungus softly. He put his finger to his lips, cocked his head to one side and listened carefully. From far below, above the hissing and humming of the stonecomb, there came the faint noise of what sounded like movement. Then nothing. 'Probably just a minor shift in the rock,' he said at length. 'After all, the stonecomb is growing all the time.'

The pair of them continued their descent in silence. All round them, the ominous humming grew louder and, as they approached the heartrock, so the deep red of the tunnels grew more intense. Beneath their feet, the incline was becoming less and less steep until, all at once, the passage emerged at a junction with a broader, flatter tunnel.

'This is it,' Bungus announced quietly. 'The Great West Tunnel.' He turned left and set off. 'It's this way. Follow me.'

Now that the going was flat, they made their way along the passageway more quickly. Each time the tunnel divided, they took the left-hand option – as Linius had instructed. Maris's heart was thumping. With every step she took, she was getting closer to the Ancient Laboratory. What would she find there? Was Quint, even at this moment, struggling to open the door? Or were she and Bungus already too late?

In front of her the tunnel abruptly split into three. Bungus stopped, raised his lantern and shone it down each passage in turn. 'This must be the dead-end that Linius mentioned,' he said at last, and pointed to the rocky obstruction in front of them.

'Let's go and see for ourselves,' said Maris. 'I . . .' She grasped Bungus's arm. 'L . . . Listen,' she whispered.

But Bungus had already heard it. From the middle passage came an unmistakable sound: a spinechilling slurping and snorting, drawing steadily closer.

'Not again. Please, not again,' Maris whispered, dread lacing her trembling voice.

'Hold your nerve,' said Bungus. 'Remember, it can sense your fear.'

At that moment, the cause of the disgusting noises rounded the corner and came into view. Maris screamed. It was the blood-red glister – and it wanted revenge.

'You must go on, Maris,' Bungus said, his voice icy calm. 'I'll join you as soon as I've dealt with the loathsome creature once and for all.'

But Maris was frozen to the spot, unable even to blink. The glister barrelled closer, its eyes rolling, its tentacles flailing, its great amorphous red body wobbling as it moved. Bungus seized her by the shoulders and propelled her towards the left-hand tunnel.

'Find Quint,' he told her.

At the entrance to the tunnel, Maris paused and glanced back. She saw Bungus stride forwards, his great stave raised before him. The blood-red glow of the approaching glister was reflected in his face. He reached for his pocket – and caught sight of Maris out of the corner of his eye.

'Are you still here?' he roared. 'Go! Go NOW!'

Maris turned on her heels and scurried into the tunnel. Behind her, she heard Bungus shouting. 'Baneful and damnable abomination!' he cursed. 'Prepare to return to the foul air from which you came!'

Maris went further into the tunnel. When she reached the rockfall she raised her lantern. Sure enough, just as her father had said, there was a narrow gap between the rocks and the wall. She began to squeeze through.

Behind her Bungus's voice grew softer, more muffled. 'For years I have tracked you and tried to destroy you. Now, at last, it is time . . .' The words faded away completely.

'Sky protect you,' Maris murmured as she continued to the end of the narrow gap in the rock. '*And* Earth, too,' she added.

By the time the tunnel opened out again, the only sound was the deep humming of the stonecomb itself. She hesitated for a moment, wondering whether to wait for Bungus or go on alone.

'Go on,' she told herself. 'I must find Quint.'

As she rounded the next bend, Maris stopped in her tracks. There it was. The great carved stone door of the Ancient Laboratory.

Heart pounding, Maris walked towards it. As she did so, she noticed something – something which made her pale with foreboding. There was a line of light running down the right-hand side of the doorway. Since the light was coming from inside, it could mean but one thing. The door was not completely shut.

'Oh, no,' Maris murmured. 'Quint?'

She stepped closer. The reason the door had not closed became clear. There was a length of glass pipe wedged into the corner of the doorway, jamming it open. Heart in her mouth, Maris looked in through the narrow gap. The cavernous laboratory was just as Linius had described: the pipes and tubes, the lectern and stool, the curious nest-like collection of parchments. And the damage . . .

'Quint,' she called. 'Quint, are you there?'

Apart from the broken pipe which was preventing the door from closing, there was shattered glass all over the floor. Maris poked her head into the gap and peered round. There were more broken pipes, and smashed spheres and bell-jars; there were lengths of coiled wire, and scrolls – some intact, some torn into countless pieces which covered the floor like confetti, and . . .

Maris gasped. Sticking out from the shadows behind the door were two legs. They were clad in familiar leggings and boots.

'Quint!' she cried out, and slipped through the gap in the door.

Quint was lying motionless on the floor. He had blood on his face. His eyes were closed.

Maris dropped to her knees and pressed her ear to his chest. And, yes. There it was. A heartbeat – faint and irregular, but a heartbeat nevertheless. She leant forwards and stroked his cheeks gently, whispering all the time.

'I came back for you, Quint,' she whispered. 'I would never have left you here. You know that, don't you?' But the youth did not move. 'Oh, Quint!' she cried. 'I'm so sorry. This is all my fault. Please don't die. Please . . .' She bent down and planted a small, light kiss on his forehead. 'Please wake up, Quint.'

Quint's eyelids flickered and opened. He looked up, confused. 'Maris,' he said drowsily. 'What are *you* doing here?'

'We came back to rescue you,' said Maris. 'Bungus and I . . .'

'Bungus?' said Quint. He peered round the gloomy laboratory. 'Bungus is here?'

'He's in the tunnel,' said Maris. 'That terrible blood-red glister reappeared . . .'

'The glister is back?' said Quint. He sat up, and put a hand to his head. 'I'd forgotten about the glister. The last thing I remember was talking to the creature . . .' He hesitated. 'And then something strange happened . . .'

'So you've seen the creature?' said Maris. 'Did it float in mid-air. Did it have horns? And hideous blistered skin?'

Quint frowned. 'No,' he said quietly. 'None of these things. It was small, quite weedy, and with great big eyes, until . . . until it changed . . . to look like me!'

'Like *you*!' Maris exclaimed. 'Of course!'

'What?' said Quint.

'The creature can take on any appearance it chooses,' said Maris. 'Father explained it all. It is a shape-shifter!'

'A shape-shifter?' said Quint.

Maris nodded miserably. 'My father created a gloamglozer, Quint,' she whispered.

Quint stared at her, wide-eyed and open-mouthed. 'I don't understand,' he said at last. 'A gloamglozer?' Surely they are only characters in myths and fairy-tales. A gloamglozer doesn't really exist.'

Maris swallowed hard. 'One does now,' she said.

As Quint struggled to his feet, he remembered the hand reaching towards his chest. He looked down – and gasped. The Great Seal was no longer there. He turned to Maris.

'It's taken your father's Seal of High Office,' he said. 'What am I going to tell him? I've been so stupid. It tricked me, and I believed it . . .' He chewed into his lower lip anxiously as he remembered all the things the creature had said about Linius. 'Maris,' he said quietly, 'the gloamglozer hates your father.'

'My father!' Maris cried. 'We'll have to return to him at once and warn him that the gloamglozer is free!' She shook her head miserably. 'He tried so hard to make sure it couldn't escape. Oh, Quint, I wish we hadn't meddled. This is all our fault. And now his life is in danger!'

'If only we'd known,' said Quint. 'And there we were trying to help.'

With a shake of her head, Maris straightened up and strode back to the door. 'Come on,' she said. 'We must get back as soon as we can.'

'But what about Bungus?' said Quint. 'And the glister?'

'Dear brave Bungus,' said Maris. 'He fought the glister so that I could escape and find you. We must go back to him. Hurry, Quint!'

Maris left the laboratory first, with Quint following close behind her. Being bigger than her, he was not able to slip through without touching the door, and as he did so, there was a sudden splintering sound as the pipe wedged in the gap began to break.

'The pipe!' Quint cried.

Maris spun round, grabbed Quint by his outstretched hand and tugged. The pair of them tumbled backwards and fell to the ground. Behind them, the door of the Ancient Laboratory slammed to.

'Shut for ever,' Maris whispered.

'But too late,' said Quint, his voice sombre. He picked himself up and helped Maris to her feet. 'Let's get out of here.'

Back through the narrow gap between the fallen rocks and the wall they squeezed, and along the tunnel on the other side. When they reached the four-way junction, Maris looked around, surprised.

'Bungus was here,' she said. 'The glister came from that way. I heard them fighting . . .'

'We'll keep looking,' said Quint. 'Perhaps Bungus gave it the slip.'

They tip-toed on along the gloomy tunnel. Maris led the way, the lantern raised high in her shaking hand. All at once, flickering light fell across a small figure lying on the ground up ahead, its bony arms outstretched.

'Bungus?' breathed Quint.

They approached anxiously. The body was face-down on the ground. Maris looked at the familiar papery clothes, and at the stave with its carved lullabee-tree pommel clasped in the skeletal hand.

'Oh, Bungus,' she groaned.

Quint crouched down. 'I recognize this place,' he said. 'We're at the entrance of the tunnel which leads to the glister-lair.'

Maris looked up, puzzled. There was no hole to be seen.

'There's been a rockfall,' said Quint. 'Yes, look.' He pointed to a length of carved wood jammed into a crack in the rock. 'It's the end of Bungus's stave. He must have broken it dislodging that great slab of rock.'

Just then, a soft, hissing sigh emerged from the folds of the baggy jerkin. Quint shifted forwards and tried to tilt the old librarian's head back. As his fingers made contact, a sudden spasm shot through the scholar's body, twisting it right round. His head shook, his arms and legs jerked, and his back slammed down hard against the ground. Quint cried out and fell back. Bungus looked up, as if surprised.

Quint gasped and Maris let out a small, horrified shriek – for the face before them was not the face they had known before. The cheeks were hollow and the jaw-line gaunt, the skin stretched tightly over the bones. The lips – once full and expressive – had become tight, narrow bands, so shrivelled that they had been pulled back to reveal the yel-lowed teeth behind, now fixed in a sinister grimace. Worst of all by far, however, were the eyes. Creamy-white, with trace of neither pupil nor iris, they stared up blindly, sending icy shivers shooting up and down Maris and Quint's spines.

'Rogue-glister. Blood-red fiend . . .' Bungus murmured, his voice choked and rasping, every word a struggle. 'Must stop creature. Must save daughter of Linius . . .'

Tears welled up in Maris's eyes. 'You *did* save me,' she sobbed. 'Don't try to talk any more.'

But Bungus paid her no attention. 'Upon me . . .' he croaked. 'The fear, the terror . . . Tentacles gripping . . .' His right arm twitched. 'Must fight . . . Chine. Need chine . . . Where is it? Where has it gone? *Where is the chine?*'

All at once, his back arched as if an electric charge had surged through his body. His fingers flexed, his hair stood on end. The next moment it was over. Bungus slumped back, his tongue lolling from his mouth, and a dry, rasping last breath rattling at the back of his throat.

'No!' Maris howled. 'Oh, Bungus! Bungus! I'm so sorry. I'm to blame for this . . .'

Quint wrapped his arm around Maris's shoulder and squeezed her tightly. 'It's my fault, too,' he said. 'Bungus gave his life protecting both of us.' He leant forwards and closed Bungus's eyes. 'His last act was to imprison the glister in its terrible lair. Although he didn't kill it, he'd be so proud to know that he sealed it up for ever.'

'I know,' Maris sniffed. 'Oh, he was so loyal. And so brave . . .' She turned to Quint, her face racked with remorse. 'But we set the gloamglozer free! What are we going to do, Quint?'

'We must tell the professor,' said Quint. 'He'll know what to do.'

Maris shook her head woefully. Her father was too weak even to walk. When she'd left him, he'd been fast asleep in his bed. He'd seemed so frail, so exhausted. Would he really know what to do? For the first time in her life, Maris was having doubts about her father, the Most High Academe of Sanctaphrax. What could *he* do against the gloamglozer? Yet she mustn't let Quint know her fears; she had to be strong.

'Yes, Quint,' she said bravely. 'He'll know what to do.'

·CHAPTER EIGHTEEN·

THE CURSE OF THE GLOAMGLOZER

The late afternoon sun was low in the sky. It shone lazily on the floating city of Sanctaphrax, turning its grand stately buildings to gold and casting long dark shadows down its alleyways and avenues. The air was perfectly still, yet in all the great schools and colleges across the city, the sky-scholars – be they mistsifters or raintasters, cloudwatchers or windtouchers – were all drawing the same conclusion from the readings they were taking. This was the lull before the storm. Every dial and every gauge of every measuring instrument in the city confirmed it.

High up at the top of the Loftus Observatory, the Professor of Light looked up from his stationary anemometer. 'We didn't complete that Inauguration Ceremony a moment too soon,' he said. 'The Great Storm will be passing over Sanctaphrax in less than an hour.'

His colleague, the Professor of Darkness, nodded solemnly. 'Sky willing, Garlinius Gernix will manage to chase the storm and return to Sanctaphrax with the precious stormphrax she bears.'

'Sky willing,' the Professor of Light repeated. He turned and looked out through the windows. Being at the highest point in Sanctaphrax, the professor had a view of the entire floating city – of the School of Light and Darkness, of the Great Hall, of the Central Viaduct and the East and West Landings ... 'Sanctaphrax,' he breathed, his voice quavering with awe. 'The finest city in all creation.'

The Professor of Darkness joined him at the window. 'It is truly magnificent,' he agreed, then added softly, 'yet a city must be well ruled.'

'Indeed,' said the Professor of Light, and the pair of them found themselves staring down towards the Palace of Shadows.

With the ancient building crouched in the shadows behind the ostentatious College of Cloud, even from their vantage point, high up in the observatory tower, only the top of the highest palace turret was visible.

'I'm worried about our old friend, Linius,' said the Professor of Darkness. 'He has been looking so dreadful recently.'

'Worse and worse every time I see him,' said the Professor of Light, and shook his head. 'Sanctaphrax deserves better from its Most High Academe.'

The bed-chamber of Linius Pallitax, Most High Academe of Sanctaphrax, was swaddled in darkness. Night came early to the rooms within the Palace of Shadows.

Linius himself was curled up in a ball beneath the bed-covers, fast asleep. His face looked at peace; his breath came in soft, rasping sighs. He hadn't noticed when, at lunch-time, Welma had entered the room to check on him. Nor had he stirred when Tweezel – still anxious about his master's state of mind – had returned to the room at sundown to close the shutters and light the bed-side candles. Even now, as the door handle shifted and the door creaked open for a third time, his heavy, dream-less sleep continued.

The newcomer crossed the floor silently and leant down over the sleeping professor. 'Wake up,' he whispered and, when there was no response, he reached forwards and shook Linius gently by the shoulder. 'Professor,' he said. 'I'm back.'

Linius's eyelids flickered for a moment, then snapped open. 'Quint,' he said, his voice drowsy from the sleeping-draught Bungus had given him. 'You're safe.'

'I came as quickly as I could,' said Quint.

'And thank Sky for that, Quint,' said Linius. He looked round the room and his brow furrowed with concern. 'But . . . but where's Maris? And Bungus? Didn't he find you?'

Quint's nostrils quivered. His tongue darted round his lips. 'Maris and Bungus?' he said. 'Oh, yes, they found me all right.'

Linius sat up. 'Maris went too? So where are they?' he said, his voice shrill and anxious. 'Are they all right? Tell me, Quint, please.'

'I don't know how to say this,' said Quint, staring at the floor. 'Maris woke me. Bungus ministered to my wounds. We left the laboratory, and then . . ' He paused and, in the flickering candlelight, Linius saw the expression on his face. 'Then something *terrible* happened,' he said.

'Tell me,' Linius gasped.

Quint turned away. His tongue flicked out and tasted the air. 'There was nothing anyone could do . . .' He stopped. 'It happened so quickly.'

'What?' Linius demanded, his heart thumping furiously. He pulled himself up and climbed out of bed. 'You *must* tell me.' He stepped towards the youth, his limbs aching, his gait unsteady. 'Quint, please,' he implored. 'This is all my fault, I know it is. Why did Maris go too? Why wasn't I strong enough to stay awake and stop her? What sort of father am I . . . ?' He slumped back onto the bed, his face twisted up with misery. 'Don't tell me the blood-red glister got her.'

Quint turned and smiled. 'It appeared out of nowhere,' he said softly.

'No!' Linius exclaimed. 'Oh, Maris! *Maris!*' He stepped closer to Quint, stumbling weakly as he moved. 'What happened to her? *Tell me!*'

'The creature grasped her,' came the reply.

Linius shuddered fearfully.

'By the throat.'

Linius hugged himself tightly. His head was swimming, his heart thumping louder and faster than ever. 'Her face turned red. Her eyes bulged . . .'

'No! No!' Linius cried out in dismay. Once again, Quint's tongue flicked out and licked at the air. Looking up, Linius met his apprentice's gaze. There was a barely disguised look of contempt on Quint's face. Linius recoiled as a terrible thought occurred to him. 'Quint,' he said. 'Is it really you?'

Quint frowned. 'How could you doubt it?' he said. 'Of course it is.' He smiled slyly and opened his cape. 'Look,' he said as the Great Seal of High Office around his neck came into view.

'My seal!' said Linius, relieved. It *must* be Quint. He scratched his head. 'And Maris?' he whispered.

'That's what I'm trying to tell you,' said Quint. He shook his head. 'Maris was in a bad way. I feared that it was all over for her. But I did not give up. I . . . I fought back and managed to beat the creature – the blood-red glister – off her. I drove it away.'

Linius sighed with relief.

'But then it returned,' Quint said. 'Bigger and uglier than ever before.' His voice grew louder. 'And with a rage blazing so violently inside it that there was nothing I could do to prevent it attacking her a second time!'

'No!' Linius howled. 'Tell me it can't be true.'

'If only I could, Professor,' said Quint. He paused, and when he spoke again, his voice was soft, trembling. 'She fell to the ground. The creature was on her in an instant. I was powerless to do a thing . . .'

'And what of Bungus?'

'Bungus?' said Quint, and spat on the floor. 'Don't talk to me about that . . . that barkslug!'

Linius trembled with fear. 'Why?'

'Because the cowardly creature took to his heels and ran,' said Quint. 'That's why. I've never seen anyone move so fast.'

Legs shaking, Linius gripped the bed-post for support. There were tears in his eyes when he spoke. 'Please, Quint. Tell me what happened to my daughter,' he whispered, scarcely daring to hear what his apprentice had to say.

Quint lowered his head. 'She never stood a chance,' he said.

Linius gasped. 'You mean . . . ?'

'Yet even in those final moments, she remembered you, Professor,' said Quint softly.

'She d . . . did?' Linius said, his voice breaking with emotion.

'*Oh, Father, if only you were here with me now!* Those were her words, Professor.' And as Linius shivered with horror, Quint continued. '*But you never had any time for your only daughter . . .*' He paused. 'It was heartrending, Professor, believe me, tragic . . .'

'Stop, Quint,' Linius pleaded. He turned away and closed his eyes. 'I've heard enough.'

'But she would have wanted you to know her final words,' said Quint. He stepped forwards. His tongue glistened in the candlelight as it flicked out into the air. 'Even now, I can hear her voice . . .

He abandoned me! He is ashamed of me! . . .'

Linius clamped his hands over his ears. 'Enough!' he moaned.

Quint continued. *'Father!* she screamed. *FATHER!'*

'No more, I beg of you,' Linius cried out. 'For pity's sake . . .'

'But there's more,' Quint interrupted, his eyes blazing. 'Her final words, as the life drained out of her.'

The professor froze. 'F . . . final words?' he said. 'What did she say?'

Quint looked back, a smile playing over his lips. 'Are you sure you want to know?'

'Y . . . yes,' said Linius uncertainly. 'Tell me.'

Quint stepped forwards again. The smile vanished. *'Father, I curse you!'* he roared.

Linius gasped, and staggered backwards across the floor, arms flailing as he struggled to keep his balance. 'No,' he whimpered. 'No . . .'

He banged heavily into his bedside table. The candelabra toppled this way, that way, before keeling over and falling silently onto the bed. Two of the candles were extinguished at once. The third sputtered – but did not go out.

Linius buried his head in his hands. 'It's all my fault,' he sobbed. His body trembled. 'My darling Maris!'

Behind him, a thin spiral of dark smoke snaked its way up from his smouldering pillow.

'I *curse you*!' Quint screeched. 'I *curse you*!' And he threw back his head and cackled with evil, raucous laughter.

Linius's jaw dropped. He looked up. 'Quint?' he gasped. 'You're not Quint at all. You're . . . you're . . .'

Before him, his apprentice's familiar features changed. His eyes turned yellow and sank back in their sockets, his back hunched, his neck disappeared beneath a thick growth of matted hair and from his brow two knobbly curving horns emerged.

'Don't you recognize me, Professor?' the creature said. 'I am your creation! You weep over your *darling Maris*,' it went on scornfully, 'and yet you have no tears for me, but only hate instead . . .' The gloamglozer raised a scaly hand. '*You* did this,' it hissed menacingly. It touched a talon to its scarred and scabby face. 'And this . . . Just as I discovered my true form, Linius, you scarred me for ever. You burned me, your own creation!' it screeched. 'Now it is *your* turn to burn!'

As the gloamglozer's voice echoed round the high ceiling of the chamber, there was a sudden crackle and hiss and the smouldering pillow burst into flames.

Linius spun round, to see pink and purple ribbons of fire spreading out rapidly in all directions: to the heavy blankets and quilted counterpane, to the velvet bed curtains – until the entire four-poster bed was ablaze and thick, choking smoke was filling the room.

'Burn, Linius! Burn!' the gloamglozer shouted, as it flew up into the air.

Linius seized a rug from the floor and tried desperately to beat out the fire. But his futile efforts served only to fan the flames, spreading them across the blistering floor and up the tapestries on the walls. The smoke filled his eyes, his mouth, his lungs.

'C . . . can't breathe,' he groaned. He fell to his knees.

'You gave me life,' the gloamglozer shrieked. 'Then you left me to die. Now it is my turn to return the compliment.' For a second time, the chamber echoed with the terrible cackling laughter. 'Die, Linius, you pathetic failure!' the gloamglozer roared. 'DIE!'

Although exhausted after their long climb back through the stonecomb to Sanctaphrax, neither Maris nor Quint considered resting – not even for a moment. They emerged from the Great Library and hurried immediately towards the Palace of Shadows. Unlike the atmosphere in the stuffy underground tunnels, the night-air outside was cool and refreshing, and as they ran, they gulped down lungful after invigorating lungful.

Maris screwed up her nose. 'What's that?' she said.

'What's *what*?' Quint panted.

'That smell,' said Maris, slowing down.

Quint stopped beside her and sniffed the air. 'Smoke,' he said. 'Something must be burning.'

'Yes, look,' said Maris, and pointed up ahead to where the mist in the sky was stained a deep yellow. 'Something *is* burning. Something big.'

Maris was gripped by a sense of foreboding. From behind them came the sound of running footsteps. Three sub-acolytes with their gowns hitched up around their waists hurtled towards them.

'What's happening?' Maris shouted out.

'Fire!' one of them shouted back breathlessly. 'The Palace of Shadows is on fire!'

Maris gasped. The palace? On fire?

'Father!' she wailed, and broke into a run. Rounding the corner of the Central Avenue, she saw broad flickering sheets of yellow flame before her, lapping at the night sky behind the College of Cloud. Quint caught up with her.

'This can be no accident,' he muttered grimly.

All round them, academics and apprentices, servants and guards were streaming towards the blazing building. Maris and Quint joined the growing throng. The closer they got, however, the slower the crowds became. By the time they reached the narrow alleys and archways between the buildings which surrounded the ancient palace, everyone was all but at a standstill, and Maris and Quint had to barge their way through the gawping onlookers.

The small fountain-square below the marble staircase was full of countless Sanctaphrax citizens, standing shoulder to shoulder and staring open-mouthed at the terrible conflagration before them.

The heat was tremendous. It blasted fiercely like a foundry furnace, roaring, scorching, turning the upturned faces crimson and drenching them in glistening sweat.

None of those who stood there watching the blaze had ever seen the Palace of Shadows illuminated so brightly before. Centuries had passed since it had disappeared behind the newer, taller buildings which had cast it in perpetual shade. Tonight, for the first time since then, it had earned its former name: the Palace of Lights. Every feature of the magnificent building stood out in stark relief against the blazing incandescence – every ridged pillar and turned colonnade, every turret, every statue, every wrought-iron balcony and ornately carved lintel.

Sadly, it would also be the last time the palace would shine out like a great beacon. Even now the west wall and turret were beginning to crumble as the ancient wooden beams inside were consumed by the roaring flames.

'My home,' Maris whispered hoarsely. 'Welma ... Digit ...' She looked up at her father's bed-chamber where great jagged flames were pouring from the window. 'Father,' she murmured.

Rigid with terror, Quint heard nothing. All he was aware of were the anguished screams inside his head – the screams of his mother and brothers as they had fallen victim to the voracious flames all those years ago.

Maris turned to those standing closest to her. 'Does anyone know what has happened to Linius Pallitax?' she asked urgently. 'Has anyone seen my father, the Most High Academe?'

Without taking their eyes off the fiery spectacle before them, several onlookers replied. 'No,' they said. 'Neither hide nor hair.' 'Neither sight nor sound.' No-one had the faintest idea where Linius Pallitax, the Most High Academe, could be.

'What now?' Maris wailed. 'Oh, Quint, I ...'

Just then, there was a piercing shriek behind them. It cut Maris short and roused Quint from his terrible reveries.

'THERE HE IS!'

The pair of them looked round to see a gnokgoblin in basket-puller garb jumping up and down and pointing up towards the far corner of the High Parapet, just below the now blazing East Turret. As one, the crowd crooked their necks back as they followed the line of his outstretched arm.

And there, far above their heads, silhouetted against the flames and surrounded by swirling smoke, was the unmistakable figure of the Most High Academe. A cry of recognition went up.

'It *is* him!' 'There he is!' '*YES!*'

Teetering dangerously close to the edge of the parapet, Linius was clearly in trouble. He was waving down at them, frantically, desperately. Then, as they watched, his foot slipped and for a moment it seemed that he was about to hurtle down to certain death on the paving-slabs below. The crowd breathed in as one and the square echoed with the loud, horrified gasp – followed by a groan of relief as he managed, just, to hold on.

'That was a close one,' someone muttered close by.

'He was lucky indeed that time,' said another, 'but I fear his luck is about to run out.'

Maris turned on them. 'Then someone must rescue him before it does,' she said.

The two who had spoken shrugged and turned away – but others took up where they had left off.

'He's had it, so he has.'

'No doubt about it, he's on his way out.'

'We'll be looking to choose a new Most High Academe before the night's done, you mark my words.'

Maris rounded on the crowd, her eyes ablaze with anger. 'We must rescue him!' she cried out.

'And how do you propose to do that, missy?' came an insolent voice. 'Even the goblin-guard couldn't save him now.'

Quint elbowed his way to the very front, turned and confronted the crowd. 'Shame on you!' he cried. 'The professor is worth a thousand of any of you. *You* might be able to stand by and watch the Most High Academe of our great city die, but *I* can't!'

As he strode forwards, he felt someone seize him by the arm. 'Quint,' came a voice.

He turned. Maris was standing before him, her eyes welling up. 'Oh, Quint,' she said, 'aren't you forgetting something?'

Quint paused. His indigo-dark eyes widened questioningly.

'The fire, Quint,' said Maris, the tears running down her cheeks. 'You know as well as I do that flames terrify you. You wouldn't stand a chance. No, if none of these *brave*

scholars will save their Most High Academe, then *I* must.'
She shot a contemptuous look over her shoulder at the
gawping faces, and strode towards the palace entrance.

Quint's hand shot out and grabbed her elbow. 'I'm a
sky pirate's son,' he said. 'If there's one thing I can do, it
is climb.'

'But the flames, Quint!' Maris insisted. 'What about
the flames?'

Quint swallowed hard. 'Let me worry about that. Your
father needs me.'

He turned quickly away and ran up the steps to the
front entrance, two at a time.

'And so do I,' Maris whispered after him.

At the top of the staircase, instead of going through
the door, Quint shinned up the fluted column to its right.
Higher and higher he climbed. The crowd below began
to murmur. There was an embossed cap at the top of the
pillar, directly beneath one of the second-storey balconies. Gripping on to it with his legs, Quint reached up.
The moment his outstretched hand made contact with
the ornate railings above, he gripped them tightly,
released his legs and pulled himself up.

'Bravo!' a voice cried out.

'Now climb up to the balcony above you!' someone
advised.

'Rubbish!' shouted another. 'It's too high. You want to
use that drainpipe and head for the Central Turret.'

But Quint had his own plans. Without hesitating even
for a moment, he picked himself up off the floor of the
balcony, skirted round the flames billowing from the

broken window and climbed up onto the surrounding balustrade. The next moment, a cry of disbelief echoed round the square as the young apprentice performed a gravity-defying leap onto the neighbouring balcony.

Maris gasped in amazement and blinked away her tears. Even though he was so terrified of fire, Quint's life on board a sky pirate ship had indeed left him with unmatched agility and a fearless head for heights.

For a second time, he leapt across the gaping void below him to the next balcony. And again. And then one last time.

'But what's he doing?' the crowd was asking itself. 'Why doesn't he simply go straight up?'

Their questions were answered a moment later when Quint reached the balcony closest to the corner of the building. Although it looked like all the others, it had one thing none of the others had. A flag-pole. Not that Quint was interested in the signal-banners which fluttered in the rising breeze, but rather in the rope which had raised them. Without his sky-pirate grappling-hook, he had to improvise. Hopefully, with a perfectly executed clamp-knot and a steady aim, he would be able to navigate the overhang at the top of the building.

Having removed the rope from the pulley wheels, wound it round in a coil and slung it over his shoulder, Quint was off again. He leapt up, grabbed and heaved himself on to the Low Parapet. Then, using a sunken lightning-rod for support, he climbed over the arch above the windows and from there, up to a broad plinth which jutted out from a shell-shaped alcove.

'He's nearly there,' said someone in the crowd excitedly.

'The most difficult part is still to come,' cautioned another.

'What's he doing?' asked a third, as Quint suddenly jerked forwards and tossed the end of the rope up into the air.

'Isn't it obvious?' came an impatient reply. 'He's trying to lassoo one of the parapet urns. He's going to pull himself up.'

Maris could barely dare to look as the rope flicked up over the top of the parapet wall. Twice, three times, four times it flew over the wall, only to drop back down again the next moment.

Come on! she willed him on. You can do it!

Five times. Six times – and still the rope did not catch. Then, at the seventh attempt, the pear-shaped loop dropped down so smoothly over the sculpted roofpot that it seemed almost as if it had been teasing before. Quint tugged on the rope. The knot tightened.

The crowd held its breath. Maris mouthed a silent prayer. The next instant, everyone gasped in unison as Quint swung away from the plinth and dangled there, high up in the smoky air, his cape flapping in the gathering wind. No-one watching from below so much as blinked as, hand over hand, Quint inched himself slowly upwards.

Above him, they saw the professor flapping his arms more desperately than ever. The flames were getting closer. Valiant though he undoubtedly was, if the young apprentice wasn't quick, then both he and his master would surely perish.

Maris closed her eyes. She simply couldn't bear to watch any more. A moment later, however, a joyous cheer rang out, and she looked up again to see Quint pulling himself over the balustrade.

'Thank Sky,' she murmured gratefully. She strained to see through the smoke. 'But where is my father?'

She scoured the whole of the High Parapet, but there was no sign of him now. He must have slipped back, away from the edge and out of view.

At that moment, there was a crack and a crash and, a large triangular section of burning wood and shattered masonry broke away from the top of the palace. As it tumbled down, a dazzling sheet of flame and a billowing plume of thick, black smoke exploded on to the parapet.

Maris stared up, unable for a few seconds to see anything at all. Then, as the smoke cleared, her pounding heart missed a beat. Quint, too, had disappeared.

'It's all right, Professor,' said Quint softly. 'But we don't have much time. Just come over here and I'll tie the rope around your waist. We'll soon . . .' He paused. 'Professor?' he said. 'Professor, come back!'

Without saying a word, Linius had turned and was heading off behind the turret. Quint swallowed nervously. The heat from the flames was intense – it burned his face yet chilled him to the bones. Any anxiety he'd felt climbing up the front of the great palace was nothing compared to the terror which gripped him now.

Quint glanced down over the balustrade. Far beneath him, he could see Maris staring back up at him. He couldn't fail her. Not now.

'Professor!' he called out. 'Wait!'

Just then, there was a violent explosion. Quint ducked down as fiery debris flew past him and the air filled with a thick, choking smoke. With his eyes streaming and his throat burnt raw, he staggered towards the side of the tower.

'Professor!' he rasped. 'Professor, *please* wait.'

As the smoke cleared, Quint saw him. He was leaning, almost nonchalantly, against the tower wall.

'Professor, you must listen to me,' said Quint, as he wiped away the stinging tears from his eyes. 'We must get out of here at once.'

But Linius was unmoved by the urgency in his voice. 'So soon?' he said. 'But you have only just arrived. Sit down and catch your breath at least, my lad.'

'You don't understand – the building could collapse at any moment,' Quint insisted.

The professor shook his head. 'Come now, Quint,' he said. 'Take the weight off your feet and warm yourself this chilly night at the fire.' He raised his hands and rubbed them theatrically by the flames. 'Ah, but the flames . . . I sense fear, Quint. They fill you with horror, do they not?'

Quint shuddered and turned away. The professor's tongue flicked out and tasted the air greedily.

Poor Linius, Quint thought in despair. After every-thing he's been through, this fire must have finally pushed him over the edge. With his heart hammering in his chest, he turned back to console him. 'You're not yourself, Professor. But it'll be all right. I promise . . .'

As their eyes met, however, he was so startled by the expression on the academic's face – a keen, almost hungry look – that it took his breath away. And as he gasped, he saw the professor's tongue lap at the air.

He noticed something else, too. Something which

glinted brightly in the flickering light: the Great Seal of High Office of Sanctaphrax.

'No,' he breathed. 'No, it *can't* be.'

Down in the small square in front of the blazing Palace of Shadows, the atmosphere had changed. Neither the Most High Academe nor his apprentice had been spotted for ages and, with the increasing amount of blazing debris tumbling down through the air, waiting for their return was becoming more and more perilous. What was more, as the wind got up, pieces of flaming material were being blown to the surrounding buildings and beyond.

Already, there were rumours coming in of minor blazes breaking out in both the School of Light and Darkness and the Raintasters' Tower, while a third fire had been reported on the roof of the Great Hall. Although none of the sky-scholars felt any great sadness about the Palace of Shadows burning to the ground, the thought that their own colleges and academies might be in danger soon sent panic buzzing round the crowd.

A group of apprentices and sub-acolyte raintasters sped off back to the College of Rain, faces white and gowns flapping. The Sub-Dean of the School of Light and Darkness ran back and forth like a headless woodcock. While at the back of the square, numerous apprentice cloudwatchers and assorted volunteers had formed a long line in front of the College of Cloud and were passing bucket after bucket of water up the stairs – twenty flights in all – to the roof, where a second contingent of helpers was pouring it down every time a stray spark from the blazing building opposite threatened to start a fire.

All round the square, the academics, servants and guards were abandoning the Palace of Shadows to its fate and the air resounded with their shouts as they streamed away.

'We don't have time for that old place!'

'We must preserve our own buildings!'

'Let the palace burn to the ground. And good riddance!'

Maris alone stood still as the chaos continued all round her. She stared up at the High Parapet. 'Please let them be all right,' she whispered grimly. 'Please let them be safe.'

But no matter how hard she peered into the smoky fire far above her head, she could find no sign of either her father or Quint. An icy fear gripped her.

'Oh, Quint,' she murmured. 'What have you done? I . . .'

At that moment, there came the sound of sudden activity from the top of the palace stairs. Anxious voices. A bolt sliding. A key turning . . .

The door flew open and a small, rounded figure emerged from the entrance. She was wearing slippers and an apron – and had a small blue-furred creature perched on her shoulder.

'Welma!' Maris cried out, and dashed up the stairs towards her. 'Digit!'

Welma and Maris fell into one another's arms and

hugged each other tightly while the wood-lemkin –
caught up in their excitement – chattered loudly and
jumped about on their shoulders.

Behind her, Maris became aware of shouting. The line
of bucket-bearers had seen something. She pulled away
from her nurse and looked back into the doorway. And
there was Tweezel the spindlebug, the great gangly old
retainer of the Palace of Shadows, emerging backwards
from the smoky hall so as not to knock the load he was
carrying so carefully in his front legs. Outside, he turned
slowly round.

'It's him!' someone shouted.

'Old glass-legs has saved him!'

Maris could hardly believe her eyes. 'Father!' she cried
out and ran towards him.

Linius turned his head. Maris flinched. His skin was
blistered, his hair singed. His lifeless eyes stared
unblinking into mid-air.

Maris turned to Tweezel. 'Will he be all right?' she
asked.

'I shall take him to his former chambers in the School
of Mist,' Tweezel said stiffly. 'Welma will dress his

wounds. We will put him to bed. And then all we can do is wait. But what about you, young mistress? Are *you* all right?'

'Yes . . . no,' said Maris. She frowned. 'Where's Quint?'

The spindlebug's antennae trembled. 'The Most High Academe's young apprentice?' he said. 'I'm sure I wouldn't know.'

'But didn't you see him?' she said. 'He was up there on the roof with my father. He . . .'

'I found your father in his bed-chamber, not on the roof,' said the spindlebug. 'Curled up in the corner, he was, while all around him the terrible fire raged . . .'

'But you *can't* have,' Maris murmured.

The spindlebug tilted its head and looked round at the Palace of Shadows. 'Oh, that it should ever have come to this!' he wailed and trilled with despair. 'I blame myself. I should have been more vigilant. I should have taken more care.' He hung his head. 'Now it is all gone. Everything. Centuries of tradition and learning wiped out . . .' He clicked his claws. 'Just like that.'

But Maris had not heard him. If my father never left his bed-chamber, she was wondering, then who had she seen on the roof? Who had Quint risked his life to rescue?

Her face fell as the terrible truth suddenly struck her.

'You,' Quint groaned. 'It was you all the time.'

Before his eyes, the professor transformed into a creature with loathsome mutilated skin and long, coiling ridged horns. It hovered in front of him.

'Very astute, *Master* Quint,' the gloamglozer hissed scornfully, and raised the Great Seal with a scaly hand. 'It was this that gave away my little secret, wasn't it? The Most High Academe's seal of office.' It threw back its head and cackled with laughter. 'It won't do him much good now.'

Quint glanced round him. There seemed to be no escape.

'I see you are beginning to understand,' said the gloamglozer, jangling the chain in Quint's face. 'This little trinket is of no use to him, for Linius Pallitax is dead. Roasted to a crisp,' it shrieked and cackled all the louder. 'You thought you were saving him, didn't you? But all the time, he was downstairs in his bed-chamber, the surrounding flames coming closer, growing higher, hotter . . .'

'N . . . no.' Quint trembled.

'You failed!' the gloamglozer roared. Its eyes flashed gleefully as it tasted the air with its quivering tongue and smacked its cracked lips. It moved closer to him and fear rose like a stone in Quint's throat.

'Can you imagine how he must have suffered,' the creature continued and its eyes narrowed. 'Ah, but I see you can imagine it *exactly*,' it purred. 'How his skin must have blistered and his hair caught fire? The terrible heat. The appalling stench of burning flesh. Oh, and the cries he must have let out as the flames consumed him – louder and louder . . .'

'Stop it!' Quint begged. 'Haven't you done enough?'

The creature hesitated for a moment. Then it turned

and fixed Quint with its yellow eyes. 'Enough?' it shrieked. 'I haven't even started. Just you wait and see.'

Despite the blistering heat, Quint gave an involuntary shudder. The gloamglozer pressed its hideous face into his own.

'I shall spread mayhem and chaos,' it said. 'I shall lure. I shall cheat. I shall lie. I shall tempt and deceive. And feed off the pain and despair I create.' As icy shivers ran up and down Quint's spine, the creature trembled with pleasure and licked its lips. 'And off the fear,' it whispered.

Quint backed away nervously – only to be beaten forwards again by the terrible encroaching inferno.

'That fool, Linius,' the gloamglozer continued, 'never had an inkling of what he was unleashing. He summoned *me* from the emptiness and then actually believed that he would be able to control what he had created, that I should be grateful to him, that I should obey him – vain and pitiful creature that he was!'

As it spoke, a massive flaming beam tumbled down from the blazing turret. It missed Quint by inches, struck the stone floor and exploded in a great shower of white and yellow sparks. He looked round him desperately. If he could just get back to the rope . . . But which way *was* it? With the flames high and the blinding smoke being driven this way and that by the rising wind, he was becoming disorientated.

'He summoned me up, only to imprison me in that underground laboratory,' the gloamglozer went on, 'too frightened of his creation to realize what I could become, if only he would let me. But I fed on his fear and I liked the taste. And I grew, and I studied, and I schemed – and at last . . .' It raised its arms in triumph and flapped its tattered robes. 'Here I am!' it roared.

Quint shuddered. If retreat was not possible, then he had no choice but to attack. His hand closed round the handle of his knife. The gloamglozer's nostrils quivered as it breathed in deeply.

'It is even better outside than I ever dared imagine,' it continued softly. 'I sense such confusion all round me – such fear, such pain and distress. It strengthens me. It empowers me. I exalt in its boundless misery.' It looked down at Quint. 'And I owe it all to you! *You* were the one who released me from my prison. *You* unleashed me on to an unsuspecting world.'

'And I shall also be the one to rid it of you!' Quint bellowed.

In a blind rage, he lunged forwards and stabbed at the hovering creature again and again. But the gloamglozer merely sneered as it dodged the blade and darted back out of reach.

'You can't destroy me!' it roared above the sound of the howling wind, and cackled with bloodchilling laughter. 'So long as the strong pick on the weak, so long as fear is valued above tenderness, so long as hatred, envy and mistrust divide the various creatures of the Edge, then I am indestructible!'

As its ranting continued, the gloamglozer had edged towards Quint. With its final defiant words, it lashed out. The dagger Quint was holding was knocked from his hand and sent scudding across the floor where it disappeared into the smoke and flames. Quint's heart hammered in his chest. The gloamglozer smacked its lips.

'The fear of the vulnerable is so much sweeter than the strong,' it purred. 'But the sweetest taste of all,' it went on, its voice growing rougher, more menacing, 'is surely at *the moment of death*.'

Quint quaked in his boots. His legs had turned to jelly.

'And that moment,' the gloamglozer roared, 'is now!'

It swooped in close to the youth, driving him back into the advancing wall of fire. Quint darted to the left. Immediately, the gloamglozer was there before him, blocking his escape. It bared its teeth grimly.

'Back you go,' it chided. 'Into the fire.'

Quint groaned with horror. He could feel the flames lapping at his back, burning his neck, singeing his hair. In a desperate attempt to stave off the inevitable, he raised the collar and wrapped the cape protectively around him. It rustled, paper dry, as the flames licked at its hem.

His hand brushed against something hard in one of the pockets. His fingers investigated. It was a small leather pouch tied up with a drawstring.

Of course! He was wearing Bungus's cape, not his own. Bungus had wrapped it round Maris, who had dropped it in the narrow tunnel and he, Quint, had put it on. This meant that the pouch must belong to Bungus!

'Oh, Bungus,' he murmured fearfully, as he remembered the old librarian's twisted body lying dead in the stonecomb. When the blood-red glister had attacked, he must have reached for the pouch himself, only to find that it was not there. 'I'm so sorry,' he whispered.

The gloamglozer's tongue flicked out into the air. 'It is time, Quint!' it announced, its yellow eyes flickering malevolently. 'Time for you to die in the fire!'

Quint returned the creature's evil gaze. His hand fumbled desperately with the pouch. With a jerk, his fingers prised it open and he felt the grains flow into his palm like soft sand. His hand closed into a fist round them.

'Time to die!' smiled the gloamglozer.

'Die!' echoed Quint, pulling his hand from the cloak pocket and flinging the precious chine into the creature's leering face.

The gloamglozer threw back its head and screamed out in agonizing pain as the tiny crystals landed on its hands, its face. It bucked, it twisted, it writhed. The gold Seal of Office slipped from its scaly neck and fell to the floor.

'My eyes! My eyes!' it cried, and clutched its head in its hands.

Quint stepped forwards and raised his other, empty fist menacingly. 'I have more chine,' he shouted at the moaning creature. 'Lots of it. Buckets and buckets full, all over Sanctaphrax! And I'll use it, I swear!' He shook his fist at the gloamglozer. 'You aren't safe here – you never will be. I'll hunt you through the streets! You'll see!'

The gloamglozer hovered above him, its eyes blood-shot and its face half-molten. It gnashed its teeth. 'You miserable excuse for an apprentice!' it snarled. 'You pathetic little creature! You dare to threaten me with your foul firesand! It burns! Oh, how it burns . . .'

'I'm warning you!' Quint shouted. 'Go. Go now!'

'Oh, I shall go,' the gloamglozer sneered. 'But mark my words and mark them well, Quint. Though you have banished me today, I shall catch up with you one day.'

Above its head, the expanse of billowing black and purple clouds of the Great Storm swirled across the sky. Lightning flashed; thunder crashed.

'I *curse* you, Quint, the apprentice!' the gloamglozer raged. 'You, and all your kind! You think you're safe with your chine to protect you, but I can smell your fear. I curse you all! And I shall find you and deal with you – as I shall find and deal with all those other weaklings out there in the world.'

It flapped up higher and raised its vicious taloned hands. 'For I am the gloamglozer, and you shall live with my curse every day of your life. The curse you cannot hide from. The curse of knowing that you, Quint the apprentice, have set me loose on the world!'

The gloamglozer howled with scornful laughter.

'Heed my curse, Quint!' it screeched as it flapped off into the night sky. 'Heed the curse of the gloamglozer!'

Quint stared into the gloom long after the gloamglozer had disappeared. 'Gone,' he murmured at last and opened his empty fist. 'The gloamglozer has gone.'

The next moment, his relief turned to terror. He might have driven the gloamglozer away with the chine, but no Riverrise crystals could help him combat the fire. If he was not to be swallowed up in the terrible flames, he must somehow escape.

His eyes streamed with the smoke as he battled his way across the parapet to the outer balustrade. Rocks and burning chunks of wood from the blazing tower dropped all round him. The wind howled. The thunder roared.

Suddenly Quint saw it. The rope. It was still there, attached to the sculpted urn and, even more wonderfully, untouched by the fire.

'Thank Sky!' Quint murmured as he dashed forwards.

He seized the rope, and was just about to ease himself over the top of the balustrade when there was an almighty crash behind him.

The East Turret had finally surrendered to the fire and come crashing down, bringing the roof of the palace with it. Before he had a chance even to wonder what to do next, Quint found himself hurtling down through the air in a torrent of blazing wood and shattered masonry.

He closed his eyes. Countless pictures flashed before him. His mother. His brothers.

Wind Jackal and the *Galerider*.

Maris.

The Palace of Shadows. The Fountain House.

Maris.

The blood-red glister.

The gloamglozer.

Maris . . .

Then nothing.

*

THE SCHOOL OF MIST

Three days later, Bagswill, the former treasury-guard, was sitting in the austere reception-room of Seftus Leprix, the Sub-Dean of the School of Mist, gazing out through the open window.

'Some sapwine, Bagswill,' said Leprix, 'to toast our great success in finally saying goodbye to the Most High Academe of Sanctaphrax.' He removed the jug from the tray and poured the green liquid into the first of the two waiting glasses.

'Yeah, who'd have thought it?' said Bagswill. 'He survives the sabotaged sky cage, he survives the poisoned cordial, and then finally dies as a result of a great fire – something we had nothing to do with.'

Leprix nodded. 'I was beginning to think he had a charmed life,' he said, as he turned his attention to the second glass. 'Particularly when I heard that Tweezel had rescued him from the flames.'

'He's taking it bad, is Tweezel,' said Bagswill. 'He was in tears when he told me his master had died of his injuries. He blames himself – for not acting sooner, for not having had better medicines at his disposal . . .'

'Thank Sky he didn't,' said Leprix, laughing unpleasantly. He placed the half-empty jug down. 'With Linius Pallitax finally out of the way, and the dean's most unfortunate accident, I – as most senior mistsifter – am now entitled to become Most High Academe. For, as the *Great Tome of Skylore* so clearly states, if a Most High Academe dies in office, then his successor has to come from the academic school where *he* originated.' Leprix grinned nastily. 'And there's nothing those accursed

Professors of Light and Darkness can do about it!'

'And me?' said Bagswill excitedly. 'What about me?'

'You, Bagswill, will be my Head Guard.' He smiled. 'With your very own torture-chamber.'

The two of them raised their glasses.

'I would like to propose a toast to the bearer of our wonderful news,' Leprix announced. 'To Tweezel!'

'To Tweezel!' Bagswill echoed and the pair of them downed their glasses in one.

'My word,' said Leprix, wiping his mouth on the back of his hand, 'that's good stuff. Another, Bagswill?'

'If I may,' said Bagswill.

'Of course you may, old friend,' said Leprix warmly. 'We are celebrating a great victory.' He poured two more glasses – which disappeared as quickly as the first two.

'Quite remarkable,' said Leprix. 'Jervis,' he called. 'Jervis!' He shook his head irritably. '*Jervis!*'

The door opened and a stooped, middle-aged individual entered the room and cowered by the wall. His eyes darted round the room anxiously. Everything seemed to be the way the master liked it – the windows were open, the curtains drawn, the pictures were all straight on the wall. His gaze fell on a silver object which lay on the sofa . . .

'Jervis, you will come when I call you,' said Leprix.

Jervis frowned. It looked almost like . . . like a *nose*.

'JERVIS!' Leprix roared.

Jervis looked down, and began bowing his head over and over. 'Yes, sir,' he mumbled. 'Sorry, sir. You called me and I await your instruction, sir.'

'Indeed I did, Jervis,' said Leprix angrily. 'I . . .' Then, as he remembered the reason for summoning the servant, his voice softened. 'I wondered which wine-maker supplied us with this excellent sapwine-cordial,' he said. 'Whoever it was from, you must order some more.'

'It . . . it . . . it didn't come from a wine-maker, if it pleases you,' Jervis muttered softly. 'Leastways,' he added nervously at the sight of Leprix's dark eyebrows drawing together ominously, 'not one that I know, though I could probably find out . . .'

'What are you blethering about?' Leprix demanded angrily. 'Where is the sapwine from?'

'From . . . from Tinsel . . . Twizzle . . .' Jervis said nervously. 'You know, that spindlebug from the Palace of Shadows . . .'

Leprix gasped. '*Tweezel*,' he breathed.

'That's the one,' said Jervis. 'He gave me the sapwine and made me promise it got to you. He said that, since his master would no longer be needing it, you should have it back – and he thanked you both kindly for your thought and concern.' He nodded appreciatively. 'Seemed like a really nice creature, he did – despite his weird appearance which, I for one must admit, is most alarming . . .'

'You gave us the spindlebug's sapwine?' said Leprix. His voice was low and trembling.

Bagswill grabbed his arm. 'You mean we've been drinking our own . . .'

They turned and looked at one another.

'. . . cordial,' said Leprix.

'. . . hover-worm venom,' said Bagswill. He stared at Leprix helplessly. 'Your face!' he cried. 'It's beginning to swell up.'

'So is your body!' said Leprix. 'The poison is taking effect.' He turned on Jervis. 'See what you've done!' he roared. 'You imbe . . . *blmfff.*' Cut off in mid-sentence, the sub-dean clutched desperately at his swollen face.

Jervis cowered in fear while, in front of him, the two creatures grew larger and larger as they inflated from within. Their clothes split. Their bellies swelled. They were turning into grotesque carnival bladder-balloons, unable to speak, their limbs stubby and their eyes nearly popping out of their skulls. Then, as Jervis continued to stare, the two massive, swollen bodies floated up from the floor.

Jervis had seen enough. With a horrified squeak, he raced from the room and slammed the door shut behind him. He would have to find himself a new master, that much was clear. Refectory gossip had it that there were openings in the Faculty of Raintasters.

On the floor above the sub-dean's rooms, the sound of the slamming door echoed round the state apartment of the Professor of Mistsifting. Seated at a desk in his great bed-chamber, Linius Pallitax looked up questioningly – before drifting back to his reveries.

In the room across the corridor, Quint stirred.

'Quint!' Maris cried. She leapt from the chair in which she had spent so many hours over the previous three days and nights, waiting, hoping, praying . . . 'Quint, can you hear me?'

The youth's eyes snapped open. He stared ahead of him wildly. 'Fire!' he screamed. 'Gloamglozer! Falling . . . falling . . .'

'Hush, now, Quint,' said Maris. 'You're safe now. It's all right.'

Quint blinked and focused in on the kindly face looking down at him. It was smiling and there were tears streaming down the flushed cheeks. 'Maris,' he whispered.

'Oh, Quint,' she sobbed. 'Three days you've been unconscious. I thought we'd lost you for ever . . .'

Quint looked round him. He was lying in a bed with soft pillows and clean sheets. 'Where am I?' he said.

'This used to be my nursery,' said Maris. 'With the Palace of Shadows destroyed, Father and I had to return to the School of Mist. Our former apartments have once again become our home . . .'

'Your father is alive?' Quint gasped. 'But I thought . . .' He fell still. So, the gloamglozer had lied to him.

'Yes,' said Maris. 'He is alive. Of course, his experiences have left him scarred, both physically and mentally. But with patience and understanding, he will improve. In the meantime,' she went on hurriedly, 'the Professors of Light and Darkness will continue to govern Sanctaphrax with him . . .' She smiled sadly. '*For* him, I should say. Until he is back to his old self . . .' Her voice trailed away.

'And they can be trusted, can they?' said Quint.

Maris nodded. 'The Professors of Light and Darkness are my father's oldest friends and allies,' she said. 'What's more,' she went on, '*you* have not escaped their attention.'

'*I*?' said Quint. 'What do you mean, Maris?'

'The Professor of Light has been particularly complimentary about you,' she said.

'He has? But . . .'

'He wants to sponsor you to go through the Knights' Academy,' she said. 'You would be his protégé.'

'His protégé,' Quint whispered. He sat up in the bed. 'But my father, Wind Jackal . . . I always imagined that, like him, I would be a sky-pirate captain.'

'As a Knight Academic, you might one day have the opportunity to go stormchasing,' said Maris.

Quint's eyes gleamed. 'Like Garlinius Gernix,' he whispered, 'Garlinius Gernix and all those other valiant knights who set sail after a Great Storm in search of stormphrax.'

'And you could be one of them,' said Maris. She smiled uncertainly and hung her head. 'That is, if you stayed here in Sanctaphrax for just a little bit longer, Quint.'

'I'm not sure,' Quint began. 'It's certainly tempting, but . . .' His eyes opened wide. 'What was *that*?'

'What?'

'At the window!' he gasped, continuing to stare out.

Maris turned, and ... 'There!' Quint yelled. 'There's another one! What *are* they?'

'They looked like huge weather-balloons,' said Maris.

'But they were making a noise,' said Quint. 'They were groaning.'

Maris rushed to the window. By the time she arrived there, however, the massive inflated objects had both been whisked away on the wind.

Maris and Quint weren't the only ones to see the vastly

inflated sub-dean and former guard rising up into the sky. From their vantage point at the top of the Loftus Observatory, the Professors of Light and Darkness had witnessed it all.

'Look there!' the Professor of Light had cried out. 'Emerging from that window in the School of Mist. A luminous object. And another ...'

'Upon my soul!' gasped the Professor of Darkness.

'What can they be? Fog-clusters?'

'Or charged hover-mist?'

'Or cloud-spirits?'

'Or some curious form of ball-lightning?'

Before either of them could decide, the two mysterious shimmering spheres – each getting larger by the second – soared up into the night sky. They shone like two new stars for a moment, before growing smaller and smaller, and finally being extinguished completely.

'Remarkable,' said the Professor of Light.

'Extraordinary,' said the Professor of Darkness.

'We must record every detail at once,' the Professor of Light said.

'Indeed,' agreed the Professor of Darkness. 'And we must compare our findings with existing records to discover what we have just witnessed.'

Despite all their work, the professors never did learn what it was they had seen that night, although they – and the others who had also witnessed the curious starry spectacle – came up with many wild theories. Subsequently, more wild theories arose as to the curious disappearance of the sub-dean of the mistsifters, Seftus Leprix, and a renegade guard by the name of Bagswill. Countless conspiracies were mooted, and various bits of gossip became gospel. But in all the intricate guesswork and speculation, no-one connected the two events.

Alone among the citizens of Sanctaphrax, only Tweezel and Jervis knew that the brief appearance of the two new stars and the disappearance of the sub-dean and the guard were linked. And they weren't telling anyone. Ever.

Back at the window of the old nursery in the School of Mist, Quint and Maris gazed out together at the dark night-sky. The stars twinkled above them, as bright as polished black-diamonds.

'It's so beautiful,' Maris breathed.

'It's more beautiful still when you escape the sky-glow of the city lights,' said Quint. 'Oh, Maris, I cannot begin to explain to you how wonderful it is to go skysailing across the Deepwoods on a night such as this. Or to drift across the top of a swirling sea of snow-white fog. Or to follow in the slip-stream of passing rainbow-clouds.' His eyes glazed over. 'To feel the sun in your face and the wind in your hair . . .' He paused and turned to Maris. 'And yet,' he said, 'I have never been stormchasing. If Sanctaphrax is prepared to teach me how to, then perhaps I should take up the Professor of Light's offer.'

'You mean, you'll stay?' said Maris.

Quint nodded. 'For now,' he said. 'But not for ever. This place is not for me, Maris. One day I shall leave Sanctaphrax with its plots and intrigues, and never come back.'

'Quint,' said Maris, taking hold of his arm. 'When you do leave, take me with you.'

Quint smiled, but said nothing. He turned and stared back outside into the wide beyond. Far out there were the sacred Twilight Woods and, beyond them, the dark

Deepwoods which stretched out for ever. A warm glow spread through his body. He longed to explore the great wide world out there, a world full of wonders. . .

The gloamglozer's voice filled his head with no warning. It sent shivers throughout his body.

'I curse you, Quint the apprentice . . . And you shall live with my curse every day of your life. The curse of knowing that you have set me loose on the world!'

No, no, he told himself, and shook his head. The gloamglozer was gone. It would never return to Sanctaphrax – and what were the chances of ever running into it again? The Edgeworld was so vast. No, it was all over.

Wasn't it?

'Well?' he heard Maris saying. She sounded impatient. 'Will you take me? Yes or no?'

Quint turned back and, seeing the earnest little face of his friend, burst out laughing. 'I'll tell you what,' he said, 'if I had you with me, the gloamglozer would never dare to come near!'

'Is that a *yes*, then?' said Maris.

'Yes, Maris, it is,' said Quint. 'When I leave Sanctaphrax you will come with me. You can stand beside me at the helm of a great sky ship and together we shall sail to the furthest corners of the sky.'

Maris nodded. 'And perhaps,' she said dreamily, 'even further than that.'